Revenge is Sweet?

First Edtion Group Ltd

Progress Centre

Charlton Place

Manchester

M12 6HS

www.firsteditiongroup.co.uk

First published in Great Britain by First Edition Group 2015

Copyright © Lynn Evans 2015

Lyn Evans asserts the moral right to
be identified as the author of the work.

A catalogue for this book is
available from the British Library

ISBN: 978-1-84547-241-2

This novel is entirely a work of fiction. The names, characters and incidents portrayed in it are the work of the author's imagination. Any resemblance to actual persons, living or dead, events or localities is entirely coincidental.

All rights reserved. No part of this publication may be reproduced, stored in a retrieval system, or transmitted, in any form or by any means, electronic, mechanical, photocopying, recording or otherwise, without the prior permission of the publisher.

Acknowledgements

My thanks go to my family, my mother Joan, my daughters Jody, Jacqueline, Jennifer and Josephine and all my wonderful friends for their valued support and input whilst writing this book, in particular, Henry and Rachael who helped the dream to come true.

1

The Bombshell

'Hey! Careful Mrs! Ya nearly took me eye out ya did,' pointing to my great grandmother's unwieldy, five foot tall Umbrella Tree that went by the name of Fred after her late husband. I mumbled an apology to the stranger and clutched the plant, rocking precariously in its heavy ceramic pot, tightly to my chest whilst endeavouring to bury my blushes in its overgrown branches. Then I waited patiently with the rest of the thong for the doors of Ward 18 to be opened on the dot at 2 pm.

Most normal people were happy to receive a bunch of grapes or a bouquet I reflected, when they were admitted to hospital not a tree! There was no way my Great Granny Wilhelmina could ever slip into that category, I thought recalling her strange request. 'Mary, dear don't bother bringing me flowers, I would much prefer to have my Fred beside me. He's my pride and joy; I talk to him every day. Left in your hands he will no doubt wither and die.' Eccentric, old, embarrassing, defined my great grandmother, definitely the latter recalling how often I had wished for the floor to open up into a huge chasm and swallow me out of sight, not unlike now.

I was suddenly jolted from my memories by an impatient push, as the crowd surged forward. Holding on tight to Fred we made our way over to my great granny's bedside, blissfully unaware of the earth shattering skeletons she was to shortly tip out of her closet. Before I even had chance to sit down and give her the customary peck on her hairy cheek she took my breath away.

'My dear Mary, I have been on this planet nigh one hundred years and am certainly no saint; prostitution, violence, sadism, extortion, I have seen it all. Oh, and falling in love of course experiencing incredible moments of sheer euphoria only to be later plunged into utter desperate heartbreak. Yes, I have had my fair share of men too but Wilhelmina Potts has witnessed things you would not believe, has done things you would not believe and is ashamed of things you would not believe.' She said with a slightly mischievous glint in her eye.

'Mary, if your great grandmother has learned one lesson, albeit the hard way, it is that the dish of revenge can never be sweet not even served cold. Indeed, how can it when vengeance leaves a legacy of hatred, bitterness, a twisted mind obsessed with a desperate urge to commit whatever it might take to satisfy that all consuming lust? Rape, torture, even one's own flesh and blood forced to suffer indescribable agony, 'an eye for an eye will make the whole world blind' and I was to remember those time honoured words of that great Indian Statesman, Mahatma Gandhi, more times than you could ever imagine.' She suddenly stopped to take a much needed breath, before continuing.

'Now dear, I may have passed my sell by date but while there is still a spark in these old embers I wish to record for posterity how I spent my days on this earth and Mary I would like you to take some notes. Umm… you maybe shocked at what I have to say but say it I must. My final curtain call could be just around the corner, that Grim Reaper could come for me tomorrow so there is no time to lose.' She looked away wearing a sad expression and allowed herself to daydream. If she could only turn back the sands of time. If only she had never chased after Horace Fortescue, a vile apology for a man, and ran into those dark woods. If only she had not driven Fred, the love of her life, away. Well one of them, and seen the hurt in his eyes when she had later trampled on his fragile ego, if only they could have grown old together.

All she had now were just memories, wistfully recalling when they were first wed how she loved to feel his strong, protective arms wrapped tightly around her while he passionately kissed her lips and whispered sweet nothings in her ear as he took her to the heights of ecstasy. That was before he had discovered her dark secret.

Sitting there beside her, I was completely unaware my Granny Wilhelmina had an ulterior motive behind her request and that a can of worms was waiting to spring out when she lifted the lid off her Pandora's Box.

With my back straight and pen poised to write, staring at this mysterious woman, a spirited but outwardly frail old lady with her elegantly placed arthritic, wrinkled hands upon her lap, appearing to study them with intent. It was not her hands she was seeing but her past. Whilst waiting for her to speak I studied her face observing how old age had ravaged her once arresting beauty. Gaunt cheek bones now jutted from a sallow complexion, a repulsive large, brown, scaly wart sprouting two wiry hairs was sitting on her chin. Her deep blue eyes were now hooded and thin wisps of silver hair had been scraped into a tight bun clinging to the nape of her neck.

I knew my great grandmother was no ordinary woman, indeed I was soon to discover Granny Wilhelmina had more skeletons hidden in her closet than most old folks had had hot dinners! Courage, determination or, was it just plain obstinacy and stupidity were being revealed as I intently listened to her travels down memory lane, as she slowly unwrapped a gripping tale. A melange of tragedy, remorse, anger, humour and irony peppered with scandal, sex and passionate lurid love affairs keeping me riveted to my chair.

That was until now, until today's earth shattering bombshell! What on earth! Was she insane? Had I heard her right? Unbelievable! Just…' 'Well I did try to warn you Mary. Now for Goodness! Sake! Close your mouth before you catch a fly!' Unable to stomach any more I hastily rose from the old woman's bedside, made a feeble excuse and made my getaway fighting to overcome waves of nausea and revulsion as I walked down the long hospital corridor oblivious to the throng pushing their way to the exit. Her words rang in my ears. I tried to shut them out. What that woman did was sheer, calculated evil, nothing more and nothing less. Indeed some would have said 'lock up the bitch and throw away the key!' Shuddering I tried to block out vivid, hideous, unbearable images laid buried for over half a century in dark recesses of Wilhelmina Potts' mind. The more I had listened to her pathetic excuses the more nauseated I had become feeling almost ashamed to be even related. But then I reflected who knows, maybe I might have been driven to react exactly the same way under such gruesome circumstances inwardly praying I had not inherited any of her genes. Maybe, just maybe, she had conjured it all up perhaps to seek attention for some obscure reason known only to her, although knew deep down in my heart she had spoken the truth for Great Granny Wilhelmina Potts never told lies, not even little white ones. A pillar of virtue, keen church goer, always there to lend an ear or a helping hand, this was the Great Granny Potts I had always known and loved who clung tenaciously to the old values of life. Had she been putting on an act all those years? Repentance perhaps in a desperate attempt to conceal the shocking truth I had momentarily been allowed to glimpse? Overtones of that notorious 'Profumo affair' that had rocked the country in the sixties sprang into mind then just as quickly discarded the notion. This was Granny Wilhelmina not some ex War Minister involved in espionage accused of betraying state top secrets to a prostitute, even, if decades later he had shown remorse by helping the poor and homeless in the East End of London.

I stopped just outside the building, with my back pressed against a rough bricked wall to keep me upright while I struggled to regain my composure. As the cold wind whipped across my face, my thoughts carelessly wandered back to when I had sat with Granny Wilhelmina. She had taken pains to explain her pet project, as she called it, was about Wilhelmina Potts' life, her family, her dreams, fears, joys, her achievements, her failures and, now that vile confession she had planned to take to her grave. What's worse is that she had hinted there was something else equally grave, equally dark, lurking in her past, but before I could ask any questions, she had quickly changed the subject refusing to resurrect another carefully concealed memory.

I dared to even think what that might reveal. What was it she had said 'my life was never a bed of roses, far from it, but I firmly believe Mary everyone rich or poor has a cross to bear because in some way, at some point, adversity will test every soul? We were all put on this earth to help others less fortunate and, at the end of the day what goes around will always come around. Never ever forget those words my dear because I … I did you see and I have lived to rue the day. I was foolishly stupid and if I had only known then what I know now.' Then lost in the realms of memory lane she had emitted a long deep sigh, stroked her wart and muttered 'so many hopes and dreams and not one came to fruition!'

As I sat waiting in anticipation for more jewels of wisdom to drop from my great grandmother's mouth I was alarmed to see her suddenly slump in her chair, a deathly pallor masked her face and her bottom lip began to quiver. A tear threatened to roll down her cheek. Embarrassed she had hastily brushed it away saying sharply under her breath 'Wilhelmina Potts pull yourself together, you know you have to do this whether you like it or not so just get on with it. They have to know and it is best it comes from you not idle gossip when you're 'pushing up the daisies!' she said as she regained her ironclad composure and with a back straight as she could muster, she took two deep breaths and resumed her incredible story.

'Many moons ago I was born into a totally different world, indeed it is hard to believe it was the same planet so much has changed. Nowadays of course it's the Technological Revolution, in my early days the Industrial Revolution was still shaping the globe. There was obscene luxury at one end of the scale and dire poverty at the other. Sadly, as always, disease also reigned, frequently claiming young lives before they could blossom, targeting unfortunate souls forced to lived in overcrowded hovels in polluted cities where the dreaded Tuberculosis, Cholera, Typhoid and Diphtheria were commonplace, rampaging through the land leaving a trail of devastation in their wake.

'More is the pity they didn't cart off Agatha Fortescue into her coffin!' Those latter words mumbled under her breath which were clearly not meant for me to hear, but unable to resist, I questioned 'excuse me Granny, umm... cart who off, what did you mean?' 'Oh! That is none of your business Mary! Now if you don't mind we must get on; I have already told you time is very precious so I shall thank you not to interrupt me.' She snapped, whilst giving me a piercing look that could turn people to stone.

Then with a softening of her expression she returned to memory lane depicting its stark contrast to the grinding poverty of the lowest of the low. There were to be found the cosseted, wealthy landowners sitting in their great mansions on their sprawling estates. 'I suppose you could say they were fat cats of their day, born with a spoon in their mouths, idling away their time playing games and sport often involving and enjoying the kill of some poor, defenceless creature. That sadly is something that still goes on today.' Then with anger in her voice she spits 'I'd like to take a pot at those folk, I would, with their double-barrelled shot-guns. They make my blood boil; all God's creatures with a right to be here I say.'

Great granny had this annoying habit where she would suddenly go off at a tangent, get on her soapbox and then having spoken her mind, she would turn to you with a puzzled stare and say 'now what was it we were talking about before dear, it has completely gone out of my head?' and with a small frustrated sigh I replied 'I believe you mentioned the aristocracy.' 'Oh yes! Those ladies were more concerned keeping up with the latest fashions, barking orders at their servants and spending hours just changing their clothes umpteenth times a day. Of course I never came from wealthy stock, but suppose I figured somewhere in between, as my father was an optician. Though later I did get a taste of life in service, but I shall save that tale for another day. Now I am feeling rather tired Mary; I think I shall have a little snooze so run along dear. I will see you tomorrow.' She said in a dismissive tone.

Though ever since she had dropped that bombshell I debated whether I could continue with her project, but then curiosity won out. There were certain questions that needed answers, so the following day I once again returned to the hospital and sat by her bedside.

This time I found granny tucking into a large bag of fruit jellies, carefully picking out all the red and green sweets, lining them up like a child. 'Now then Mary', popping one into her mouth, 'just remind me dear where we were again.' 'I believe you were about to speak of your father?' 'Oh Yes! Him! Edward Crabtree, a typical Victorian, spare the rod, spoil the child was his motto and believe me, you couldn't sit down for a week after he ...'

Stopping mid-sentence she cleared her throat and reached for a drink in her haste to dismiss extremely uncomfortable memories that had been safely buried away. 'Now, that's quite enough of that, I'm sure we can find more pleasant topics,' she said as she put a careful smile on her face, attempting to change the subject back to safer ground. 'He used to have a practice in London, if memory serves me, although according to gossip he spent more time with his whores in the capital than ever actually practising. I remember he often used to look down his nose at people, belittling them with his harsh words; he was a most unpleasant little man, was my father. I failed to understand what my mother ever saw in him, they say love is blind. Kathleen Crabtree could have captured the heart of any man, with her dark tumbling locks, porcelain skin and eyes which were as blue as the forget-me-not's that bloomed in the summer and were framed with long sweeping lashes that left shadows on her cheeks. She had a gentle, compassionate nature, making sure she always had time to help the needy and less fortunate. Salt of the earth is what you'd call her.' She stopped with a soft smile as she dabbed her eyes with a clean handkerchief, before returning to her memories.

'Now, my father was a different kettle of fish, small in stature, with a heart made of stone, cold impenetrable stone. A man so cold he could not even relate to his own children, would you believe! We were his cross to bear, he said, a burden to him, nothing more, and nothing less.

There were four of us, Hector, Harry, Charlotte and me, the baby of the family, all gone now, except me of course, and I don't expect I will have to wait too long before I join them.' Collating her thoughts she stared down at her gnarled, aged hands, stroked her wedding ring, then took a deep breath and looked away, gathering the strength to continue. After a few minutes of silence, she began to speak again.

'As long as I draw breath I shall never forget that day. The clock in the nursery had just struck eleven when we received an order from father to go downstairs and wait in the parlour of our small but neat Victorian house; we all huddled in a fever of anxious anticipation. Outside a strong, gusty, cold March wind howled and moaned while rain beat down hard on the windowpanes. Childish intuition warned us something terrible had occurred as an unusual eerie silence had befallen the household that day, an oppressive, melancholic atmosphere enveloped it. Earlier that morning Charlotte had heard the maids whispering to one another, 'what will become of us if the master throws us out on to the streets? Where will we go? What will become of the bairns?' She noticed that their eyes were red from weeping. Nothing escaped my sister you see, for it was she who had once witnessed father shout and curse, hurl a glass into the fireplace then keel over having hit the bottle for three days. She was only seven years old then, I believe, but wise beyond her years. Anyway, there we stood lined up in the parlour each of us dreading his entrance.

I can still remember that room as if it were just yesterday. It was usually adorned with a vase of fresh flowers or sprigs of evergreen and was my mother's special place, her retreat. She would often sit in there engrossed in a favourite classic. If she wasn't reading she would be industriously making clothes for some waif and stray she had found on the streets. On the far wall hung a portrait of a young blushing bride in white lace and satin. I recall staring at the warm, kind face as she lovingly gazed down at the little dog in her arms which, in turn, was looking up at her with dark brown, adoring eyes. She had named the spaniel Lucky, a Cavalier, I believe, although my mother could not have chosen a more inappropriate name as time would reveal. On the opposite wall was a painting of her husband in his youth though, even then, it was plain to see he had an air of arrogance about him. Underneath it was a photograph of my brother Harry as an infant sat on his mother's lap dressed to look more like a girl than a boy, such being the custom.

I can still see him trembling at the knees as we waited for father to appear, for Harry knew no matter how innocent he was, he would still find some excuse to beat him. Hardly surprising, Harry had developed a terrible stammer that infuriated Edward Crabtree whose response was to painfully humiliate his son by comparing him to his younger brother Hector. Chalk and cheese they were, one brother keen to take on the world, the other looking for the nearest corner to hide in it.'

Granny's voice suddenly began to falter falling to a barely audible whisper. 'Many... many decades have passed and... much water has flowed under the bridge but I can still recall every single detail of that scene, played it over in my mind so many times you see. My father entered the room in his customary fashion, barking orders 'stop slouching, no talking, pay attention!' the silence so profound you could have heard a pin drop, not one of us dared to move each of us standing up as straight as possible, with our shoulders back so far that our chests puffed out. Each set of eyes focused on the floor listening to the loud thud of our beating hearts as he proceeded to inspect the line as if it were soldiers preparing for drill.

Suddenly Harry shrieked as he felt the sting of a birch twig aimed without mercy on the seat of his pants being unjustly accused of fidgeting, but even he was struck dumb by father's next words. 'If you are all wondering why I have ordered you to come here today, well it is to inform you that your mother has been found dead, burnt to a cinder apparently in a fire along with some old woman she had gone to visit. It was entirely her own fault of course, I forbade her to go but she disobeyed me. Anyway she has now gone to the Lord's Dominions and her remains will be put in the ground as soon as I have made the necessary arrangements. As the bible says 'The Lord giveth and the Lord taketh away'. Then totally ignoring the fact the sky had just fallen in on us, he cleared his throat and declared. 'I shall shortly be closing the house and moving to London. My sister, Aunt Matilda, has very kindly offered a roof over your heads, as long as you earn your daily bread of course and do not shirk your duties. You will be leaving tomorrow. That is all I have to say, dismissed' then with a sharp turn he marched out of the room.

I still remember Charlotte whispering in my ear 'it's probably some other woman's body they found, mother will soon be back with us Wilhelmina, you'll see,' voicing a forlorn hope as we left the room. I was left wondering how could this have happened and what, and where, were those Dominions, I wanted to know?

You see, like most children at the tender age of five I had regarded my mother as being clothed in immortality refusing to believe I would never again hear her silver voice, look into those beautiful azure eyes or, feel her loving embrace and, something else, something that only a mother's love can give to protect her young from the evils of a cruel, unforgiving world. I can still remember, even to this day, the floor swayed or so it seemed, and this lump in my throat that I couldn't swallow. I wanted to scream out, 'NO SHE IS NOT DEAD!' but no words would come. I was screaming from within, only able to gasp like a fish pulled from water, only aware of the gnawing, searing pain that seemed to reach into my body ripping it apart and leaving a gaping hole. I was struck by grief mixed with fear, fear of the unknown. I turned to search Charlotte's face and saw the tears she had been fighting to hold back, as she too struggled with this new reality. She couldn't let father see her cry, he hated tears with a vengeance, you see. To him they displayed weakness and in his book visible emotions were never featured on any page. He lived by the stiff upper lip that must be seen to rule at all times, this included funerals.

A week later I stood beside the open grave with my siblings at the service, clutching my handful of earth to sprinkle on to the coffin, allowing the endless stream of tears to roam freely down my cheeks. I suddenly felt my sister's fingers curl tightly around mine before tugging me back, away from the six foot precipice on which I teetered. Had she foreseen what I was about to do? I just could not imagine a world without those maternal loving, protective arms and this way I would not need to, they would be wrapped around me for eternity.

I remember looking up at the sky that day, it was not grey and miserable to match my mood. Instead there were patches of blue, almost forget-me-not blue and I felt a soft breeze gently touch my face while a bird soared high above. It was as if she was trying to say to me those famous words -

> Do not stand at my grave and weep
> I am not there; I do not sleep.
> I am a thousand winds that blow
> I am the diamond glints on snow.
> I am the sunlight on ripened grain
> I am the gentle autumn rain
> When you awaken in the morning's hush
> I am the swift uplifting rush
> Of quiet birds in circled flight
> I am the soft stars that shine at night
> Do not stand at my grave and cry
> I am not there; I did not die.

And I can still hear Charlotte whispering in my ear 'Wilhelmina have you forgotten 'what the caterpillar perceives is the end, to the butterfly is just the beginning?'

Then with a sudden abruptness, Granny turns away from me. 'Now Mary that's quite enough talking for today, I'm going to have a nap now and I really must pay a little call, so if you don't mind dear'... I took the hint, but as I was gathering my things to leave, I caught her staring at the ceiling and heard her mutter under her breath, 'please, Lord, please give me the courage to tell them. Help me make them all understand, particularly Mildred and Amy, and please spare me some more time.' And with that I left her alone, to remember her mother, in peace, telling myself those unanswered questions still buzzing round my head could wait, unaware their incredible responses would later make me wish I had never asked them in the first place.

2

Agatha Esmerelda Fortescue

The following day after the doctor's routine visit usually around half past ten each morning, I returned to the ward only to find Granny Wilhelmina's bed empty. Fearing the Grim Reaper had decided to take her in the night, overwhelming relief swept over me when a nursing assistant struggling to manoeuvre a wheelchair, that had a mind of its own called out 'Mrs Potts has only gone down to X-ray. She should be back soon dear.' With a wave of thanks, I took my usual seat and waited for her to return.

About 10 minutes later, I greeted her with a cheery smile and my typical 'Good morning Granny'. Only to notice the disgruntled expression upon her face and wondered if I should come back later. 'No! It most certainly is not, a good morning!' She retorted. While trying to stifle a wide yawn she announced 'the doctors still refuse to let me go home and I've not had a wink of sleep thanks to her in the corner there, snored and snorted her head off all night she did. That woman could wake the dead! I do declare! It is hard enough doing my little project without needing match sticks to prop my eyes open! Would you believe she still carried on making that unearthly racket after I dragged myself from my nice warm bed to give her a poke with my stick! Really, some people have no consideration, none whatsoever!' Resisting an urge to raise my eyebrows, turning my head I inquisitively strained my neck to see 'her in the corner there' spotting a little obese, middle aged lady enveloped in a fluorescent lime green bed jacket, clicking furiously away with a pair of knitting needles. She then held up the unfinished garment as a nurse approached her bed and in a loud broad Scottish accent heard her say 'it's going to be a wee matinee coat for our Maggie's brand new bairn, a wee lassie finally after seven lads. Och! She had a terrible time though, practically four days in labour, then her husband went and passed out at the birth, would…' 'Mary! Stop staring and do not listen in to other people's conversations it is extremely rude,' Granny suddenly intercepted as if reprimanding a small child. 'Anyway, I am talking so kindly pay attention. Now where was I again dear?' Before I could reply 'Goodness knows when I shall be seeing my own bed now they have decided to do some more tests and stick needles in me as if I were a pin cushion. I shall have to call Mildred to come and get me out of this dreadful place but, in the meantime Mary we have work to do.' Why Mildred, her niece I wondered, had she forgotten they had not even spoken properly to one another for years? 'Now pass me my stick dear.' With that she slowly endeavoured to lift her aged frame from her chair then leaning on her walking aid, refusing my assistance I watched her slowly pick up a large, well worn and capacious black handbag from her locker. What secrets I wondered did that hold?

'Now if you recall I told you earlier that father had arranged for his sister to take charge of us but it so happened that not long after mother passed away Aunt Matilda was taken ill so we were passed like a parcel to another of father's relations an Aunt Gertrude or, was it Geraldine? Anyway she was a funny old stick and reminded me of a mouse scuttling about the place with little beady eyes that never missed a thing. Would you mind just passing me my other spectacles dear? I believe I have a picture of her somewhere in this bag. Umm…That's rather odd I was certain it was in here. Ah! Yes! Here it is,' handing me a faded brown photograph bearing a crease down the centre. 'There she is. Do you see her? She's stood at the back,' pointing to a stern faced, scowling woman probably in her forties, wearing a long plain dark dress and wide brimmed hat. 'You know, I used to think as very young children naively do, she had some secret eyes tucked away in between all the hairpins in the back of her head and, she was father's spy. I never trusted her not for one minute but, neither had I appreciated that old saying 'better the devil you know than the devil you don't.'

I believe I mentioned earlier my father had a voracious sexual appetite for the fairer sex, considered himself an Adonis, Charlotte used to say, God's gift to women, I believe you would probably say nowadays. Ignoring my shocked expression at her words she went on 'so I was not surprised to see him escorting a woman when he arrived to pay us a visit one day not long after my sixth birthday, I believe.

There he stood in my aunt's drawing room with his arm entwined through hers reminding me of the proverbial cat that had swallowed the cream or, maybe I should say had just pounced on its prey held tight in its clutches. My father never ever took 'no' for an answer you see. On first impressions I recall wanting to giggle. They looked such an odd pair, father being barely over five feet, not a single hair to his head, rather stout and sported a long handlebar moustache whilst his companion was huge, maybe eleven or twelve stone definitely not a spring chicken and towered over him. She was part African part Jamaican if I recall and had dressed in fashionable finery of lace and taffeta but my instincts told me she was most definitely not a lady. There was something else, something that ran shivers down my spine and made the hairs stand up on the back of my neck besides the cold glint in her eye.

Beside her stood an unkempt small boy with one finger pushed up his nose as high as he could reach whilst another poked and picked an ear then to my further disgust he next placed the digit he had inserted into his nose straight into his mouth. Sniffing and snorting he presented such an obnoxious first impression I have never forgotten and never shall. 'Horace Oswald!' His mother suddenly shrieked at same time launching her right hand to box her son's ears. 'Remember your manners!' At that point my father quickly intervened to introduce the newcomers saying 'this is Miss Agatha Fortescue and her son Horace, come and shake hands children,' he sternly commanded. Utterly repulsed by both mother and son I remember watching as she slowly extricated from a long black glove a claw bearing long, scarlet painted fingernails. Then a thunderbolt struck, icy waters of reality washed over me as I realised the gossip had been true the servants had been whispering for there was the evidence staring me in the face. Feeling sickened to the pit of my stomach I wanted to scratch her eyes out and yell 'How Dare You!' You see Mary, glinting in a shaft of sunlight from the afternoon sun was a large emerald stone on her left hand. Anger, shock, fear, hatred welled up inside me. I was longing to shriek 'Traitor' at my father. My reaction had not gone unnoticed however, by Miss Fortescue who looked me straight in the eye and said 'aint it the most beautiful thing you ever did see? Your father and I got betrothed.' She said as if it was the most wonderful thing in the world. In my eyes, the sheets had not even gone cold before he had found her to warm his bed and to add to my misery it was my mother's engagement ring that had been squeezed on to her grubby fat finger. 'Children, Miss Agatha is going to be your new mother and you will be living under her roof,' he told us. 'Now come, give her a kiss and pay your respects.' All you heard was deafening silence! That was until my sister, throwing all caution to the wind, exuding all her pent up emotion suddenly shouted at the top of her voice 'NO! I would rather kiss a toad! Who does she think she is? I'll tell you, she is nothing but a cheap ugly slut, one of father's whores. I've seen her before leaving their bedroom, when mama was alive. She's a scary old hag I would sooner see her dead than ever be our mother. Miss Fortescue and her horrid, disgusting son can go and burn in hell for all I care!' And, on those words, tears cascading down her cheeks, she flounced out of the room and up the stairs leaving everyone standing with gaping mouths. Nobody, you see, ever flouted father's authority let alone dared to criticize his behaviour unless they were prepared to take the consequences, being none too pleasant I might add. Taken aback by my sister's open hostility I recall Agatha Fortescue suddenly gasped 'Well! I have never been so insulted in all my life! What a monstrous child, that girl needs to be punished one that she will always remember Edward. Your daughter needs to learn some respect.'

'Agatha dear I can assure you Charlotte will receive the whipping of her life then her mouth washed out with vinegar and a bar of soap for such insolence.'

'And you think that will be enough do you Edward? Well I do not! I most certainly do not! Did you hear what she said about us and that is all you intend to do Edward?' I saw Agatha Fortescue's thin lips curl and those cruel eyes narrow as they glared up towards the staircase. There was something vicious, hideous and petrifying in that face, something unforgettable. Suddenly she grabbed my hand in a vice like grip saying to her husband to be 'I think your children and I need to have a little talk Edward. We need to get a few things straight.' As she grabbed my hand I felt her long nails deliberately dig into my palm, snake eyes bore into my very soul and hairs prickle on the back of my neck. Eyes wide with fear I felt the earth tremble as she hissed and spat something that will stay with me until my dying day.

'This is a warning to all of you, listen carefully because I shall not tell you again. Anyone who dares to cross Agatha Fortescue does so at their peril. Should anyone try they will sorely live to regret it for the rest of their life, because you see children I believe in taking an eye for an eye, a tooth for a tooth or a hand for a hand, and I can assure you that before the next solstice your sister will be dearly wishing she had held her spiteful little tongue.' She then started to cackle emitting a ghastly, eerie noise. I remember childish instincts screaming out 'danger, run away!' But there was nowhere. Venom, sheer unadulterated venom from every pore that woman oozed and that was why I... umm... I...' Granny Wilhelmina suddenly began to tremble and shiver. 'Oh! Someone has just walked over my grave, she whispered. 'I have no wish to discuss the subject any further, not the likes of her, that's for sure.' Did this scary woman hold some posthumous, awesome power over

Granny Wilhelmina, I wondered? The old lady refused to discuss any more dark secrets in her past asserting 'that woman has long been dead and buried and I have no wish to dig her up, let her rot and may her soul burn in the devil's eternal flames.' An uneasy silence ensued between us. A few seconds later granny surprised me by saying with a heavy sigh 'no! I have changed my mind. There are certain things people should know before it is too late but, not now, it is almost time for my dinner so if you'll excuse me my dear I must tidy my hair and pay a little call.'

I stared at the green, watery soup, which a busy nurse had placed hastily in front of her. 'Asparagus is it?' 'No, Mary it is pea and I believe that could be a speck of ham floating on the surface.' I soon found my thoughts turning from Granny's green, unappetizing lunch once more to Agatha Fortescue. Treading on eggshells I ventured on 'do you remember saying to me the other day that you could never find it in your heart to forgive? What did you …' I stopped mid-track having suddenly witnessed the old lady's expression, a long hard icy glare. 'Let me get on with my soup Mary; I do not like to see my food going cold. Anyway that is none of your business; you ask too many questions.'

A familiar awkward silence followed as she finished her first course then dabbed her mouth with her serviette and pushed the bowl to one side. 'You must forgive me Mary my bark is worse than my bite my dear. Some things are best left alone for one never knows what can happen even from beyond the grave when things get disturbed. You see Agatha Fortescue was a dangerous, nasty piece of work, Satan incarnate folks whispered. They talked of strange happenings in the woods. Black cloaked figures, stone circles, chants, a sacrificial table bearing the remains of a chicken or some other wretched creature that had had its throat cut and died an agonising death. She had been followed, you see. Everyone knew she worshipped the Occult for the pendants around her neck bearing the symbols of a scarab, an inverted pentagram and the all seeing eye of Lucifer, king of hell, were plain evidence for all to see. They feared her power knowing doom would befall he who dared to speak out against her. Wild, gruesome rumours abounded, tales of black cauldrons containing blood and gore, guarded by old, toothless hags chanting indiscernible sounds. Some I believe told of a heinous, secret ritual involving a coffin and razor blades, and others just whispered to one another 'the beans!'

They meant the African Calabar beans known to kill. I remembered reading about this bean in a newspaper which also went by another name, the Ordeal Bean. Originating from the capital of Cross River State in south eastern Nigeria, the plants, sometimes reaching up to fifteen metres tall, bore a brown bean containing an alkaloid. Similar to a nerve gas this alkaloid disrupts communication between nerves and muscles resulting in seizures, copious salivation, paralysis and ultimately death. Apparently in the early Middle Ages in ancient trials these beans were administered to any unfortunate soul accused of witchcraft the belief being if the victim died it was because they were guilty but if the bean was rejected by the stomach then the accused would be declared innocent. Also the Calabar bean had no bitter taste nor did it have a characteristic smell and bore nothing to distinguish it from any harmless legume. What's more, it could not on forensic examination be found in the body. I was beginning to see why Granny Wilhelmina had feared the wrath of Agatha Fortescue whose spies I was to learn crawled out of the woodwork.

Having eaten less than a sparrow she turned her attention once more to her pet project saying 'well Mary, I've now opened this huge can of wriggling maggots so I may as well continue. Where were we again? Let me see.' Stroking her wart whilst trying to collate her thoughts she looked away and emitted another long familiar sigh then returned to her intriguing past.

'I recall not long after Agatha Fortescue's eventful introduction, father quickly set the date for his second wedding spurred on by his fiancée, late August I believe or, was it the spring? Anyway, whenever it was, it frequently figured in my nightmares but certain things still remain clear as day, despite the passing of the decades, like the need to pinch my nose as I entered the church. There was a foul stench you see, a sour fusty smell resembling old mothballs, rotten eggs and rancid milk that permeated the nostrils soon as we stepped into the building which incidentally, in those days, stood alone in the middle of a field. I remember having to traipse across muddy, swampy ground trying to avoid the earth swallowing my shoes or tripping over a rabbit hole whilst feeling crushed with despair, anger and boiling resentment, until suddenly inspiration dawned.

A hasty plan began to form in my mind as I remembered a conversation I had overheard one day. Dare I do it? I asked myself. Dare I really do that? The answer was, you have to Wilhelmina; what other way is there? The voice of the Reverend droned on and on extolling the virtues of love and obedience until suddenly he had arrived at the dreaded moment 'if anyone here knows of any impediment as to why Edward and Agatha should not be joined together in holy matrimony let them speak now or forever hold their peace?' Here was my chance. It was now or never. I had to act before it was too late but just as I was picking up some shreds of courage to stand up, a scratchy voice in the midst of the congregation suddenly shouted 'I do! It's a charade, it aint legal, 'er, pointing to the bride, is still married to me brother see and he aint gonna give 'er a divorce. She can whistle 'e told me till cows come 'ome and she's tried to bump… '

'Umm… thank you madam,' the Reverend suddenly intervened as the sea of faces in the congregation sat there open mouthed, some who had a penchant for gossip clearly enjoying the little spectacle. Emboldened by this dramatic revelation I decided it was time to add my two penny worth into the pudding, so I then stood up and announced in a voice as loud as I could muster 'Agatha Fortescue is a wicked, horrid, evil woman.' A thousand eyes seemed to fall upon me. 'They say she killed her first husband. She's a witch you see and she casts spells, real horrible spells that make bad things happen to people she doesn't like. And she strings up animals,' adding as an afterthought before sitting back down.

There was a stunned silence until from somewhere in the church a loud guffaw rang out echoing in the rafters. 'For pity sake, get on with it man,' my father, red faced with both embarrassment and anger, curtly instructed the vicar. 'Of course there is no impediment. Ignore the stupid child; I shall deal with her shortly.' A dark, fierce glare shot my way and two minutes later I was unceremoniously thrown out amongst the gravestones that told me in no uncertain terms he would keep his word. 'As for her, pointing to the owner of the scratchy voice, 'she cooked all that stuff up because she's just plain jealous. You see she wanted me to wed her instead of my beautiful bride standing beside me who I adore and will for eternity my dear,' looking into Agatha's eyes as he spoke who was eyeing him with anger and suspicion. 'I am telling you if she, pointing again to the woman in the congregation, was the last woman on this earth I would not touch her with a barge pole. Now Reverend, hurry up and wed us man. I have not got all day.' Amid a buzz of recriminating whispers the vicar hurriedly raced through the ceremony but now I had cause to fear Agatha Fortescue all the more.

After the honeymoon, I believe it was Paris they chose, he stuck to his plan and ensconced us all into her abode being more spacious than his own in London. It was rumoured to be haunted. I hated living in her old house, I believed it dated back to the sixteenth century with its tortuous dark passages many culminating with long black heavy curtains that eerily moved sending my childish imagination wild. What monster lurked behind? Cold as the grave, oppressive and unwelcoming it made a mockery of the old tapestry that hung in the parlour depicting 'Home Sweet Home.' Another picture meticulously worked in thread hung nearby read 'Home Is Where the Heart

Is' but this house had no heart. It never echoed to the sound of children's laughter. There was no music or singing. No one walked into its rooms or down its long corridors with a light spring in their step, for the devil was at work within and fear stalked those four walls. Apart from a handful of servants who had one by one packed their bags, those left were mostly her old cronies whose joints had slowly stiffened up from the cold, arthritis having paid them a visit and refused to leave. Aged protruding veins on the back of their hands resembled a gnarled tree. There was one such tree, an ancient oak whose branches proudly reached for the sky, that had been planted behind the west wing of that old, grim house. One day I decided to explore that wing which had been long ago closed off from the main hubbub.

I found the rooms had all been securely locked, that is, except one. Peering inside I let my imagination carry me away. Furniture draped in white covers became hideous ghostly shapes in the dim glow of a flickering solitary candle with the dark curtains being tightly shut. Was this the room that Gladys Pritchard walked the boards emitting a pitiful, eerie wail when the clock tower struck midnight? Legend had it that Gladys had broken her neck having fallen down the narrow, stone staircase nearby on her way to meet her lover. Was she pushed? Did someone murder her? Nobody knows and never will - only Gladys! If only the dead could talk. I was to discover that the ghost of Gladys Pritchard would pale in insignificance, compared to what awaited me.

3

The Prisoner

True to her words before the next solstice Agatha Fortescue took her pound of flesh, but it was some time before I learned the truth of what actually happened that day, for my sister never spoke of it to anyone. She had kept a secret diary which she later sent, via the local vicar, to me hidden between some letters. As I leafed through it I remember coming across a certain page which had been turned down at the top corner, but as I struggled to read my sister's hieroglyphics, I felt a huge lump come into my throat and tears prick my eyes. I couldn't believe what I was reading.

The Diary of Charlotte Crabtree

'Today I was summoned to stepmother's room. I had no choice, but to go. On the way Annie, our parlour maid, stopped me in my tracks and whispered in my ear 'take care Miss Charlotte, remember to hold your tongue dear, that she-devil's got a bee in her drawers today, make no mistake!'

'That woman doesn't scare me,' I told her. I knew only too well, I had humiliated and insulted Agatha Fortescue and despite the welts and bruises father had administered, she was still seeking her own revenge. Biding her time waiting until her husband had conveniently left the house for a few days.

I could feel my heart pounding in my chest, aware that every step was taking me closer and closer to the lion's lair. Then, having reached the threshold, I stood for a few seconds, mustering up some courage, whilst staring but not seeing those strange carvings of two conjoined snakes intertwined, with their long protruding tongues circling the heavy knocker. I lifted it, let it drop with a 'BANG!' then waited. After what seemed like an eternity, a familiar sharp rasping voice bid me enter.

If only I had listened to that little voice in my head telling me 'turn back Charlotte; it's not too late! Don't go through there. You'll be sorry.' I ignored it having no time for cowardice. Instead took a deep breath, placed my sweaty palm around the handle then pushed open the heavy creaking door and passed through the black curtain into her chamber. In the dim light I almost knocked over a large urn. Panic pulsed through me, as I reached out to grab it terrified the vessel might shatter into a thousand pieces spilling ghastly remains over the floor.

Then I saw her, dark and formidable, framing the window, standing in stony silence, with her back to me like a thunderous black cloud ominous and threatening. She suddenly spun around to face me, still said nothing, letting the silence increase my fear. Like two blades of steel her eyes flashed towards me. Ugly, flaccid features were contorted with rage whilst clenched white knuckles tautly gripped something by her side, something that could only be seen in the very worst of nightmares. I decided to make a run for it, but with lightening speed, she grabbed my arm then violently pushed me over as she rushed ahead to lock the door. Looking me straight in the eye, forcing me to watch in horror, she next let out an eerie cackle as she undid the top button of her dress and slipped the key into her bosom. I was trapped!

There was no escaping from the lion's den. A wave of hysteria swept over me and I screamed at the top of my lungs 'Help! Help Me! Help!' it was only then I remembered no-one ever lingered near Agatha Fortescue's quarters. Instinctively I looked around for something, anything I could use to defend myself then remembered the urn, I had carefully tried to rescue only a few minutes before. Every time I tried to get up from the floor to reach it she would raise the cat o' nine tails high into the air then bring it down with a sickening crack onto my back, shoulders and legs. Emitting a familiar, horrible, unearthly cacophony that rang though my ears as searing pain overwhelmed my body.

Out of desperation I curled myself up into a tight ball, trying to protect my head with my arms. It was only later that I saw the deep cuts and bloody welts her vengeance had wrought. For now I was at her mercy. Then a seething anger suddenly exploded within me and I decided I wasn't going to take this without putting up a fight. Like a vicious wild cat I threw myself at her, lashing out with claws, scratching, biting and even spitting, whatever I could do to survive. Within seconds I was overpowered and again pushed to the floor, hitting my head hard on the boards, the whip remained unyielding with its hunger for my blood and flesh.

My heart almost stopped as I looked up at her face, for it didn't seem human; it made my blood run cold. Once again she threw her head back and let out that horrible, raucous laugh that I detest. With the lash hovering over my head, she then started to circle me whilst chanting strange words. I truly believe she was calling for Satan to unleash all his power into her body so she could…'

Granny Wilhelmina suddenly fell silent wearing a troubled expression as she pulled her lace handkerchief from her sleeve and wiped away the tear trickling down her cheek. It was a few minutes before she spoke again, then with passion and deep conviction in her voice she said… 'And Mary what happened next to my poor dear sister I can't ever forgive nor forget. Indeed I swore on my mother's grave that as long as I drew breath Agatha Fortescue would be made to pay for her heinous crime . Even now when I close my eyes I can still see my sister's shaky handwriting, as she tried to describe something so horrific, so appalling, and so inhuman that ever since has been indelibly imprinted on my mind.'

The harrowing memories, almost too much to bear, made the old lady begin to tremble as she tried to stop her tears from falling. After what seemed like an eternity, but in reality probably was only two, maybe three minutes, I waited for Granny to continue, watching her with her head in her hands staring down at her lap, as she struggled to find the right words. I wondered if instead I should leave her to rest, but before I could voice my concern, she swallowed hard and continued on in a strained whisper.

'Mary, I almost passed out when I read Charlotte's words on the next page of her diary. To think how my poor sister must have suffered, it just breaks my heart to even contemplate it.

'That she-devil, that sorry excuse for a human being, then grabbed me by my hair and proceeded to drag me across the floor. For a few horrific seconds I was gripped in sheer, paralysing terror. Then just like a dam bursting its wall a sudden wave of adrenaline surged through my body and I desperately put up another violent struggle, resisting the intense pain from my scalp. It was to no avail, once again her massive strength overpowered me. I was just a child and it was like fighting Goliath, hopeless.

Between piercing shrieks of 'HELP ME!' sobbing, screaming, I begged for mercy, apologising for having insulted her. With a smug smile twisting her evil face she spat 'No-one can hear your screams Charlotte, I gave explicit orders we were not to be disturbed. You are simply wasting your breath my dear.' No words can ever describe that tidal wave of panic and hysteria that swept over me when she reached the fireplace then pinned me down to the floor with her knee on my chest and removed a white hot poker from the flames. 'I warned you!' she hissed 'it would be perilous to cross me, that you would live to regret it. You see my dear I believe in taking an eye for an eye or, maybe I should say a hand for a hand.' She suddenly swooped and viciously grabbed my tightly clenched fist, piercing my skin with her long sharp talons forcing it open and then… pain, agonising, excruciating pain, the likes I have never known and the smell of burning flesh, … my flesh …'

Overcome with emotion Granny stopped to brush away another tear running down her face and hurriedly tried to unravel the lace handkerchief she had once again wrapped tightly around her finger. Whilst dabbing her eyes, she struggled to speak, in broken sentences, as she tried to describe how that barbarian had slowly branded her sister's tender young palm, with the symbol of an inverted pentagram, used in the Occult to attract sinister forces.

I must have fainted, everything went black' Charlotte had written, 'even losing consciousness, gave me no merciful respite from my agony, a bucket of icy water was thrown over my head. Through my intense throbbing pain I heard the viper spit 'nobody ever crosses your stepmother, not without dire regret. At every corner you turn Charlotte Crabtree, when they see that mark on your hand you will be shunned, by every man, woman and child for the rest of your days. I am not finished with you yet' and as she spoke she allowed the poker to slip from her hand and drop on to Charlotte's arm. Completely ignoring my sister's screams the Jezebel then spat 'you shall be locked up for five days, allowed only bread and water, whilst you sit in the dark and reflect on my words.' Another stab of pain shot through me as the witch's boot delivered a hard blow to my ankle, demanding that I get up from the floor.

'My whole body felt on fire yet I was shivering, having been drenched from head to toe. Feeling nauseous and totally exhausted I had absolutely no strength left to fight Agatha's iron grip. I lay sobbing and writhing in indescribable suffering, trying to protect my arm and burned palm. With the whip still in her grasp, she then dragged me, by my wounded hand, down badly lit steps, through a dark corridor, until we reached the bowels of that horrible rambling house.'

Granny turned to look at me with a distressed expression saying 'Charlotte was flung into that room as if she were nothing but a rag doll, she was left lying on the cold, wet floor of her dungeon fighting to remain conscious. I remember in her shaky hand my sister had scrawled … 'after a while I became aware of something else, something that made me take a sharp intake of breath. I realised to my horror that I was not alone. Just when I believed my life could not get any worse I was suddenly confronted with something that made my skin crawl. A large black rat was scavenging in the corner of the dark and dirty cellar that was infested with cobwebs and spiders.

Through sheer terror and determination I dragged myself to my feet and stumbled over to the door, although I knew in my heart that it was pointless. It was firmly locked. I tried hammering on it with my left hand, only stopping when my knuckles became covered in blood. I kept shrieking 'HELP! Someone Help Me, I am locked in the cellar. Please, Please Help Me,' but only silence answered my calls. It wasn't long, before I yielded to the excruciating pain that held my entire body in its jaws. I began shivering and shaking, my teeth chattering, as I was enveloped by waves of nausea. With my spirit broken, I slowly slumped back down to the floor until a sudden movement in the far corner of the cellar spiked my adrenaline levels yet again. Drawing my knees tightly up to my chin I tried hard to focus on the rodent in case heaven forbid it ran towards me.

As I hung my head in despair I suddenly noticed my dress; a large, dark, wet stain had appeared temporarily making me forget the fearsome creature. I tried to lift up my frock to investigate but found to my horror that the material had adhered to the deep, ugly gash in my thigh, where the whip left its mark. Very slowly and very carefully I endeavoured to peel the threads away whilst wincing in pain but as I fumbled in my pocket for a handkerchief, in an attempt to staunch the blood, I found something else that was to send me reeling into panic and hysteria. Instead of crisp, clean linen I pulled out a crumpled note on which someone had earlier scribbled some words. As I struggled to read them I gasped, my pain being momentarily forgotten shock having replaced it. 'There's a plot to kill you Miss Charlotte. Please, meet me tonight in the old cemetery at midnight. Don't be late. It's your only chance'. It was signed 'Well wisher.'

Who was this? How could they save me from this place? I knew somehow I had to escape; my life depended on it. Once again I fought the urge to pass out as the room started to spin, my vision began to cloud and everything started to fade into darkness. As I put my head in my hands, I could feel a large swelling on my temple. Another reminder of the evil Agatha Fortescue could inflict.

Desperately I tried to form a plan however the throbbing pain in my head made it impossible to think. Then I heard a voice saying 'Charlotte lift your eyes up to the Lord my dear from whence cometh your help.' I knew it was my mother talking to me from beyond the grave. What was the use? Nobody ever went near the old, dark cellars rumoured to be haunted by the ghost of Gladys Pritchard. Overwhelmed with despair, squeezing my mutilated, burned hand in an effort to relieve the constant agony I slowly fell on to my knees and said a silent prayer. Then with the last of my energy, I slithered to the floor and let the tears flow, sobbing and shaking.

It was sometime later that I heard a noise. What was that? …. Had my prayers been answered? Could it be … I strained hard to listen, I felt my heart miss a beat as I recognised the unmistakable sound of footsteps, heavy footsteps coming closer and closer. I waited with baited breath, terrified they might belong to Agatha Fortescue, hungry for another pound of flesh.

Silence! Had they turned back? I stared at my dungeon door and prayed waiting to hear them again. This time they were running down what sounded like a flight of stairs. Still holding my breath, I waited as a key was being hurriedly tried first one way then the other in the rusty lock. The heavy wooden door opened slowly with a menacing creak. I could hear heavy panting then someone urgently calling me, but when I tried to answer I found my voice was but a whisper and my legs threatened to fold under me as I tried to stand. With supreme effort I managed to half stagger, half crawl over to the door and squeeze my body through the tight gap, only to discover whoever had risked life and limb to help me had quickly disappeared.

I was free. Which way, do I turn left or right? Go straight ahead an inner voice answered seeing a steep flight of stone steps to the right. Renewed optimism had produced a hidden strength and not daring to pause for breath I bravely tried to ignore the pain and ran as fast as my legs would carry me, until I was stopped in my tracks. To my dismay facing me was a large ebony door, an imposing wooden structure which many decades before had been skillfully carved by craftsmen, now long gone. Looking upwards with pleading eyes, I struggled with just one hand to pull back the creaking bolt unaware a dreadful shock awaited me on the other side.

To my surprise I found myself inside a tunnel, my gateway to freedom and safety I told myself. The sheer darkness made me stumble frequently and I almost listened to the little voice saying 'turn back Charlotte; it is dangerous in here'. Something urged me to keep on going deeper and deeper through the dark passageway, though I had no sooner convinced myself it was my best option, when … Oh! My! Lord! What was that? I knew it was not my imagination; something had definitely brushed my shoulder. Consumed by fear, I slowly turned to look behind me.

In the darkness I was left blind, but I sensed that something was there, something twisted and macabre. I could feel its eyes watching me. Was it the ghost of Gladys Pritchard? As my eyes slowly adjusted to the dark, I noticed something moving, swinging to and fro in a grotesque, sinister, eerie fashion. Shivers tingled down my spine, every hair stood up on the back of my neck, my heart was pounding furiously and my forehead was glossed with beads of cold sweat. I clenched my knuckles, fighting desperately not to faint, for hanging from a large hook embedded in the tunnel wall I could dimly make out its outline. A disgusting, putrid smell filled the air making my nose wrinkle.

Covering my face with my hand, I quickly turned away and in doing so kicked something lying on the ground. Bending down to pick it up I discovered it was a dog collar. Fumbling carefully, I prayed I would not find a miniature cow bell that Harry had one day found in the woods and attached, but there it was. In that instant I knew I had unwittingly discovered the fate of our mother's favourite pet, a little brown and cream spaniel dog called Lucky, still just a pup when she had mysteriously disappeared.

Then a hideous, familiar cackle together with the sound of raised voices sent my adrenaline levels spiralling through the roof. Consumed with numbing terror I froze, pinning my body into a niche in the wall, trying to remain as still as a statue, hardly daring to breathe. Until a gasp of shock almost gave my position away, having learned something I had long suspected, something so repulsive I…'

Granny Wilhelmina's next words were suddenly drowned out on account of loud peals of the ward bell announcing that visiting time was over for another day. Startled and agitated Granny almost leapt out of her chair. 'Oh! Goodness! Gracious! Just look at the time Mary and I have not yet even scratched the surface. You must come back tomorrow; run along now dear, do not be late.' As I turned to leave she grabbed my wrist and said 'you must not judge me, no matter what you may hear.'

4

Horace Oswald Fortescue

The following day I rushed to my great grandmother's bedside not because she was ill, but because I was burning with curiosity to hear the next instalment. After grabbing a chair from the neat stack at the far side of the ward, I sat with my notebook and pen poised only to be reminded, 'now remember Mary no interruptions even if you sit there aghast! Now where was I?'

'Your sister's diary,' I prompted. 'She was hiding in the wall of the …'

'Oh yes! That! Well, you see, Charlotte was clever as well as beautiful, a winning combination, so she managed to escape from the tunnel. In fact it led to an old priest hole in the local church where a kindly vicar had found her and on hearing her story, he arranged for her to go overseas to France, where he had distant relatives. If only she had never set foot in that country, but you will see why later. Anyway the vicar had also witnessed the fear in folks' eyes, when they heard the black witch's name and knew Agatha Fortescue was indeed a force to be reckoned with, but he decided to leave that to the mysterious ways of the Almighty. However, in order to cover Charlotte's sudden disappearance Agatha fed us a lie, she said that Charlotte had been sent away to a convent to learn some manners, warning us if we tried to look for her we would be horse whipped to within an inch of our lives and I knew she meant every word. Although come to think of it, she must have wondered how my sister had escaped from the locked cellar. Of course none of us knew then, that she was living abroad.

It was at that point I suddenly became aware that my stepmother was watching my own every move; her narrow snake eyes seemed to be studying me as if she were waiting, biding her time. What was she plotting, I wondered? It wasn't long before I discovered that somebody else had also been watching me from the wings…'

The old lady fell silent, closed her eyes and swallowed hard. 'Oh! Dear! I am afraid this has all been a terrible mistake Mary; I can not go on with this project. I should never have started it in the first place; this was a bad idea, I should forget the whole thing. It's hard opening up old wounds that time had healed. I tried to bury the pain, you see, the rage, the hatred and bitterness long ago and now I …' Her voice trailed off, as she searched for her handkerchief, blew her nose like a trumpet and said, more to herself than me, 'no, they need to understand everything before they judge me. I have to do this.' As I sat in silence waiting for granny to continue, I wondered what else her pet project was going to reveal, she then turned to me and said out of the blue 'did I mention earlier dear that my father kept horses? No, perhaps I did not,' winding her lace handkerchief tightly round her finger as she spoke. 'One of his so called lady friends offered him a paddock and stables on a farm she owned, you see. I believe he went over to the Emerald Isle periodically to buy the ponies if my memory serves me. Anyway one day, one horrific, tragic day, when I was around fifteen, I went to the stables to tend a sickly foal that my father had threatened to shoot if it didn't improve, saying 'it's no good to me Wilhelmina; a sick animal cannot be sold for profit.' I asked if I could keep him and was told 'it will be dead by morning; you'll be wasting your time girl.'

My heart went out to the little creature I named Star, on account of a mark shaped as such on his right flank. He had a beautiful silky, jet coat; he would have made a handsome…'

She suddenly looked away, not wanting me to notice a tear threatening to roll down her cheek, then closing her eyes, biting her bottom lip she began to speak again. 'How long he had been there waiting I have no idea for I never heard a sound. Maybe I had been too engrossed talking to Star pouring out all my woes, to be aware of the stealthy footsteps that had been slowly creeping up behind me. Until I was suddenly thrown to the ground and a knife pressed against my throat, 'Scream and the foal dies' he spat. Ice cold fear swept over me as I realised to my horror the identity of my assailant, for there was no mistaking the stale, alcoholic breath as I struggled to wrench off his mask or the foul stench from unwashed sweat. He tore at the bodice of my dress, ripping it open exposing my heaving chest, my heart thumping violently from within. Then like a cat playing with its prey before going in for the kill he began to trace his blade over my breasts. Petrified for the foal's safety knowing he would have no qualms and, indeed would enjoy sadistically stabbing the little creature I struggled to grab the weapon but he held the blade aloft and began teasing me, sniggering, saying 'Come on then, catch it! Ah! You missed!'

A stream of blood ran down my arm as he suddenly swiped the blade into my hand. Like a bull teased with a red rag, my fear momentarily evaporated replaced by an overwhelming surge of anger, giving me renewed strength to fight. I aimed a well placed knee jerk, just where it hurt his male pride.'

The old lady suddenly paused, spotting my astonishment, and then she smiled and winked. 'Well, Mary isn't that any man's Achilles dear? That was a mistake, a very grave mistake. Incensed with rage he launched his steel capped boot into my shin then my ankle before pinning me down to the ground once more with his obese, foul smelling body. Then he said something that filled me with sheer unadulterated terror 'now Wilhelmina the horse gets it.' Tossing back his long, filthy black hair, no doubt covered in lice, he suddenly let out a hideous laugh as he lunged at the foal forcing me to watch helplessly as spurts of bright red arterial blood shot out of the animal's leg and I heard Star whimpering pitifully as his short life slowly ebbed away. Oh Mary, that dreadful sound still haunts me…. worse, far worse was yet to come. My step brother,' she spat, 'still had unfinished business. In those next few minutes I was about to find out how depraved, obnoxious and dangerous Horace Fortescue truly was.

Still holding a knife to my throat he then, to my utter horror and intense disgust, threw his head back and aimed a thick globule of green phlegm straight into my face smearing it down my cheek almost into my mouth and whispered five words in my ear. Five words which made my blood turn to ice in my veins and my heart pound furiously 'now it be your turn!'. With his filthy hand clamped over my lips and his knee pressing into my stomach, he suddenly wielded his blade into my chest, cutting, tearing into my flesh. No words can describe the intensity of that pain. Struggling with all my might to escape I sank my teeth deep into his fingers, almost to the bone. That was another blunder, a grave error, but this time, this time …'

Wilhelmina Potts voice trailed off again, as every emotion from that hideous scene sprang back to life making her eyes brim, her voice falter and her body tremble once again. She turned away trying to regain her self control by drawing slow, deep breaths and bowing her head. Then in broken syllables she whispered 'that son of the devil, an apology for a man, took his vile, cruel and cowardly revenge. While holding my jaw and body in a vice grip, forcing me to witness, he then did something that was so abhorrent, so repulsive, and utterly barbaric, I can not bear to even think about it. I didn't believe even he was capable of such a heinous act but I was wrong. The demon grabbed the foal knowing the poor creature was too ill to even stand … and…with his rusty blade carved a deep bloody welt along Star's back but then he… he…' Wilhelmina fell silent. Staring down into her lap she let out a sob, as she brushed away the tears spilling down her cheek while she battled to find her words mumbling 'another maggot in the box.'

I waited while she fumbled with her handkerchief, blowing her nose as she tried to compose herself. We could resume the project later, I suggested, but ignoring my words she said 'no Mary it has to be said. And only I can say it nobody else can!' After a deep breath she continued, 'He… he grabbed hold of the foal's ear and started hacking, cackling as if he were possessed … and I was powerless to do anything except scream, but it was futile. Within seconds his hand was round my throat, squeezing hard. I honestly believed I was going to die… I remember vomiting as he waved his grisly, dripping trophy in front of my face then, between clenched teeth he hissed in my ear 'next time Wilhelmina I shall take one of yours!'

Again I tried desperately to escape writhing and twisting my body like a snake but, it was useless. 'I've been watching you Wilhelmina', he spat 'been waiting for this moment for a long time. Now I'm going to savour every single minute' with a smile on his face and laughter in his voice he continued 'why, I do believe you're a little scared of me, how sweet.'

Paralysed with fear, I watched his filthy finger slowly trace a strange symbol on my blood soaked chest. Then the digit moved up to my face pretending to caress my cheek, whilst the sharp tip of his knife jutted into my throat. Terrified I retched with trepidation witnessing a crazed look in his eye, the look of a mad man intent on acting out his sick, perverted fantasies. Suddenly he emitted another high pitched cackle, just like his mother's, sniggering before spewing out something else, something that always accompanies my worst nightmares and something that has haunted me ever since. 'Wilhelmina Crabtree you are now the daughter of Satan and you belong to the devil. When your time comes, maybe today, maybe tomorrow, he will claim your soul. There will never be rest in peace for you, when you lie in your grave. You shall walk the road to hell, you shall fall down into its flames and you will burn forever.' Then he told me 'Satan will always be there watching you because now you bear his mark.'

I was to discover later on, Horace Oswald Fortescue had scarred me with a strange sign bearing the outline of an eye. Again I put up a violent struggle and managed to utter a weak scream only to receive another painful blow from his fist. Mutilation was not the only thing he had on his mind. I could feel his hot stinking breath on my face when he violently grabbed my head and tried to plant his thick slavering lips on my mouth, tightly clamped, then finding his advances rejected, felt the sharp tip of his weapon scratch my ear, drawing blood, before hissing into it his vicious, hideous threat. In desperation I fought with all my might to escape, clawing the monster with my nails, spitting into his eyes, mustering every last ounce of strength I possessed but, it was hopeless. He whispered in my ear 'go ahead Wilhelmina I like a good fight. It excites me, turns me on and nobody can hear ya' then slobbering and panting heavily with perverted excitement, he undid the belt holding up his trousers. Utterly exhausted and trapped, all I could do was grit my teeth, close my eyes tightly and pray that the horrendous ordeal would be over in a few seconds. Crazed with lust and possessed by demonic spirits he raped me again and again and again, his knife all the while being just a hairs breath away from my jugular, constantly repeating his ugly threat, to slice off my ear just as he had done to the foal if I didn't obey his obscene demands. Until finally, all his perverted energy was spent. I knew he had won; I had no choice, absolutely no choice.

As each year had passed Agatha's vile son had grown even more obnoxious, graduating from being a vindictive liar, thief and bully, to rape and torture who got immense obscene pleasure from seeing others suffer, whether they were human or animal was immaterial as long as he could feed his sadistic urges. I had no doubt my mother's dear little dog had also suffered at his hands as well as his mother's. Now that he had reached puberty testosterone surged through his veins giving him a voracious, dangerous sexual appetite and, whatever he lusted after he took, not caring how as long as he benefited. A chip off the old block his motto in life was 'if an injury has to be done to a man it should be so severe that his vengeance need not be feared.'

Eventually after what seemed an eternity he released me. Then pushing his face into mine, his foul breath making me retch even more, threatened 'if you choose to tell anyone of this Wilhelmina, Satan will ensure you never speak again. He will cut out your tongue; force it down your throat. You wouldn't want that now would you Wilhelmina?' Enjoying his power he threw his head back and laughed emitting a horrible evil sound that haunts my nightmares sending shivers down my spine. My body felt so dirty and violated I almost scrubbed it till it was raw.

I'm sure you can imagine my appalling horror, when I later discovered I was carrying his child. Of course I desperately tried all the old wives remedies to get rid of it, you know gin, hot baths, etc. but it was not to be. Neither did it take long for tongues to start wagging when the servants noticed me vomiting in the mornings but as the child grew within me it became harder to conceal and it was not long before my father intervened with a whip as well as words. Poking me in my belly, he screamed for the entire house to hear 'Wilhelmina Crabtree, you disgust me. You have brought shame to this family. Who is the father?' I tried to tell him I had been raped, but he would not listen. 'Your mother would turn in her grave if she could see you. Well! I'll not have you or your brat under my roof you can pack your bags and live on the streets for all I care. I have my reputation to consider. Now get out of my sight you whore. You are no daughter of mine and you are never to set foot across this threshold ever again. Get out and never come back!'

As it happened, Annie, one of our parlour maids, had heard the others gossiping and came to my aid, saying she knew of this woman who could help. 'Go and see old Mrs. Rogers, Wilhelmina. She's a midwife, helped my sister she did. You'll find her living in that old farmhouse at far end of Badger's Lane.' So with what few possessions I had, packed in an old, cloth bag, tucked under my arm. I set off to Badgers lane.

A woman in her late forties, looking weather-beaten and tired, was hanging out some sheets to dry in the yard, when I arrived. 'Ah! You must be Wilhelmina. Annie's told me all about you.' She said, as she approached. 'Now you can stay just till the child comes then you'll have to leave. Can't afford another mouth to feed, got eight already.' She led me towards the old house, picking up the empty wicker basket, on her way.

'You can help me with a few chores around the farm in the meantime. Don't expect you to milk Daisy mind, that cow can give you a good kick' she gestured at the large animal grazing in the nearby field, 'but you can help in the kitchen with the cheese making and run a few errands. Miriam, idle hands make for mischief, my mother used to say, God bless her.' She smiled and looked up to the heavens. 'Now come with me and I'll show you to your room. You will see a list of rules on your door and I shall expect you to obey them to the letter. Is that clear?'

I nodded in agreement and apprehension but decided her bark was probably worse than her bite. 'Just keep your head down Wilhelmina, work hard and she'll have no reason to complain', I kept saying to myself. I was forgetting that pregnancy had its own demands like sheer fatigue, nausea, and that annoying need to rush to the toilet every few minutes, all while my belly was growing bigger and bigger.

Three months after my arrival I gave birth to a healthy baby boy. All I could see when I looked into his wrinkled little face was his ugly, evil and disgusting father and I couldn't bring myself to hold something that was part of him. In fact smothering the little mite passed my mind more than once. The squirming little bundle was trouble since the day he was born, screaming incessantly day and night almost sending me insane. I was exhausted.

Then one day... 'It's time you were on your way Wilhelmina; remember I told you just till the bairn was born' She said as we worked. I looked up from the kitchen table and hesitantly asked 'If I were to get rid of it could I stay?' a look of shock crossed Mrs. Rogers face. 'Well umm ... what exactly do you plan to do with the child?' she asked cautiously. 'I've found a young family you see who have agreed to take him in and rear him as if he were one of their own, provided I agree to help them out with regular food parcels.' She replied, 'food parcels you say, well I hope you are not planning to steal anything from my kitchen? I won't have that'.

Suddenly Granny paused and looked away, then down at her navy woollen skirt, trying to brush away the few crumbs she had dropped earlier, before letting out one of her familiar deep sighs. 'Look my dear I think I have talked for quite long enough today so if you don't mind leaving me now please. I would like to nap.'

I couldn't help but notice whilst she had been talking; she'd constantly been winding and unwinding her lace handkerchief round and around her finger and then she started twisting and adjusting her wedding ring. What else was it that she had hidden all those years and was too scared to resurrect? Perhaps some things are best left alone; you never know what can happen when they get disturbed. The old lady looked tired and drained, it was clear that she'd had enough for today. 'Good night Granny, sleep well. I shall be back again tomorrow to help you.' I patted her hand as I got up. She looked off into the distance and murmured 'Goodnight Mary, don't be late dear.'

The following morning I returned to granny's bedside to be greeted with 'now where had I got up to Mary? I am afraid this old brain just isn't what it used to be. Dearie me! I had a marvellous memory in my youth I did, nowadays, I can't even remember what I had for my dinner yesterday!' she huffed. I pulled my pen and note pad from my handbag whilst reassuring her, 'don't worry it happens to us all Granny and I believe you were...' Before I had a chance to finish, she exclaimed 'Yes that's right, I remember now I was coming to... Oh no! I can't tell them that.' As she paused to think, I hastily asked 'what... what can't you tell them Granny?' Instead of answering, she gave me a dismissive hand wave 'Oh, none of your business Mary and please don't interrupt me, your job is to write what I tell you and not to ask impertinent questions.'

In an attempt to smooth her ruffled feathers I gently suggested that we continue after a nice cup of tea, that British panacea for all ills. 'No, there's no time for that dear. I am sorry if I was a little sharp with you Mary, there's something preying on my mind, a heavy burden I have been carrying ever since that day when... Anyway never mind that, we must get on.' I knew she wasn't really talking to me but herself as she struggled to erase the disturbing images flooding her head. Deciding she needed a slight prompt I said cautiously 'umm... I believe you mentioned something about leaving your baby son with a family who would....'

'Yes, that's right. You see once a fortnight Mrs Rogers allowed me a couple of hours off from my chores and I would go to the old cottage, little better than a hovel really, tucked deep into the woods off the beaten track. Every few yards, as I made my way along the muddy path, I would stop and listen anxious someone might be following me ready to slither away and tell Agatha Fortescue what they had witnessed. My instincts told me it would be wise to keep the whereabouts of the child a secret, though a small part of me wanted to hand him over to his father fearing my son had inherited his vile genes. However, my protective maternal instincts wouldn't allow such a thing.

On this particular day, fate was to extend its hand out to me in such a way that... Anyway, blissfully unaware of what was about to unfold, clutching my bag of bones, a few carrots and turnips which would make a hearty broth, I hurried along stopping occasionally to collect a few primroses next to a nearby stream, as a small thank you token for the lady of the house. It was a crisp spring day and I remember the woods were alive with birdsong, trees were bursting into bud and the sky was a deep halcyon blue that you would expect to find on a hot summers day.

I had a light spring in my step as I walked up the path of the little white house with just two rooms, one for the five children to sleep in and the other to cook, eat, wash, etc. Both were kept immaculately clean, but displayed little furniture except for basic necessities.

A familiar face etched with lines before her time and a kindly smile greeted me at the door, bidding me enter whilst inquisitive eyes watched me remove my coat. 'Arnold' she called, addressing one of her offspring as she picked up a pot and placed it over a struggling fire, 'go out and get some more wood, we have a guest.' The child groaned, but soon scurried off catching his mother's stern glare. I went and sat down by the hearth on a little wooden stool, listening to the children's chatter, punctuated with heated arguments, their mother intervening when necessary in case fists should suddenly fly.

I talked with her for a while, about my mother, siblings and life on Mrs Rogers's farm. There was one subject never discussed for I did not care to know if my son had cut his first tooth, said his first word or even taken his first steps. Indeed every time I saw my child, it brought an ever deepening intensity of revulsion, try as I might to overcome it.

On this particular visit, I sensed that something was not right. Why will she not look me in the eye, I wondered? What was she hiding from me? She had barely said two words except for the fact that my son was fast asleep in his cot and she didn't want him disturbed. I did not have to wait too long to find out why she was so tense, for suddenly the bedroom door was flung open and the gruff voice I detested vehemently said 'hello Wilhelmina!'

Aghast, I leapt back in horror. In the doorway stood a man holding my writhing and screaming infant in his arms. It was his next words that pierced my body like cold steel. 'I came to get my son; it is his time. Did you think you could keep him hidden away from me forever? You must be more stupid than I've given you credit for.' My maternal instincts reared up and fear for my baby's safety overwhelmed me. I leapt to grab my child out of Horace's arms, but he just laughed as he held him high above his head, ignoring his son's loud pitched cries. Fear and panic could be seen in the small infant's eyes.

I turned to the woman, who had taken him to become one of her own, searching her face when I saw the coins she was clutching in her hand. 'I'm so sorry Wilhelmina', she whispered, 'he told me there would be more, many more from where these came from, if I handed over the boy. You see the bairn's grandmother wants him to live with her. She's got plans for him you see' she said desperately. With the woman's betrayal stuck in my throat like a fish bone, for I had stupidly given her my trust, I yelled 'Did you know his mother is a black witch? That woman is pure evil. She worships Satan… and him' pointing to Horace, 'shall I tell you about his hideous, perverted, obscene ways?' Images of the foal's appalling abuse shot through my mind. 'Well did you? No! Greed reared its ugly head didn't it?'

'I'm so sorry', she repeated, but I wasn't listening as I made another lunge to grab my son, only to be rebuffed by a sharp kick and a familiar short bladed knife. Then while holding the weapon to his son's throat he rushed to the back door threw it open and hurriedly left the cottage, his hideous cackle ringing in my ears as the woods swallowed him out of sight. I struggled to my feet and chased after him, but of course, he had disappeared. I ran through the trees and the mud, letting my instincts guide me, determined to rescue my son aware the next solstice was fast approaching.

As I brushed those thoughts aside, too horrible to even contemplate I suddenly heard a blood curdling scream. Quickly I followed the sound as it rang through the trees and discovered that fate had dealt my step brother a timely blow. He had only become entrapped by one of his own snares, a horrible evil device designed to inflict agonizing pain so severe that one poor creature had actually half gnawed through the bone of its own leg to escape the torture.'

A slight smile appeared on Granny's face as she carried on. 'I can still see my step-brother looking up at me with pleading eyes begging me to help him, but I just laughed in his face, for I am ashamed to say, a mixture of relief and malice surged through my veins. As I slowly approached, savouring the moment I told him 'no Horace Fortescue you can stay there and rot! May vultures peck out your eyes and strip clean your evil bones.' Without saying a word, glowering, his face purple with fury and pain he threw his head back and spat straight into my face just as he had that day in the stables.

Just at that point an infant's loud piercing screams suddenly filled the air jolting my latent maternal instincts once more. I did not have to look far before I discovered that my son had landed safely into a nearby bush, albeit covered in thorns, having been flung out of his father's arms, when he had tripped and fallen into razor sharp claws set to pounce on some poor unfortunate animal. When I turned to rescue my screaming baby, Horace suddenly made a lunge for my leg. Out of desperation I grabbed a large stone and threw it with all my might, aiming for his head. A trickle of blood ran down from his temple.

Flashbacks ran through my mind, of his horrific abuse, the indescribable agony I felt when he cut me, the torture he bestowed on beloved family pets, all served to give me a surge of strength as I managed to release his grip. Then I pelted rock after rock at his skull, circling him, enjoying seeing him cower and beg for mercy. Fired with adrenaline I heard a voice in my head saying 'go on Wilhelmina, here is your chance to take an eye for an eye and make him suffer!'

Then just as I was about to aim another rock he slumped forward. Was he unconscious or could he be dead? I needed to know. Very carefully and with baited breath I poked his body with a stick – no reaction. The voice in my head kept repeating 'finish him off! Kill him! Kill him, bludgeon him to death. Remember what he did to Star? Go on Wilhelmina get rid of the piece of scum. He would take your life if he could.' I knew I had to act fast, suppose someone had heard Horace's unforgettable screams or maybe my child's loud wails? So with a pounding heart and beads of cold perspiration running off my forehead, I dragged his heavy, inert body still trapped in the hideous snare, to the edge of the deep gorge where there was a spectacular waterfall, stopping every few minutes to listen to the quiet, petrified that someone might witness me.

To my horror just as I was about to heave him head first over the abyss, he suddenly moved his hand, let out a ghastly moan and opened his eyes - he was not only alive but conscious. I felt my adrenaline levels go sky high as I hung him over the cliff holding on to his feet. He was begging, screaming, sobbing and pleading for me to spare his life. I just laughed and told him 'this will be our little secret Horace but I shall ensure folk will think you were drunk, as indeed you frequently are and just toppled over the edge to a watery grave. Everyone knows to keep away from the dangerous waterfall in Black Gorge Woods, and everyone knows that rocks near running water can be very slippery, and everyone knows you must take care or you could have an accident. Everyone knows that Horace Fortescue but it would appear you forgot.

The woman in the cottage would have noticed the whisky on your breath and saw me chase after you to grab my son back. After all they witnessed the knife you held at his throat and what mother would not do everything in her power to help her own flesh and blood? You were stupid, you ran towards the cascade then played one of your sick games, balancing on the edge of the cliff taunting me and holding the child over the abyss when I tried to reach for him just as you did in the cottage remember? You see, fate then dealt you a bad hand and you slipped … backwards … then ... goodbye Horace Oswald Fortescue. So simple, and after all nobody is going to weep over your grave you made sure of that when you were alive.

Of course I shall tell them how you let your son fall and by some miracle I managed to grab him and just in case someone might have heard your ghastly screams I shall say 'would you believe he stood on one of his own evil traps and you could have heard his yells ten miles away! Serves him right I say. Anyway that's my story Horace Fortescue and I shall be sticking to it. Let us say an eye for an eye or maybe I should say an ear in your case. And now Horace Fortescue, prepare to meet Satan, he waits for you in hell.'

Then with no more ado and one final push I watched him hurtle down the waterfall into the ravine bouncing like a ball against the rock face before landing in the torrent below, a thin strip of deep water concealing hidden currents renowned for taking lives. I told myself Mary, as time passed on ' he only got no more than he deserved and, who knows how many others would have suffered at his evil hands were it not for my actions. I was justifying my mortal sin to myself for, in my eyes, I had saved the world from a monster. Eventually I tried to blot it all out, but try as I might I could not. It was not someone else who had broken the Lord's sixth commandment 'Thou shalt not kill.' It was me!' she said as she grasped the cross on her necklace.

'What happened next Granny,' gently squeezing the old lady's hand as she fell silent for a few minutes, we were both emotionally drained. I had just listened to my great grandmother telling me she was a murderer. Unlike her, I could not justify or excuse her actions; it appalled, sickened and disgusted me. Maybe in a French court it might have been called a Crime of Passion but it made me want to retch. It was pure luck that she had not been caught then locked up in some high security gaol for the rest of her life.

Overwhelmed by it all, I turned to the frail old woman and stammered 'I am sorry Granny may we continue this project tomorrow please? I need some fresh air.' To my utter relief she replied 'Umm… yes Mary if you wish' then she tightly grasped my hand, 'but do not forget I may not have much time left dear and I must finish what I have begun. There are certain things that certain people should know and I have barely scratched the surface. It is important, very important that I complete this. All I ask is that you write down whatever I have to say dear without prejudice, judgment or interruption.' Then she released me from her cold hard stare and I turned to put my things away. 'Goodbye Granny. I will come tomorrow as usual,' believing that whatever lay in store in the next chapters could not shock me any more than she had today. I was to be proved wrong, so very wrong.

5

Confessions

The following morning I arrived on the ward to see Granny Wilhelmina, arms tightly crossed, having a few words with a young student nurse, who had been instructed to give her patient an injection.

'Take it away girl! Don't you dare stick that needle in me!'

'Come now Mrs Potts, don't you want to get better and go home?' the nurse calmly approached her; 'Of course I do and kindly do not talk to me as if I were a child. You're an impertinent young woman. Now I have a visitor so go away, shoo! Shoo!' suddenly spotting me as I went to collect a chair from the neat stack near the window, leaving the nurse to her ministrations which were accompanied by Granny's shrieks when she hit her target.

Ten minutes later I sat by her bedside, perusing her frowning face and tightly pursed lips, reflecting a cup of tea would not come amiss, when the inevitable question came. 'Now Mary just remind me where I finished yesterday dear?' 'Umm'... I couldn't bring myself to say 'Oh! You had just murdered your stepbrother, Granny. You chucked him over a high cliff and he drowned, remember?'

'Well Mary?' she interrupted my thoughts, 'Oh! I believe you were talking about umm... a certain event in the woods?' I said as delicately as I could, 'Ah yes! That can of worms!' As she again wound her lace handkerchief firmly around her finger, she revealed how she initially experienced an overwhelming feeling of pure relief. 'Horace Fortescue was gone forever you see, never again would he torture me or any of God's creatures. This feeling did not last long; it was quickly replaced by fear and panic, in case he had miraculously survived the fall, but not shame or guilt. No they were to appear later and have since never gone. I don't suppose they ever will now, the mental scars I mean. The physical ones healed long ago, thanks to the healing properties of plantain, aloe and calendula. Every time I undress I am reminded of that horrible eye, the excruciating pain and… and the mark of the devil etched into my skin. It sickens and terrifies me you see, because soon it will accompany me to the grave and then where? I've tried to make amends you know for my crime. I helped anyone and everyone, spent hours taking meals round people's houses, raising money for charitable causes, even tried to help those fallen by the wayside whom society had long ago given up on and locked away.'

'Granny' …I hesitated … 'what did you do after umm … in the woods I mean?' I asked, not really sure if I wanted to know the answer. 'Well I ran as fast as I could, away from that waterfall of course and then… then I believe I just slumped down in the dense undergrowth both mentally and physically exhausted. It's quite tiring dear dragging a man through woods you know.' She chuckled then turned her face away before saying slowly 'but when… when I wiped the sweat from my brow, I saw to my horror my hands and clothes were covered in blood. Feelings of utter revulsion accompanied by nausea overwhelmed me as I desperately tried to rub it off my hands in the long grass, scarcely noticing the sharp cuts from the course fibres. I heard a little voice in my head telling me 'you need to wash that evidence away Wilhelmina Potts; you need to find that little stream where you got the primroses it can't be too far away.'

I was distracted by a rustle in the undergrowth, for I had disturbed a young rabbit fleeing for safety. As I watched it disappear with speed of lightening, down a nearby warren, I wondered if its mother could be nearby to protect it. It was in that moment a huge wave of icy reality smacked me in the face, as I remembered with an almighty shock, my own offspring. Lost in my act of revenge I had completely forgotten the child. I knew I could not possibly leave the infant lying in a bush. He would surely die of exposure if not starvation, so I tried to wend my way back retracing my earlier steps or, so I thought, but I soon found myself going round in circles. My obsession with revenge, you see, had made me lose sight of the real reason why I had chased Horace into the woods.

No! Even she wouldn't do that, as a macabre thought entered my mind recalling her ancestor's evil rituals but, then remembered my mother's dog and Gods other creatures that had ended up in her hands, having met their untimely deaths, and knew she would. I was well aware Agatha Fortescue, wicked like her perverted son, was capable of anything. Again maternal instincts screamed out as I was overwhelmed by a dark cloud of fear and foreboding, I had drowned the witch's son. Satanic as he was, he was still her flesh and blood. I realised as a heavy weight descended on me, that I would always be looking over my shoulder for the rest of my life. Each night I was forced to wrestle with tormenting nightmares, whilst waiting for his mother to take her pound of flesh, as she had with my sister. For as long as Agatha Fortescue was alive, I would never be safe. She would eventually discover that I had chased after her vicious, barbaric son, that I had been the last person to see him alive and whom she was only too well aware had made my skin crawl every time I set eyes on him.

I collapsed among the grass in a daze. Still hungering for revenge turning over and over in my mind how I could satisfy my lust, for I now knew beyond any shadow of a doubt my mother had been murdered. Apparently the servants who toiled for the sick woman my mother had gone to nurse that day she disappeared, had all left the house having been given permission to attend a local village fair. There had been a chill in the air that afternoon and one of the maids, an elderly soul, had returned for a warm shawl. On her way to the attics she had noticed her mistress's door was slightly ajar and on hearing a strange gurgling sound coming from within had decided to check on her, fearing she might have taken a turn for the worse. When the servant had popped her head around the door she had recoiled in utter horror unable to believe her own eyes.

It was not until the old woman lay on her deathbed six months later did she ever confess freely what she had witnessed that terrible day. In low, rasping, broken whispers she had slowly, revealed to those standing around her bed, how she had come across a blood bath. Barely audible at times she tried to tell how she had witnessed her employer's body dangling off the end of the bed, a deep gouge across her throat. Whilst my poor mother had been pinned to the floor, her head forced back, as one assailant knelt on her hair whilst the other evildoer sat on her chest. 'Swallow it bitch or, you'll be next, just like er see,' she heard Agatha Fortescue clearly shriek, as she yanked Kathleen Crabtree's face to the side so she could see the body of the old woman lying in a pool of blood, slowly trickling across the floor. Then following another laboured gasp the old servant had whispered 'I saw.... saw what they did... I couldn't beli....' but then the maid had closed her eyes in exhaustion and those gathered round her bed with gaping mouths, had started to leave the room shaking their heads in disbelief. It wasn't long before she tried to beckon someone over and whispered in their ear, something too horrific to even contemplate, something that upon hearing her lone audience paled then hit the floor in shock. Between long gurgling gasps, the dying woman had revealed that Agatha Fortescue aided by her wicked accessory forced open their victim's mouth, grabbed hold of her tongue then sliced into it with a pair of scissors saying 'you see Kathleen Crabtree the dead cannot talk, nor can the dumb and very soon all that is yours will be mine, all mine' she cackled. Next the barbarian grabbed an oil lamp, eerily lighting the macabre scene and hurled it across the room. It landed on the bed bearing the corpse and within minutes the bedclothes, curtains and body were all ablaze. Fearing for her own life the old maid had fled down the stairs and hid, waiting for the murderous pair to flee, sadly by then the roof had begun to collapse and although she had managed to raise the alarm, it had been too late to battle the intense flames to rescue my mother. After hearing this, I was unable to get out of my mind, the tormenting images of that dear, kind, sweet lady, mutilated and in agony, trapped and left to burn alive. 'Forgive thine enemies' was something I could never do. I wanted revenge, sweet revenge served cold, an eye for an eye or perhaps a tongue.'

I had to take a break from listening to Granny, I was in such shock. What more would she reveal? How much more could I take? I made the excuse of needing a cup of tea and rushed out of the room. Ten minutes later I returned a little calmer, and Granny carried on as if I hadn't left. 'It reminded me of a passage in Charlotte's diary that revealed a heated conversation she had overheard that day in the tunnel, between her stepmother and an accomplice, discussing their barbaric crime. She was reminding her accessory that she would cut out her tongue if she ever spoke of it again.

I was suddenly jolted out of my thoughts by a noise, a sort of wailing, moaning sound. Could it have been a child's cry? I stopped and listened but it was only the wind whistling through the trees. As I looked down to avoid stepping into another muddy puddle I saw grass that once had been clothed in mother nature's verdant green but was now stained red, blood red. Nearby I saw the bush where the infant had earlier lain; writhing among the thorns, but now there was no child. He couldn't have vanished into thin air; somebody must have picked him up, a little familiar voice in my head interrupted. A horrible thought made me want to retch and shudder, hairs prickled on the back of my neck and my breath caught. Suppose someone else had been there, watching, spying. Maybe the woman in the cottage had sent her husband to follow me, keen to be rewarded with more coins and had taken the child back to the witch and imparted the truth, the terrible truth that I was desperate to conceal. I thought of Agatha whose eyes were too narrow to see into her soul but that belonged to the devil anyway. Her inscrutable face with its thin, pursed lips, reminding me of a tightly closed door, but behind closed doors many things go on which are kept secret from the outside world. What was going on behind her door I wondered, what forces had made her wish to be the devil's advocate? What had gone on in her childhood, though it was difficult to imagine the martinet ever having been a child? Then don't they say abuse begets abuse in next generations? Perhaps she was whipped and branded in her formative years, those years that can lay down a blueprint for the rest of one's life. I can't possibly go back there, I told myself as I hastily tried to form some sort of plan. Scarab Towers, Agatha Fortescue's house was the last place on earth I wanted to see. But suppose the child was lying under her roof, being a pawn in some ghastly inhumane ritual? Much as I could never love this scrap of humanity I had brought into the world, neither could I see him suffer such a cruel and barbaric death. How could I rescue the child whose life I was convinced lay in mortal danger if, I did not return to the den of iniquity, I argued with myself?

'It is his time,' Horace had said that day when he abducted the infant. Could I return to work for Mrs Rogers and carry on as normal, while fearing the whole time that the Police might suddenly swoop one day and lock me away forever? My head was spinning I didn't know which way to turn Mary. Naturally I wanted to get as far away from the area as possible. Maybe I should find my brother Harry or write to him and tell him everything, every sordid detail for he would know how to advise me I reflected, remembering the close bond we shared. In the meantime that familiar voice whispered in my head 'you must hasten back to Mrs Rogers before she sends out a search party, try to carry on as normal to avoid suspicion.'

I knew Harry had joined the army ranks at the start of the Great War but I had forgotten in his last letter, I had received in the spring of 1916, he said he expected to be sent to the frontline to France to fight. I knew little of the war, except that it devoured lives. It was all a long way away and didn't really concern me until the day I had found Annie our pretty young parlour maid, given to flirting with anything in trousers, tucked into a corner in the kitchen weeping bitterly. 'It's my brother Will, he's dead' she managed to say in between the sobs. 'They made them all go over the top you see and they were just blown to smithereens.' In her trembling hands she clutched a letter written by a close comrade of Will's named Edwin Backhouse who, like Harry, had joined the 4th Battalion Grenadier Guards. Edwin had depicted a desperate and horrific picture of the horrors of trench warfare the soldiers were forced to suffer on those bloodied battlefields of the Somme. 'I was lying in a shell hole badly wounded with a large piece of shrapnel jutting out of my shin when some courageous soldiers seeing my plight risked life and limb to rescue me and ensured I was returned safely to our lines. If they hadn't, I don't know what would have happened to me. Sadly it was too late for Will, I remember him showing me your picture Annie saying how much he adored you and should anything happen to him he wanted you to know from me, not merely a cold telegram from the War Office. He also wanted you to do something for him. Inside the envelope you will find a flower, a poppy he picked, saying how can something so beautiful come from a place of utter hell? Please tuck it into a wreath and put it on his grave.'

'Apart from the constant fear of being killed by an enemy sniper or being hurled into the air from an exploding German shell the soldiers had come face to face with other appalling terrors. Imagine being forced to share overcrowded trenches often flooded with freezing muddy water sometimes as high as a man's chest, with dead bodies who were once friends and colleagues, along with a population of huge rats, slugs and spiders not to mention the flies and maggots which thrived on the remains of decomposing human and animal corpses. Or, imagine being buried alive by collapsing trenches or suffering from Trench Foot from being forced to stand in filthy water for endless hours, resulting in infection. Then imagine being covered in body lice another common tribulation as it was often weeks before the soldiers at the Front could bathe or, having to march for days, subsisting on meagre rations of only bully beef and a few hard baked biscuits for they were often all we got given some days' Edwin had written.

I often lie awake at night thinking of Harry, Edwin and Will. Letters to loved ones and illegal diaries written on the bloodied battlefields of the Somme had revealed a shocking, insight of hideous things being done under the cover of frontline war. No longer perceived as glorious but seen for what it truly was totally abhorrent, men's lives being sacrificed for gun fodder. Even upper class ladies insulated from life's grimmer aspects could no longer hide from the messy realities of war like bloodshed, pain and suffering as unimaginable scenes of carnage in a godforsaken place called 'No Man's Land' had come to light by the famous war poet Wilfred Owen, in a letter to his mother. Many soldiers became trapped in the quagmire while high explosive shells fell all around and machine guns spluttered every few minutes. Like lambs to the slaughter those brave young innocents had been sent into battle many ne'er to set their eyes upon English shores again. I believe they say over nineteen thousand perished on only the first day and those whose lives had been spared at Armageddon suffered horrifying, traumatic images of shells blowing away limbs, hearing blood curdling screams, and being forced to shoot their own comrades for deserting their posts, a sick game of Russian Roulette being played with bullets.' Granny paused and looked away. A tear was starting to trickle down her cheek. Hastily she brushed it away and blew her nose in an effort to regain her self-control having resurrected extremely disturbing pictures of Harry running away, too traumatised to fight any more, only to be captured and face a firing squad. In a faltering voice she whispered 'they died in hell. Why? What was it all for, it was proclaimed it would be the war to end all war? Whoever said that had not reckoned on the weakness of man because persecution and war still continue to tear nations apart and bring untold suffering. No! Man still hasn't learned his lesson and I doubt ever will. Such appalling terrible waste, so many fine young men, like Harry and Will cut down in their prime. Some were barely sixteen, having lied saying that they were seventeen and therefore old enough to enlist, even they paid the ultimate sacrifice giving up their today, so that we might have our tomorrow. Anyway, my dear that's enough talk of war. 'Granny' I interrupted, she never answered, just got down from her soap box and stared at me with a vacant expression. Then looked away and muttered under her breath 'poor Harry, he never had much of a life before the war snuffed it out, never able to conquer his stutter, too shy to talk much and never to a woman if he could avoid it.'

6

The Curse

'Granny' I interrupted again, endeavouring to bring the topic back to that fateful day in the woods, feeling she had said more than enough about war. 'What did you do after … you know? …' For a few seconds Granny just stared at me without saying a word then out of the blue said 'well a little bird, believe it was a blackbird or was it a thrush, anyway it suddenly swooped down from its perch in the trees to grab an unsuspecting worm. Black Gorge Woods was a feast for wild life. I noticed that every few seconds it would stop and listen fearing a stealthy predator was preparing to pounce, it was then I realised I too was not unlike that bird. My instincts still told me I would find my little son in my stepmother's possession, but they also told me it would be folly to go there on my own. I thought of asking my brother Hector for help but my stepmother had sent him hundreds of miles away, to somewhere in Ireland, I believe, not long after Charlotte's dramatic escape. I had not heard from him for some time. And how could I tell him, indeed how could I ever begin to make anyone understand? Like a black pall of smoke my shame began to choke and engulf me. Had Horace not been punished enough by fate or maybe some higher power, when he almost had his leg severed, suffering unrelenting agony of his own making? Each night in my sleep I'm tormented by Horace's pleading eyes, begging me to release him from his torture, the blood trickling down his face as I give the final push, except he does not fall down to the cascading rapids, instead he recovers. Then I find myself desperately holding on to the cliff face by my fingertips, dangling over the abyss until he drops a large stone, crushing each finger, before finally stamping on them, sending me hurtling down whilst the noise of his sick laughter echoes in my ears. It's at that point I usually wake up in a cold sweat, screaming until reality catches hold, you see my conscience forbids sweet dreams. Now it's time I wished you good night Mary. All this talking has tired me out dear. Maybe tomorrow I may reveal another little secret I have kept to myself; that is if the Reaper doesn't call on me first.'

The next morning I returned to Granny Wilhelmina's bedside to find her bursting with excitement, grinning from ear to ear.

'Mary I'm going home. Friday I shall be leaving or, did they say Saturday? Anyway, never mind, home it is. You must come to tea dear, but first we need to get on with my little project. Just remind me again where we had reached yesterday.' I gently reminded her, 'Granny you were talking about the Great War, Hector, and finding the child. Do you remember?'

'Oh yes of course I do dear!' A frown appeared on her face, creasing her brow as she collated her thoughts before resuming her compelling story.

'Apparently the woman with the kindly smile, who lived in the cottage, I believe her name was Emily Wilkins but cannot be sure. The one who had betrayed me, well she had been in the village and heard folk whispering to one another 'look to your animals for the solstice is nigh and the witch will be up to her old tricks.' Fearing for the child's safety, immersed in guilt, she returned home and demanded that her husband visit Agatha's house to plead for the child's return, unaware of events that had enfolded in the woods. The witch laughed in his face and told him 'you must be deluded man there's no infant living under this roof. I cannot abide children!' she then dismissed him. As he was leaving a young servant girl grabbed his sleeve and whispered 'meet me tomorrow at noon; behind the stables I have something to tell you'. So the next day determined to keep the clandestine appointment, he tethered his horse in the woods and scurried to the stable house. The girl was waiting, around the back, agitated and breathless. 'I can't tarry sir but a few nights ago I was wakened you see by this unearthly scream, sent shivers down me spine it did. Then there was this awful wailing, upset me it did, lay there rest of night tossing and turning I did sir. It seemed to be coming from the west wing too, which was real strange sir because that is all closed off you see, has been for years. Anyway sir I swear on my mother's grave it was a young child I heard. The next morning at breakfast I asked the other servants if they had heard anything but they pretended not to hear me, exchanging furtive glances with one another. Indeed all I got for my trouble was 'Dolly aint you ever heard ask no questions hear no lies?' It happened again the following night, then it stopped and I just put it out of my mind you see, that is until now.'

Not sure what to believe he decided to investigate the matter further, remembering his wife's parting words 'Lewis make sure you bring back the babe or I shall make sure you do not see my bed for the next six weeks or your stomach be filled by my good food.' Lewis Wilkins knew from past experience it was unwise to cross his hen pecking wife who ruled the roost, in both departments, so he concocted a little web of lies to keep her sweet. After all he reasoned she would never find out the truth if he were careful, so he decided to tell her 'they say the child has the pox, nobody is allowed to see him and surely dear wife you would not want our bairns to catch it, now would you?'

You see, although he would never have admitted it, deep down Lewis feared his wife whose acid tongue and aggressive manner towards him had gradually worn away his self esteem. Like putty in her hands she had tried to mould him into the subservient almost pathetic figure of the man he had become. Apparently his wife had forgotten a valuable lesson, the worm can turn. He had found the secret assignation with the girl had aroused dormant sexual urges his wife was always keen to dissipate, fearing another mouth to feed. No, try as he might, Lewis could not forget the young servant girl who, unlike his tired, haggard wife had a fresh complexion and a youthful look of innocence. Her skin was firm and tender not wrinkled and sagging, her breasts were full and pert, hair long, thick and glossy, not straggly or peppered with grey and when he looked into her deep brown velvet eyes he saw a sparkle he never found in his spouse. No, he could not get the girl out of his mind; he wrote letters declaring his undying love, which were only to be discovered by his wife! Emily Wilkins later confided in a friend of her husband's betrayal, unaware her confidante happened to have a penchant for gossip and before long everyone in the village was whispering and nudging one another including Annie our parlour maid. 'Have you heard about Lewis Wilkins, Miss Wilhelmina? I just could not believe my own ears when I heard it Miss. Talk about silent waters run deep, never knew he was a dirty old man though, but that letter was downright disgusting Miss.' Completely stunned, I asked 'What had he written exactly? Well Mary as far as I can remember I believe it went something like. 'My darling, I yearn to take you in my arms, nibble at your ear lobes and kiss your soft rosebud lips. I want to see you arch your back and toss that beautiful dark mane while you softly moan with ecstatic delight, as I gently cup your heaving breasts in my hands feeling your nipples harden, as I roll my tongue over them, then suck on each one like a babe. My dearest, every waking moment I think of you, for you, not her, I wonder are my reason for living? I lie in my bed each night and yearn to plant my seed in you to show you with every inch of my being, sheer unbridled ecstasy.'

Granny cleared her throat, 'I'm sure you get the picture Mary.' With a slight blush to my cheeks I answer, 'Umm yes Granny' wishing I had never asked in the first place. 'You know Mary I have led quite a colourful life, dear, and I consider myself to be quite broad minded, but even I was a little shocked at what old man Wilkins had written so graphically to his amour, I'm sure you can imagine the cruel taunts he received. His passionate feelings had not been reciprocated, after all, he was old enough to have been the girl's father. Not surprisingly Wilkins' wife did what many a woman before and after, faced with such humiliation, she threw him out of the house, vowing revenge. Playing him at his own game she hired a prostitute to seduce her husband, ply him with alcohol and 'give him a taste of oral relief he will never ever forget, be sure to use your teeth my dear,' she instructed the woman. Anyway Lewis Wilkins never went philandering again and I believe when the scandal broke he became a recluse. What is it they say 'Hell hath no fury like a woman scorned.'

'Granny did Lewis ever find the child? You still haven't said.' I wonder, desperate to know the truth, 'No, I have not, have I. Please be patient Mary all will be revealed in due course. I will tell you this; it came as a great shock, knocked me for six it did!' Just at that moment an authoritative voice interrupted our conversation… 'Mrs Potts needs to rest my dear. Come back and visit her tomorrow.' Said the ward sister, as she gestured towards the exit, I was suddenly reminded of Great Granny's age and failing health, so I heeded the nurse's advice and said goodbye.

On my return the following day, keen to hear the next instalment, I was surprised to see screens had been pulled round Granny's bed. Fearing the worst, I rushed to ask a nurse if I could see her. 'I am afraid Mrs. Potts had a nasty fall in the night my dear and hurt herself so she is resting in bed today.' On peeping round the curtain I saw Granny Wilhelmina lying peacefully with her eyes closed, a painful contusion on her brow showed evidence of her tumble. Believing her to be asleep, I jumped with surprise to hear her suddenly say 'now, what are you staring at Mary? I was only looking at the back of my eyelids, I could see you, you know.' Choosing to ignore her bad mood, 'how do you feel Granny? Whatever were you doing to get that whopping big bruise?' I replied. 'Well!' she exclaimed, 'If that woman in the corner hadn't been snoring like a herd of pigs again, I wouldn't have had to go and give her a prod with my stick, once more now would I and my legs wouldn't have folded under me, so it was all her fault!' she huffed, 'Anyway Mildred will be coming later to take me home, got a granny flat for me apparently, so she can keep her eye on me, she said. How cheeky is that? She has absolutely no respect for her elders that one, none at all!'

When I returned that afternoon to visit, great granny was sitting with her niece Mildred, who, like her mother Charlotte, was never afraid to speak her mind and today was no exception.

'Now Aunt Wilhelmina when I get you home, you stay put! Do you hear! You stay in your bed at night. Do I make myself clear; I'm telling you now I'm not having any nonsense or you'll go into that old folk's home down Orchard Street.' She said sternly, to my very stubborn grandmother.

'For goodness sake Mildred! It was only a wee bump and I'll not be setting foot in any home or be bossed about by you, so you can stop that right now. Do you hear me? I'll have some respect! I'm not a child!' Granny barked.

'Where have you put your dirty washing? I can't seem to find any knickers. Where have you hidden them this time Aunt Wilhelmina?' Mildred asked, ignoring Granny's angry retort, as she searched in her aunt's locker. Her reply was drowned out by loud clangs from the bell announcing the end of visiting hours. 'It's time for us to go auntie' hastily planting a quick peck on great granny's hairy face and armed with her dirty clothes, Mildred disappeared into the gaggle of folks thronging the exits of wards and corridors.

'Now then Mary I don't see your notepad or pen; I told you dear I want to get my little project completed soon as possible. I have not all the time in the world like you, you know.' I pointed to my watch and said 'Granny I can't stay. We'll continue with your little project later; you must do what they say and get some rest now. You need to recoup your strength. I'll see you again tomorrow.'

Despite her great age, it wasn't long before great granny's iron constitution returned and the doctors decided she was fit to go home. A week later once again I found myself taking notes. Looking around the little flat her niece had annexed to her own large detached cottage, I could see it had all the essentials but it was lacking a homely touch, perhaps a warm red rug or some fresh flowers. Then, I spotted a silver framed photograph next to her bed. It was Granny Wilhelmina standing next to a young man. I picked it up to get a closer look and saw his smiling eyes and cheeky grin. He was smartly dressed in a dark suit with his arm wrapped tightly round a young woman who only had eyes for him, but then suddenly a familiar voice made me jump and I replaced it quickly. 'Mary kindly don't go nosing around in my bedroom, I do not want anything to be broken. I know how clumsy you can be.' I quickly ran to her side to help her to her bed, 'Granny there's a picture here...' I queried. 'If you're wondering who that is in the photograph, it's me with my Fred.'

'Who's Fred?' I asked politely. 'Well I was coming to him, dear. He was my

Fred, my soul mate, my nearest and dearest, my lover, my rock and my first husband. He's up there now waiting for me.' She looked up to the ceiling and whispered 'not long now Fred. Please show me a sign, say you've forgiven me. These years have been so empty without you.' Her eyes started to fill. 'Umm Granny how did you meet him?' I asked, feeling guilty for making her cry. 'Well sit down Mary, start writing and I shall tell you.' the old lady didn't say a word. I knew she had travelled back into the realms of memory lane and found something else she had carefully buried, recognising that familiar faraway look in her eyes, the sad expression on her face, biting her lip and constantly rubbing her wedding ring as if hoping for some comfort from her dead husband. I knew she was being forced to confront another skeleton carefully hidden.

After a while she started to speak in a familiar strained tone. 'Well umm… after Horace's death I headed back to the farmhouse and tried to create some semblance of normality. 'Keep your head down Wilhelmina and get on with your work' the little voice in my head urged. Then something happened, something that was to be life changing though I didn't know it at the time. One day Mrs Rogers sent me on an errand to the haberdashery shop where the shopkeeper, a non-descript, grey haired little man suddenly peered over his thick-rimmed glasses and said to my astonishment 'umm… aren't you her that lived in that big house on the hill, with that old witch? Heard they've been looking for you, something about a telegram, I believe. Mr. Potts is in the post office, go and see him, he'll know all about it.' So off I went and found Mr. Potts who after rummaging in a drawer finally handed me the telegram. For a second our eyes held contact and something stirred within me but I quickly brushed the feeling aside, as I ripped open the telegram desperately trying to control my trembling hands. Then I collapsed to the floor as I read 'Hector dead. Heart attack. Funeral Church of Sacred Heart, Dublin, Wednesday 23rd March.'

With both Harry and Hector gone and my sister somewhere abroad, my mind was in turmoil, one minute racked with panic, the next with grief. Then I remembered my mother's words 'my dears a trouble shared is a trouble halved' I gradually began to unburden myself on Frederick Potts, who was a good listener, kind and empathetic. Then we began courting, he was a lovely man, one of a kind. Six months later he got down on one knee, told me how he couldn't live without me and would be by my side for the rest of his days, caring and protecting me. Well, that was true until he left one day, walking out two years after we had wed. He left me a note saying he couldn't take any more, knocked me for six it did, came right out of the blue, but I guess I had been too preoccupied with my own feelings to even notice his. I never saw the hurt in his eyes as I trampled on his fragile ego, casting aside his opinions, his emotions, his needs. Later I heard someone in the village say 'Fred never deserved that woman. Whatever did he see in her? Changed him she did, never used to be morose and bad tempered didn't Fred.'

So my rock crumbled and my marriage disintegrated into the dust. That's what happens when obsession takes over; everything else pales into insignificance. I had briefly told Fred about Horace, one night after he had discovered that hideous eye, omitting of course the fact I had thrown the tyrant over a cliff and he had drowned. The constant nightmares, the incessant weight preying on my mind led me to inadvertently spill the beans that evening. Apparently I talked in my sleep you see and it wasn't long before he looked at me as if I were a stranger in his own house. Every waking moment, I could think of nothing else except Agatha Fortescue and my nameless son. She had to pay you see, made to suffer the barbaric torture she had inflicted on others. My obsession only piled on more misery, revenge is futile and can never serve a purpose and I was to learn that lesson the hard way. 'An eye for an eye will make everyone blind' but I was so young and stupid. If only I had known what was to come… now I'm tired and I'm going to have a little nap, so don't forget to shut the door on your way out dear.' I took the not so subtle hint and left.

At two thirty that afternoon I was once again sitting beside Granny Wilhelmina with my pen poised, wondering how many more shocking revelations would ensue, when she interrupted my thoughts. 'Wake up Mary! Did you hear what I just said? Why are you not writing? Now what was I saying my train of thought has disappeared?' I quickly sat up, 'Umm something about an eye for an eye, I prompted. 'Oh yes! That!' She looked away searching for the right words, a deep furrow appeared on her brow and she started to pale, then having pulled her handkerchief from her sleeve, blown her nose and composed herself she began relating her past once more. 'It wasn't long after Fred abandoned me, I opened my door to find Agatha Fortescue flanked by her cronies. Instinctively I tried to shut it but they forced their way in. I was no match against three.

For a couple of minutes Agatha just stared at my swollen belly, I was carrying Fred's child, then she poked me hard in the stomach with her long spindly finger. Before I had time to recover I was grabbed from behind and pushed to the floor. I fell heavily, before I could catch my breath, they were on top of me pinning me down, forcing my head back and my mouth open. I could hear the rustle of a paper bag and then a scratchy voice asking 'how many shall we give her Agatha, one, two, how about the lot?' …In that terrifying moment I realised it was a bean she was holding, a paralysing Calibar bean. "One will suffice for now', I heard Agatha reply.

Then it hit me with a sledgehammer, Agatha had discovered the truth, the dreadful truth that I had for so long tried to hide. Desperately I fought to spit the bean out as her cronies holding black candles chanted and cursed my unborn child, calling upon evil spirits to enter its body, maim its limbs and send it to Satan. It was what happened next I would never ever forget. The witch suddenly bent down and whispered in my ear 'your child has been cursed and will drown before it passes its fifth birthday.' Agatha had picked her time carefully to exact her revenge.

Two months later my daughter was born, with beautiful blue eyes like my mother's. I named her Mollie and became an obsessive mother, practically smothering my child so desperate I was, to protect her. First one, then two, three, until eventually five years passed and my little daughter still remained alive. I felt free believing the evil curse would never happen. I was wrong, so very wrong, unaware that the seeds of revenge were still growing.

I remember that day, as if it were just yesterday. I recall trying to shake off an uneasy mood believing it was a bad omen, when a sole magpie had appeared in my garden that morning. You see my mother had believed in superstitions such as 'one for sorrow, two for joy', funny how things can stick in your mind. Anyway that November night the heavens opened and the sound of thunder shook the cottage whilst flashes of lightening eerily lit the sky. I believe it was just gone midnight when I was awakened by an incessant banging on the door. Hurrying downstairs I opened it to find a young girl, I mentally placed around twelve, hysterically crying and screaming that she needed my help, saying her brother was badly hurt, there had been an accident. Asked if she could use my telephone to ring for an ambulance and then pleaded I went back with her to stay with him until the Emergency Services arrived on the scene. Having checked Mollie was safe asleep I grabbed my coat and some bandages. The girl led me to a house saying Tom was lying injured in there. He was but he wasn't hurt. I'd walked straight into a trap. Just like the unsuspecting fly I was set upon, tightly trussed up by the pair and left at the whim of the spider none other than Agatha Fortescue whom they informed me would be paying a visit the next day.

Despite being gagged and bound my maternal instincts to protect my child gave me a hidden strength and it wasn't long before I escaped. Running as fast as my legs could carry me I rushed home to my daughter, berating myself for being so stupid, I threw open the door and rushed upstairs but there was no sign of little Mollie. I searched every nook and cranny in the cottage, shrieking her name refusing to believe that I had lost her to something evil. I thought of her cute little chubby cheeks, blonde locks falling in waves encompassing her face and those huge deep blue eyes full of innocence. Overwhelmed by guilt for abandoning her I ran out of the house, down the lane into the darkness for night clouds still covered the sky, heading for the village. I soon discovered on such a stormy night no-one had bothered to tarry long, and my little girl had gone unnoticed. Exhausted emotionally and physically I returned home praying that little Mollie would be there. It wasn't Mollie I found, but a note that someone had pushed under the door, laying on the mat. With trembling fingers I picked it up. I'm telling you now Mary, no words can ever describe the utter despair and desolation of that moment, for someone had scrawled 'LOOK FOR YOUR CHILD IN THE RIVER!'

That's when I knew Agatha had once again taken her pound of flesh. She had taken away my little angel, an eye for an eye. Slowly I fell into a deep depression, day passed into night and night into day, even menial tasks suddenly became impossible. Without my precious little Mollie my life held no point. Six months had come and gone since I had found that horrible note, but despite searching for her from dawn to dusk in my heart I started to believe she was lying in the river. It was my comeuppance. It was then I just gave up and not long afterwards choked with grief and blinded with tears I made my way over to the wooden bridge upstream, I climbed over the narrow parapet and stared into the deep swirling waters. Just as I was about to drown myself I suddenly heard a voice in my head saying 'no Wilhelmina turn around, you're on the wrong road again, turn around, that is not the way.' Something made me stop and listen to those words, I knew it was my mother talking from beyond the grave. I turned around, but I didn't take the right road as that would have involved a confession to the police, so finally revenge reared its ugly head. It was then I resolved that no matter how long it took Agatha Fortescue would pay for her cruel, heinous crimes. Only her death painful and slow could suffice to remove that abscess on the backside of humanity.

So I hatched my plot, but had forgotten in my fervour that I had been seen, that one day very soon perhaps, I would be judged and I don't mean by a mere mortal.

Not long after I started to put the wheels of my plan into motion, everything seemed to go awry.

First a letter arrived out of the blue from Fred's solicitor informing me the cottage belonged to his client who had decided to sell it. He had been a gambler, frequently frittering away our savings on the horses, poker etc.

and, as all gamblers, paid the price. I reckoned it was the only avenue left, to pay off his debts and I had until the end of the month to find a new roof over my head, after then I would be evicted. Though without my Mollie the house was bleak and empty, part of me wanted to uproot and move on to newer pastures. Although time had passed with no sight or sign of my little angel there was still that small voice that kept urging me to stay, to keep on searching. 'Don't give up now' it whispered.

That was how I came to meet a man who made my heart flutter and my senses giddy. I had noticed him before walking his dog, apart from the odd 'Good Morning Miss' he never really paid me much attention until one winter's day, which still makes shivers run down my spine just thinking about it. As usual I had taken my morning walk down by the riverside and was enjoying a brief encounter of sunshine. It lifted my spirits, made the river sparkle and every tree, bush and twig, summer had covered in a verdant green cloak, temporarily seemed to come to life. I believe my mind had been focused on some swans, gracefully swimming downstream with a pair of ducks in tow, when it happened. It had been raining heavily for the last few weeks, turning the earth in some parts into a swamp of thick mud. Suddenly I lost my footing, careered down the muddy bank and landed in the deep, churning torrent. Strong fast currents in freezing water soon began to overpower my strength. Floundering in the river, I saw my whole life flash before me. I began to lose the battle plunging to the depths convinced I was going to die, that it was my punishment. Then I felt a pair of strong arms grab hold of me, lift my head up and a deep manly voice say 'I've got you. You're safe now.' He was my knight in shining armour, who had seen my plight and risked his own life to rescue me.

If I recall correctly, he carried me back to his house nearby, wrapped me in a blanket and stuck me by a roaring fire and then we talked and talked and talked. Lonely you see, his wife had died suddenly leaving a deep void in his life and he missed her companionship. He told me his name was Humphrey Arthur Wilson. I remember he had that distinguished air about him. He had been a major during the Great War and had many stories to tell. Gradually a bond developed between us, two lonely souls we were and it made sense to take him up on his offer when he later asked me to go and live with him.

Of course, in those strait-laced days, it caused some folks to tittle, tattle. There was always a wild streak in me that no man could tame. 'You're my 'Kathy Earnshaw' he would whisper in my ear out of Charlotte Bronte's famous novel Wuthering Heights, and he was my 'Heathcliff.' I believe I would have walked to the ends of the earth for Humphrey if he had asked me. Sadly twelve months later my hero became very ill, a heavy cold turned to pneumonia and one night the Grim Reaper came to take him away. I was devastated as you can imagine. Around three months after the funeral, I found myself both saddened and overjoyed when I discovered I was pregnant. Soon I told myself I would have a babe to nurse and cherish. If it's a boy I shall call him Humphrey Edward Heathcliff and a girl Catherine Mary Elizabeth but my son arrived prematurely, lived for just two days, I buried him next to his father.

Shortly afterwards I turned to a young man, who first befriended me in my grief and a year later tried to persuade me to walk down the aisle. Though after Fred left I decided that marriage wasn't for me. Again I agreed to go and live with him, to share his bed and cook his meals. I guess I was lonely, vulnerable and flattered by his attentions towards me. I must have been wearing blinkers though they do say 'love is blind'. You see Edward Smythe, handsome in a rugged sort of way, turned out to be a bad apple. I soon discovered it wasn't me he wanted but my inheritance, a small sum of money that Humphrey had left me. Edward was not only a greedy, deceptive man but also a bully and a philanderer to boot. On many occasions he would return home from a public house or a lady friend's, staggering along the street screaming offensive obscenities to people he passed before falling into the gutter having hit the bottle for endless hours. Then one day after a particularly bitter row, I came to my senses and stood up to him, told him to pack his bags and leave, never return and I haven't seen him since. Should imagine he's dead now, it would be his liver that got him after all he drank.

For a long time I would look back, I suppose the ghosts of the past were haunting me, but I still couldn't forget Agatha even after... um... after I...' she paused. 'After what Granny, what were you about to say?' The moment of disclosure had passed. 'I um... I've forgotten' she said choosing to file it away in her mind's archives under 'secret - do not disturb'.

7

An Unwelcome Visitor

'Rooted to the spot and struck speechless, I stared in disbelief at the young man standing on my door step, I estimated him to be in his late thirties, looking decidedly dishevelled and a little bit smelly. He reminded me of a tramp who had spent the night on a park bench. His lank greasy hair like his clothes looked like they hadn't seen a wash for a long time, not to mention his finger nails which were yellowing and caked in dirt.

He cleared his throat, 'I'm looking for a … you all right missus, you look like you've just seen a ghost, gone dead white you 'ave?' A look of concern crossed over his face.

'Umm… yes I'm perfectly fine. What do you want?' I felt my heart drop out of my chest, he looked so familiar.

'Well…I'm trying to trace a Wilhelmina Potts, been told she knew me father; Horace Fortescue's was his name. Someone from village told me I would find her 'ere, perhaps you …' I stopped listening, overwhelmed with tumultuous shock, coming face to face with the features of the man rotting in the inky waters of Black-wood Gorge. Like a spirited stallion my past once again reared up throwing me off course. Beyond a shadow of a doubt I knew this filthy, unkempt man was none other than my nameless son whom I had long ago resigned myself to being part of Agatha's evil game plan. I could plainly see he had grown up a mirror image of his father but had he also inherited his obnoxious paternal genes, I wondered?

'No! Never heard of her,' I heard myself lying and quickly slammed the door shut, taking care to bolt it. Then I ran around the house shutting all the curtains, in a futile attempt to shut out my past.

Nevertheless, the young man didn't give up and continued to hammer on the door. 'Go away, leave me alone,' I yelled fearing he would try to break in. 'I'm expecting company any minute and if you linger on my premises any longer I'll call the law and have you arrested.' I watched him slither off, shouting over his shoulder, 'I'll be back missus, you ain't seen last of me and I want truth, you hear!'

That night I couldn't sleep, just tossed and turned trying desperately to come up with a plan, completely unaware that something was to happen the next day that would blow it utterly apart.

Having run out of a few essentials, I got up early the next morning and walked down to the village. On my way back home I impulsively decided to take a short cut over the fields, curious to see if there were any late blackberries in the hedgerow, it was then I began to feel uneasy. Is someone following me? I wondered nervously as I walked through the thick spiky grass, looking over my shoulder every few minutes to see if someone was there. A twig suddenly snapped behind me. I could feel my heart pounding; beads of cold perspiration glossed my brow and trickled down my face. I quickened my pace breaking into a run heading towards the old wooden style, practically throwing myself over it in my haste to get back to the safety of my cottage. Desperately I looked around hoping to see someone, anyone, walking a dog or perhaps enjoying a picnic in the fields. There was nobody. I was all alone.

After a few moments and a couple of deep breaths later, I started to calm down, maybe it was my imagination, 'pull yourself together Wilhelmina', I told myself as I once again looked over my shoulder. To my horror, a man was leaping over the style, running towards me and a familiar voice I dreaded, broke into my thoughts, as he tried to bar my path.

'I told you I'd be back missus; I think you know summit you 'aven't told me.' He said crossing his arms and widening his stance, ready to pounce at any second. Full blown panic swept through me, I quickly scanned the horizon praying that someone would come to my rescue, but there was no one, only him and me. With some fast thinking, I managed to side step him and ran as fast as my legs could carry me, shouting for him to 'leave me alone,' wishing in earnest I had kept to public roads. He soon caught up with me, grabbed my arm then swung me round to face him waving a small dirty, half torn photograph in front of my face saying 'Tell me have ya seen 'er? Take a look Missus!' Curious to see what he meant, I grabbed the picture from his hand and gasped with shock; I could not believe what I was seeing.

'Where… Where did you get this?' I blurted out, dread setting in.

'Why? What's it to you?' He probed, cocking his head to one side. 'Never you mind, just tell me!' I snapped, desperate for more information. His cold eyes narrowed 'so you do know summit, I knew it...' he said with a sly smile. 'Well a few months back, I went to do business with this man ya see then just as I was leaving the 'ouse a servant girl suddenly ran after me, pushed this picture into me pocket then whispered in my ear dead frantic like, 'Ask around town for Wilhelmina Potts. She's my mother. Find her, tell her that I'm alive and give her this. You can't tell her where I am; they'll kill her if she tries to see me. She'll understand. She'll know what to do.'

Anyway, I went back to the house a couple of days later, on quiet like to see the girl. She told me she would be waiting for me in the barn and had summat important to tell me. Used to have a good old romp in that hay barn we did. Knew just how to whet a man's appetite she did I can tell you with her big blue come-to-bed eyes and full rounded breasts bulging out of her blouse, begging for it she were. Yeah she knew how to ...' feeling truly sickened, I barked at him, 'for goodness sake man I really do not want to hear...' Completely ignoring me he continued 'yeah pretty thing she were and feisty like a little tiger, we made mad passionate love like it was...' running out of patience, I grabbed him by the arm and said 'I'm really not interested in your sexual exploits.' Putting his hands up in surrender, he continued 'Ok missus, keep yer hair on; give us chance. You see last time I went to see 'er she'd gone, vanished into thin air.' I never did get to 'ear what she 'ad to say.'

'Vanished?' I repeated slowly.

'Yeah gone, disappeared. When I asked folks around the village if they had seen her, they just slammed their doors in me face. Why would they do that eh? Anyway missus I'm telling you all this cos' I love her see with all me 'eart and I'm gonna marry her, that is when I find her.'

I hesitated trying to take it all in, 'and um... she has agreed to marry you then?' I ask, holding my breath, hoping the answer was no, 'Not yet but she will do, she's carrying my kid see.' Feeling trapped in this whirlpool of emotions I try to carry on, 'Your child! Oh My Lord! She can't! She can't possibly have your child!' I started to back up preparing to run, realising I'd said too much. He peered into my face and spat 'now whatever do ya mean by that eh?'

I fought desperately to subdue the waves of rising panic, determined he wouldn't sense my fear as he suddenly pushed his face up close to mine, placed his hands firmly on my shoulders and hissed between clenched teeth 'I know ya hiding summit from me. I saw ya pale yesterday when I came to door. Tell, if you don't Missus I'll make you sorry. I might just lose me temper and ya could get hurt, real hurt. Taken aback by his threat I retorted 'you don't scare me! I'm telling you nothing, you need to mind your own business. Now get out of my way, or I'll go straight to the police.'

It was clear he had absolutely no idea he was talking to his own mother.

'Ya ain't telling Police, not if ya know what's good for ya' he threatened. In a desperate effort to calm him down I asked 'That girl in the photograph you never said what her name was.' He began to relax, a look of love morphing his face into something a little more pleasant.

'Mollie, they call her Mollie Rose, real beauty aint she.' He replied with a wide smile on his face. 'Yes she is very pretty, very pretty indeed,' I mumbled quietly, forcing back the tears threatening to trickle down my face. The deep painful wound that time had managed to close had just been ripped open once again. 'You say she just vanished? Have you any idea where she could be? Any idea at all?' I begged, but never got an answer.

Instead to my horror he snatched back Mollie's photograph then said quietly while staring at her picture, 'She told me she loved me she did. I never 'ad love ya see, I grew up knowing me own mother left me in a wood to die when I was a babe, left me to starve, wanted rid of me see. Tell me what kind of woman does that? A callous, evil creature, I swore if I ever set eyes on her I'd make her pay. Me grandmother told me she was last person to see me dad alive and I want answers see. I need to find that lousy bitch and when I do…' He shouted angrily.

I quickly interrupted. 'And your grandmother …Umm… does she come from these parts? What's her name?' I asked urgently trying to avert the topic away from me. 'Agatha, Agatha Crabtree, used to be Fortescue it did.' In my eyes that woman's name would always be Fortescue. Seeing the smile on his face made me feel sick, 'Is she well, I hope …' I asked, with my fingers crossed behind my back. 'No, she's in 'ospital, collapsed she did, could die.' I struggled to control my relief as he continued, 'one minute she was looking at this ring on her finger and next she's lying on floor struggling to catch her breath see, must have been her old ticker again', tapping at his chest. 'Oh, she has a bad heart then? Well I'm sorry to hear that but I'm afraid I can't help you, I'm new to this area you see,' I lied, visualising my mother tut tutting from beyond the grave for my brazen dishonesty, 'so if I were you I would put the past right behind you, never did any good dragging up old skeletons best to let them lie. I would forget all about that girl in the photograph. I believe there's a travelling fair in the village. Why don't you go and see if they will give you a job then you would have work and a roof over your head?'

His cold, steely glare flooded my mind with memories of his evil father. I nervously recoiled back, lost my balance and fell twisting my ankle. Pain shot up my leg; I looked up for help and froze in abject terror as he pulled out a short length of rope from his pocket. 'Oh! My Lord! He's going to strangle me.' Panicking I struggled to stand up and run for my life only to be pushed back down. He grabbed my wrists and tied them behind my back, so tight the cord bit into my skin, then in a low terrifying voice he spat 'now we shall see if ya been telling truth.' With that he ripped open my blouse revealing the ugly satanic scar. His mouth fell open as he gasped 'My God! It's you! I knew it. You're the bitch that abandoned me, left me to die! Me grandmother was right she told me to look for the eye…' I pulled my knees to my chest, in a desperate attempt to cover myself up.

'No! No! It's a load of lies they have fed you; that's what they wanted you to believe. Your father did that, he cut me with his knife. I didn't… I couldn't find… I tried…' I pleaded but he wasn't listening. He towered over me and demanded, 'what 'appened to him? Why did he disappear into the woods and why 'as nobody ever seen 'im since? You know, they said you were last person to see 'im. Well I'm waiting bitch, start talking.' He ordered.

'He had an accident; fell over the cliff by the waterfall. I tried to save him I did, but I couldn't. He walked into one of his own traps you see and was trying to remove it from his leg when it happened. He liked his whisky did your father and that day he must have had a skinful.' I explained, hoping he that he believed, but no such luck, 'you're lying to me bitch. If that be true why didn't you tell someone, go and get 'elp or something?' he insisted.

'It was too late.' I cried.

'No! Don't believe a word of that cock 'n bull yarn you've just spun. They told me how you 'ated him; reckon you pushed him over top.' Aggression, malice, the evil glint in his eye, the threatening tones in the voice, it was as if his father's spirit lived within him. 'No! It's the truth,' I shouted as he yanked me painfully to my feet by the rope. I tried to kick his shins, ankles, trip him up, anything to distract him, to release his iron grip but it was useless. His physical strength far outweighed mine just as his father's had done decades before. I was a prisoner and my own son was my captor. 'Perhaps we need to jolt your memory,' he whispered cruelly into my ear. I felt sick to the pit of my stomach for I knew only too well our destination. My very worst nightmare had evolved into reality.

Hobbling painfully along the uneven ground I had no choice but to be dragged along with him. Eventually we came to a cross roads. To the left a signpost pointed to the sleepy hamlet of Briardale-on-Wye nestled in the valley, to the right was the Black-wood Gorge. We took the right. I tried to block out the little annoying voice in my head which kept repeating 'what goes around always comes around Wilhelmina. You didn't expect to get away with it did you?' After all those years my heinous crime had come back to haunt me. My nemesis had not taken into account my fighting spirit, that he would have to drag me on my back kicking and screaming before he could get me anywhere near that place. So, I stubbornly sat down in the middle of the road praying a passing vehicle would not run me over, but stop and rescue me. Of course, he soon lost his patience and started thrashing out with his fists as he endeavoured to drag me on to my feet, shortening the cord which bit painfully into my wrists, but wild horses couldn't have forced me to go there. No, when her time came Wilhelmina Potts was going to fade away peacefully in her bed.

My mind was reeling, suppose Molly had been murdered by Agatha Fortescue or one of her cronies. Maybe her body was lying in swirling, murky depths of the River Wye? Where was she? Why had nobody seen her? Not even this obnoxious human being standing next to me. What did some folks know but were too scared to tell? Why would they have slammed their doors in his face, when he had mentioned Mollie's name, maybe they recognised him and knew who his evil grandmother was. Tortured by these inner questions, I was determined to discover what had happened to my beautiful daughter.

Just at that point a young couple, their arms wrapped lovingly around each other, laughing and giggling, appeared around a corner. I was about to plead for their help, to do anything to get their attention. My son, in an attempt to allay suspicion, suddenly leaned in to my face and tried to stick his tongue down my throat, as we passed the young couple by. Had they noticed me struggling or spotted the rope my son had desperately tried to hide, I wondered? I could only pray. Risking a further assault I bit his tongue clamping down hard with my teeth. His face turned purple with rage and pain reminding me of Horace. My ugly flesh and blood lifted his hand to strike me, but then remembered the young witnesses nearby and tried to laugh. Aware that all was not quite right the young man suddenly turned around and raced back to face my captor. Having spotted the ligature binding my wrists and seen my silent plea for help. My saviour then told his girlfriend to call the Police; she had to run to the nearest call box which was a quarter of a mile down the lane.

Nevertheless my prayers were answered, although I was quite lucky if it hadn't been for the fact that my knight in shining armour was twice the size of my son and enjoyed wrestling, then things might have gone very differently. Thanks to him and his girlfriend, within fifteen minutes I was saved and he was bundled into a police car.

It turned out that my son was well known to the local law enforcement, having been partial to a bit of burglary including grievous bodily harm. There was a warrant out for his arrest. Thankfully the police were more interested in having captured their prey than bombarding me with lots of difficult questions.

So later that afternoon I left the police station with a deep sense of relief and an even deeper resolve to uncover the past until I found my little angel. With my son safely tucked away behind bars and the knowledge that Agatha was in hospital, hopefully lying at death's door, I was free to concentrate on finding Mollie and bring her home where she belonged.

'Granny' I interrupted, needing to know if what I suspected was true. 'Did you… have anything to do with Agatha's sudden collapse?' I asked trying to ignore the familiar glare, having disrupted her train of thought. She looked down and mumbled 'well I might have slipped her a little something.'

'Oh! My! God! Granny! You don't mean you tried to poison her?' I gasped.

'Kindly do not swear Mary. It is most unbecoming in a young lady dear and if you must know I did exactly what had to be done. If she writhed in agony for a few minutes so be it. It's what she deserved and more, much more.' She said with a cold frankness.

'So it was you who sent Agatha that ring.' I said, connecting the dots.

'Umm yes dear, you see I knew the stupid woman could be quite vain so letting her believe she had an admirer who wanted to send her a few gifts was so very easy.' She smirked.

'But… but you killed not just once but… but you tried to kill again' I suddenly blurted out.

'Mary kindly do not interrupt me any further, it is most tiresome. Now I really need to get this finished. Where are you going? Sit down this instant!'

I was already on my feet, still reeling from shock, my great grandmother was practically a serial killer.

'I have to go um… I've got an appointment,' I lied backing out of the room. 'I … I'll try and see you tomorrow Granny.'

'Tomorrow! I could be dead by tomorrow Mary!' I pretended not to hear.

I spent the night tossing and turning, I promised myself I wouldn't go back, I couldn't not after everything I just learned. In the end curiosity got the better of me and it wasn't long before I was sitting beside Granny once again.

'Now then Mary, where were we?' she queried.

'Umm I believe you had attempted to poison your stepmother, Granny' I told her trying to sound nonchalant about it.

'Oh yes! I remember … 'with Agatha out of the way, I decided to pay a visit to her house which I had heard had been put up for sale, though goodness knows why anyone would want to live within those four godforsaken walls. So the next morning I made my way up the hill to the foreboding fortress sitting on the top. Would it be empty, I wondered? Feeling very nervous my trembling hand lifted the heavy, ancient door knocker carved in the shape of a lion's head, and let it drop with a loud clang. No-one came. I knocked again and still nothing. Trying the door I felt, my heart leap into my mouth as with a loud creak it slowly opened. I could hear raised voices from within and knew I had heard them before but could not recall where or when. Though one thing was for sure they spelt danger. A nearby drape afforded a suitable hiding place and spy hole.

I stayed there for a good ten or fifteen minutes waiting until all was quiet again. Then leaving the safety of the thick protective curtain, I quickly tiptoed up the large winding, oak staircase intending to peep into the dark, forbidding rooms, only to find them all locked. I tried the staircase to the attics but again my search was fruitless, then it hit me maybe a clue to my daughter's fate would be in my stepmother's room.

Tiptoeing back down the creaking steps I made my way towards Agatha Fortescue's quarters, my heart thumping wildly and shivers tingling down my spine as I did. Expecting the heavy wooden door to be locked I placed my fingers around the knob and gasped as it turned. Taking a deep breath I ignored that little voice within saying 'Wilhelmina don't go in there, you're trespassing. Just get out and go home.' Instead I slithered into the blackness. As my eyes became accustomed to the dim light I spotted a table nearby covered in small animal skulls where feathers and clumps of fur lie in pools of congealed blood. I shuddered and quickly moved away. To this day I cannot say why but suddenly I felt drawn to a niche in the wall curtained off at the far end of the room. Still trying to quieten the little voice in my head, I carefully pulled back the heavy black drape and peered behind, only to take another sharp intake of breath.

Lit by a solitary candle was a large black coffin.

'Oh! My! Goodness gracious!' I whispered. Maybe Agatha wasn't in the hospital. Maybe she was dead after all and her body had been removed back to her house because nobody wanted to touch the old hag. Resisting the powerful urge to turn and run I picked up the candle resting on the coffin and looked nervously round the room. A stuffed black cat looked down at me amongst piles of thick, dust-laden volumes heaped untidily on a shelf in a large bookcase. Obeying an instinct I walked over to it. As I let my fingers run over the dusty, leather bound books wondering if they contained spells and curses, suddenly I heard a whirring noise. Struck dumb I stared in amazement as the bookcase slowly started to move towards me. Peering around I discovered a long steep flight of steps leading down to what appeared to be a heavy wooden door.

Whatever was behind that door both terrified and filled me with a burning curiosity, for I knew I had inadvertently discovered Agatha Fortescue's secret chamber. With strong trepidation I placed one foot on the narrow top step almost daring to breathe as the wood creaked and groaned under me. Fearing the noise might have alerted someone I rushed down to the bottom and quickly squeezed myself into a small recess under the steps while I tried to pluck up some shreds of courage which seemed to have temporarily flown completely out of the window. Hairs started to prickle on the back of my neck; I could hear my heart racing. What am I doing? What had I been thinking?

Instantly those thoughts were all forgotten as sheer panic set in, but it was not voices or footsteps I had heard. Oh my Lord! No! Racing frantically back up the rickety steps I was just in time to see the bookcase click tightly shut. I was trapped. After a few seconds of overwhelming horror I heard that irritating little voice in my head telling me 'well! Wilhelmina you got yourself into this fine mess now you've got to get yourself out of it. You've only got yourself to blame, shouldn't have been so nosy.' It continued unhelpfully. The candle suddenly flickered in the dim light as I unsuccessfully fumbled for the hidden switch somewhere in the shelves.

Refusing to cave in to despair I desperately tried to think of a way to get out, then remembered the secret room I discovered earlier. So I carefully made my way back down the creaky steps, one hand against the wall, the other holding the candle stick. I reached the last step then, took a deep breath, walked up to the old rotting door and slid my fingers around the cold metallic knob. My heart fluttered in my chest as the handle turned, I winced as the door groaned and squeaked open. Biting my lip in anticipation I peered through the gap, terrified of what I might find. A few heart beats later, I managed to calm down enough to realise that the room appeared empty.

Believing it to be safe I quietly slipped into the dank, windowless basement. The furniture was sparse, consisting of only an old single bed and a broken chair. The room was an icy cold, the kind that threatened to numb my bones and turn my skin blue. Or could that be Agatha's presence I could feel? It was in that moment I realised that I wasn't alone; there was a small figure on the bed huddled up in the corner. Instead of running away in fear, a wild thought crossed my mind and I had to obey my instincts but they had not prepared me, indeed nothing could have for what I was about to discover. Slowly I made my way towards the figure as I got closer the light from my candle shone across the room.

There was a woman, a young woman, bound to the bed with thick leather straps and covered by a filthy, blood-stained sheet. She was extremely thin with an emaciated face, which was barely recognisable, covered in dark bruises and open sores. I knew it was her, call it intuition or instinct, I knew after all those long, sad years I had finally discovered my beautiful Mollie. Was I too late?

Her sharp, blue eyes now lay in their sockets in dark sunken hollows. Her complexion instead of peaches and cream now had a greyish pallor. I lifted the dirty sheet, her jutting ribcage instantly reminding me of a prisoner of war in a concentration camp. She began to stir, opening her eyes but just looked at me with a glassy stare, the kind you see on someone who's been subjected to sustained abuse. Softly I whispered her name but not a flicker of recognition crossed her face.

Quickly I undid the straps wondering why she was tied down when escape was impossible anyway. I picked her up very gently, pulling her close, cuddling her to my chest. How I had longed for this moment, dreamed of it every night and never stopped believing it but never in a million years, had I expected it would be like this. In an effort to comfort her, I began stroking her face, talking to her to allay her fears forgetting for a few seconds being caught up in the moment we were both now trapped in this dungeon and in very real danger. Having no other option, I lay her back on the bed and pulled the straps back across her to prevent suspicion, on hearing a noise but it was my imagination playing cruel tricks.

If only I could give her a few sips of water but there was none to be found and like the blood stained, filthy sheet that covered her, she had not seen a wash for a very long time. As for her hair, someone had shaved off her beautiful long, blonde locks leaving her completely bald. Tears of sadness and guilt began to prick my eyes at the thought of what had happened to my little angel. There was something which shocked and disturbed me even more, her belly was swollen, I couldn't tell it was from malnutrition or, could she really be carrying my evil son's child? Surely no babe could have survived this, could it?

At that point my thoughts were interrupted by the familiar whirring noise from the top of the staircase. Desperately looking around the room for a place to hide, my inner voice whispered 'Quick, someone's coming, hide under the bed and keep calm. You know how clumsy you are when you panic'. Listening to it for the first time today, I threw myself on to the filthy floor and struggled to crawl under the old iron bedstead edging my way into the middle not realising I had company. Waiting patiently to catch its next meal was a large black hairy spider the size of a tarantula. Its web containing the remains of several disembowelled flies stretched from almost one side of the rusty bedstead to the other. Suddenly it darted out from the corner and ran across my body. I could feel the insect's hairy legs touch my skin. Desperately trying to stifle a scream I shut my eyes tightly and clamped my hand across my mouth as adrenaline coursed through my veins. Just at that point I heard the door creak and two people enter the room in conversation.

'Has she gone yet? Taking her time aint she, thought she would have snuffed it days ago. Did you remember the shroud?' said a deep gruff voice.

'Thought you said you were dealing with that.' The second whined in response.

'My! God! Can't be trusted with nothing you can't. Didn't ya listen to what Agatha said? It's time she was moved out of here now. You know the plan or have you forgotten that too, ya stupid cow? Remember Agatha asked us to finish what she started and we don't want no trouble now do we?' The first voice groaned while approaching the bed.

'She'll pay and she'll pay good I reckon once girl's ma thinks she's alive. Don't matter if she's not like and sooner she's in coffin the better. I take it you did send the letters?'

'Umm... well um... I left them in me room you see and now I can't find them. Disappeared off face of earth they 'ave.' She replied hesitantly.

'Never met anyone so damn stupid as you in all me born days.' The first one snapped.

I stopped listening to the pair arguing, my head was buzzing with everything I had just overheard. The coffin was empty awaiting its occupant, but it wasn't meant for Agatha's carcase but my own little angel's. What's more disturbing is that they didn't care whether she was alive or not before they incarcerated her body. Just where were they planning to take my Mollie lying only a few feet away so weak and wan at death's door, I wondered?

That wasn't my only problem however for the thick dust under the bed had got up my nostrils making me want to sneeze. Desperately fighting to hold it back I spluttered as I held my nose and then to my horror I heard one of them say, 'What was that?' Did you hear a noise?'

'What? I ain't heard nothing, now shut up and undo that strap. She's almost gone, suppose we could always use pillow to finish her.' She barked.

'No! I ain't touching no pillow or that coffin I'm telling ya now' the other shrieked in horror.

'Oh! Stop your belly-aching! You'll do as I say'

I lay stuck under that bed praying for a miracle waiting until the evil pair had left the room, having wrapped Molly in a dirty blanket and taken her away. My plan was to get out of the house as soon as possible, call a doctor and the police who would search the house, find my angel and I would have my daughter back and we would live happily ever after. That only happens in fairy tales.

With the coast clear and having no time to lose I struggled to roll myself out from under the bed. Then once free I rushed to the door, ran up the stairs and searched the bookcase, desperately running my fingers over it looking for the ingenious mechanism hidden within. At last, after what seemed like a matter of hours and not just a few minutes I heard the familiar click and once more the bookcase creaked open. Almost knocking something over in my haste, I ran to the door and placed my hand on the knob but this time it did not yield. Someone had locked it.

Terror swept over me choking me with its hold, I ran to the window forgetting that I was on the first floor. 'Now don't be stupid, you can't possibly jump from here, unless you want to break your neck, I argued with myself but maybe I could get on to that overhanging branch. Carefully lifting the heavy window sash I took a deep breath telling myself 'now is not the time to think of your phobia with heights, be brave Wilhelmina, don't be a baby you can do this, you have to' I then climbed out on to the narrow sill and inched gingerly towards the tree. Holding on for dear life I stretched out to grab the bough praying it would take my weight, but it was further away than I had realised. There was no turning back I just had to go for it and hurled myself towards the old elm. Somehow I made it, euphoria pulsed through me as I praised myself for my bravery, but it was to soon evaporate when I saw what was waiting for me on the ground.

My heart froze from hearing a long, deep growl followed by a vicious snarl. In my hasty plan I had forgotten Bruno, a huge black mastiff whose job was to prowl the grounds for intruders. Once again I was trapped. Bruno was circling the tree, every now and then he would stop to claw the trunk until finally he lay down and just waited. Eventually after what seemed like hours but was probably only ten minutes, I heard someone shout two magic words 'Bruno. Dinner!' The hound raced off in response, leaving the coast clear. Quickly I scrambled down from the tree, the bark scratching my skin and ran across the grounds making for the short cut leading to the town, heading for Dr. Johnson's surgery.

Adam Johnson was a middle aged man who was not exactly renowned for his bedside manner, given to being somewhat gruff and abrupt with his patients. He was sat at his desk and looking over his glasses staring at me as I begged and pleaded for his help. After a few moments of silence he spoke. 'My dear I think you're suffering from nervous exhaustion leading to paranoia and delusions I am going to prescribe these tablets and I want you …'

'No! doctor! I'm not ill.' I interrupted. 'It's my daughter Mollie who needs you. You've got to come with me before they kill her. Please, they're going to …' I begged.

'Mrs Potts just take two of these twice a day with a glass of water and....' He continued as if I hadn't said a word.

'No! You've got to come with me doctor before it's too late. We've got to get the police too.' I insisted. I don't know whether it was the desperation in my voice, but something made him succumb and finally he grabbed his bag and coat.

On the way I tried to tell him all about Agatha, babbling on about Charlotte's diary, my mother's death, witches, the note left on my mat and I could plainly see Adam Johnson still thought the woman sat in his car next to him dirty and dishevelled was definitely delusional. It was obvious he didn't believe a word I'd said nor did he want to risk looking foolish involving the police. But in case there was a grain of truth somewhere in this crazy tale, he couldn't risk his career by neglecting my plea for his help. Eventually after rounding a bend in the road I spotted Agatha's gloomy, sinister old house standing like an eyesore, in the beautiful surrounding scenery overlooking the valley. 'I am telling you again Mrs. Potts I am a very busy man; this had better be no cock and bull story.' The doctor glanced at me sternly.

'I know it might all sound a bit far-fetched doctor but it's no pack of lies, I promise.' I beseeched.

'Well we shall soon see Mrs. Potts.' Pulling himself from the car he strode up to the front door of the old mansion with me a few steps behind. He lifted the door knocker and dropped it with a loud clang three times then stood back and waited. Silence, one, two, three minutes passed but no-one answered. Running out of time and patience, I reached across the doctor and tried the handle. 'It's not locked doctor! Come on!' I demanded, storming into the place.

'Whatever are you doing Mrs Potts? That would be trespassing.' He said in shock.

'There's no time to worry about details like that doctor.' I tried desperately to pull him in. Suddenly appearing out of the blue baring its teeth and snarling, was Bruno.

'Stand perfectly still Mrs Potts. They only bite when they smell fear. It won't hurt you long as you don't look it in the eye.' Bruno belonged to Agatha who frequently kicked and mistreated the hound turning him into a vicious animal that now hated humans but I guessed this wasn't exactly the best time to tell the doctor about that. Rooted to the spot with terror, pinned against the wall we were each Bruno's prisoner. I looked at Dr Johnson, beads of perspiration glistened on his brow. He was as white as a sheet.

Bruno suddenly barked then uttered a loud, ferocious growl alerting the occupants in the house. A grumpy voice suddenly shouted 'Shut up Bruno! Be Quiet!' Just at that point one of Agatha's old cronies shuffled into the hallway leaning heavily on a wooden stick and clutching a black shawl close to her. I instantly recognised the old wizened face. How could I forget it? She was the one that had pinned me down and tried to kill me with those poisonous beans when I was pregnant with Mollie. 'Kindly call off your dog madam, I'm Dr. Johnson and if you would show me where I might find my patient. I understand someone is extremely ill in this house and …'

'Extremely ill! Nah! Dunno what you mean, no-ones ill 'ere. You've got wrong 'ouse you 'ave doctor.' She rasped.

'Please madam, please call off this vicious animal immediately.' He said, turning paler by the second. I watched with baited breath as I heard the hound growl then yelp as the old woman cruelly beat him with her stick.

'Get in ya kennel!' she demanded. Bruno was already slinking away with his tail between his legs. Then the old woman, bent with age slowly trudged her way over to the door and without a word opened it. Dr. Johnson couldn't leave fast enough.

'Come along Mrs. Potts, hurry up now! You heard her say there's nobody ill in the place' trying to usher me out of the house.

'But doctor …' I begged, but Adam Johnson wasn't listening. He was only too glad to get away, nothing would drag him back.

'Mrs Potts just get in the car and as soon as you get home take those tablets I prescribed.' Having made it perfectly clear I could not expect any further help from him I went to the police station pleading with them to search the house, however hope ended in despair when they told me they had found nothing suspicious. Then they had also spoken to Dr. Johnson too who was now more than ever convinced I was delusional.

Agatha had won. She had taken her revenge; an eye for an eye and so had I, but in doing so we had both become blinded and ultimately it would destroy both of our lives.

Despite his crimes the courts only gave my son six months behind bars and before long he was free. It was round about then the notes started arriving demanding first, one hundred pounds then two and the last asked for five hundred or dismemberment of five fingers. The first ransom note had been carefully wrapped around a stone and hurled through my window sending shards of glass flying across my living room. Who was writing them? Was it the evil pair living in Agatha's house or, could it be my son taking his revenge? After all I had told him his father had been trapped in a snare that he had fallen to his death and in one note it had mentioned the device attached to Horace's leg and the deep gorge which contained a body. I still had a gut feeling someone else had witnessed my crime that dark day in Black Gorge Woods. I looked at the last note and stared at the writing, being barely legible, then remembered the terrifying threat and shuddered. I knew this person meant business but five hundred pounds where on earth was I going to find that kind of money, earning only a pittance cleaning the local post office a couple of days a week?

'You cannot even consider going to the police Wilhelmina; that would be as good as to commit suicide, they would investigate and unearth the truth then how could you search for Mollie.' I argued with myself, but surrendering to blackmail would be unthinkable, the demands would never stop, it would never end.

Convinced it was only now a matter of time before my arrest or fingers being amputated I decided to pack my bags and leave the next day. There was only one person in the whole world in whom I could confide but she was hundreds of miles away and I had no idea of her address.

My roughly formed plan involved moving to a different town somewhere in the south perhaps, maybe on the coast as I had a special affinity with the sea, or a farm having gained plenty of experience working on Mrs Rogers' smallholding but a place where I would be completely unknown. What have you got that is worth staying for anyway Wilhelmina? Interrupted that familiar little voice. You've lost everything and you have only yourself to blame. Mollie is never going to walk through that door because of you.' That voice taunted. Yes it was time to move on and move on fast, unaware that fate was about to deal its own surprising hand.

8

A New Beginning

I was in shock. Pinching myself to check I was not dreaming I read the letter for the tenth time, taking deep breaths to calm my nerves. It was from a firm of solicitors who had been dealing with Hector's will.

Their client, Mr. Hector Crabtree, had bequeathed to me a house, situated in Cork, Ireland.

I was spinning, my imagination running wild, picturing myself as the lady of a manor. It would have grand rooms with high decorative ceilings, striking antique furniture and walls adorned with beautiful paintings by Monet or Van Gogh. Perhaps I would have a few silver ornaments on display to suggest an air of ostentation. There would be a great ballroom where I'd dance with the elite and the gentry under an array of exquisite crystal chandeliers glistening in the light. There would be music and laughter bursting through the house every night if I wished, a complete contrast to that dark, grim household of my childhood.

You see, I knew Hector had been successful and always strived for the best. So in my mind his house would be no exception.

'This has got to be a mistake, this can't be the right address.' There was no error. Bitter disappointment swept through me as I stood in front of what was now mine, nothing more than a dilapidated old building more fit for demolition than habitation. All my dreams and fantasies suddenly evaporated and I was all alone in a strange place. The ghosts of my past had reappeared once more to haunt, to punish, and to destroy any crumb of happiness I might have. Surely Hector had not been living here I thought, then remembered the little communication there had been between us. What on earth happened to my brother? I decided to try and put together the missing pieces of his life after Agatha dispatched him to the Emerald Isle.

Deeply curious to see inside the house I inserted the key into the lock, turned it and pushed. The old wooden door creaked open, flecks of its dark green paint crumbling to the ground as it hit the wall. Cautiously I walked in, worried that the house would do the same. I began to look round in dismay; evidence of Hector was everywhere. Used crockery left in the sink, the unmade bed with a stained sheet and his unwashed clothes which lay in a heap on the floor. At first I didn't believe these dirty scraps of cloth belonged to him until I searched the pockets of an old, brown jacket that had seen better days and found a utility bill bearing his name and address. There was no evidence of the Hector I'd always known the smart, neat, proud man filled with enthusiasm and ambition. Just a slob created from a deep depression which he had sadly fallen into I later learned when he had lost all the trappings he'd carefully acquired while striding along life's highroad. A glamorous wife, a son and a beautiful estate had all been his, but the Stock Market had changed all that. He lost all his money, his marriage and his child.

Nevertheless it had been a long day and I suddenly felt very weary. I went over to an old armchair by the fireplace, removed an old newspaper then patted the seat before dropping into it only to be covered in a thick layer of dust. I jumped back up coughing and spluttering. 'Well maybe I shall have a cup of tea instead and then fetch some wood. Once I've got a roaring fire going I'll feel much better,' I told myself.

When I walked into the tiny, ill equipped kitchen my heart sunk again. A thick layer of grime coated every kitchen surface including a small cracked window adorned in cobwebs and a filthy lace curtain. Black mould spores covered the walls. I reached into the cupboard above the greasy sink and found a lone mug sitting on the shelf then almost dropped it with disgust. At the bottom of the cup lay a thick coating of penicillin mould. Aghast I threw it into the bin which was overflowing with household rubbish surrounded by a swarm of flies then went in search of cleaning cloths and disinfectant but unsurprisingly none were to be found.

However, apart from the filth, cockroaches, and large spiders, not forgetting the rats I did find something. It completely knocked me sideways… but I'll tell you all about it tomorrow, I really must nap now Mary.' Pausing to yawn, 'you know where the door is dear. Don't forget to lock it on your way out and don't be late tomorrow.'

Keen to be punctual the following day I arrived outside Great Granny's flat at 9.55 am, felt for the key hanging on a string behind the door, pulled it through the letter box and let myself in only to find my great grandmother still in bed. Concerned, I enquired if she was feeling unwell as lying in bed longer than six am was something Granny never did.

'I'm fine dear; I just forgot to set my clock. I may be many things but a lazybones I am not,' she announced passionately.

'Now Mary dear would you pass me my stick and I will need you to help me put on the clothes I have laid out ready to wear today. First turn on my fire, it's a wee bit chilly in here this morning. I expect Mildred will be along shortly with my breakfast then we can get on with my little project. I can not work on an empty stomach.'

'Um Granny,' I ventured, handing her the solid wooden cane, 'what did you find in Hector's house?' She paled suddenly.

'Oh that! Such a shock, a real slap in the face, I never expected my Fred to do that, not in a million years! You see I discovered a letter he had written to Hector about six months after we were married, asking for his advice. To this day I wish I had never read.' She said with such sadness in her eyes.

'What did it say?' I asked, but as usual when confronted with a painful memory she needed a few minutes to compose herself then search for the right words . 'Fred had written;

Hector my dear friend; I am turning to you for help in a difficult situation in which I find myself. I really don't know what to do and am on the verge of leaving Wilhelmina. Indeed she is becoming more and more impossible with every day that passes. No matter how hard I try I just can not do right by her. I believe there is something troubling her deeply, about her past maybe and that is why I'm writing to you, to ask if you can get her to confide in you as she refuses to discuss it with me. Whatever secret she holds is slowly destroying our marriage. She talks in her sleep sometimes and the things she says well, it makes shivers run down my spine and my blood run cold. Wilhelmina has always been my world from the day we met, she called me her rock, but now she keeps pushing me away. I might as well be a stick of furniture in the house. To be honest my friend I'm finding it very difficult to ignore her constant irritable, bad tempered moods. After all, she wasn't the only red apple on the tree. There are plenty more out there ripe for plucking and if Wilhelmina doesn't change her ways then I may just give in to temptation.'

'Humph! Not the only red apple on the tree eh! Fred Potts! Well I never! You old devil!' I tore Hector's letter into shreds feeling a mixture of anger, hurt, guilt and rejection. How could he? He just left and now I know why. Red apple indeed!

Feeling upset and broken hearted, I looked around the room for a distraction when my glance happened to fall on the old newspaper I had removed from the chair and had intended to place in the bin. An advertisement for a lady's maid caught my eye. The paper was well out of date of course but maybe there would be another vacancy if that one had been filled.

After letting out another large yawn, I walked into the small, dirty, untidy bedroom and over to the bed telling myself after a good night's sleep I would feel able to take on the world. Having removed the stained sheet I climbed in still wearing my clothes; feeling tired enough to sleep on a clothes line. The bed dipped in the middle, creaked and groaned on every movement. I lay there tossing and turning hearing intermittent claps of thunder followed by heavy rain drops beating against the window pane. Eventually I dropped off into a restless slumber only to wake to discover the bed bugs had eaten me alive!

The following morning I tried to plan my new life. 'First I will get the house sorted seeing with dismay the half full bucket of rain water that had poured through the cracked ceiling from a hole in the roof when the heavens had opened during the night. Then I shall buy some new furniture and burn every rotting stick, I have inherited. So I will need to find myself a new man, preferably a wealthy widower, then I could also have a few posh dresses.' I wasn't endowed with pesky wrinkles or warts in those days you see Mary and a few men gave me more than just a second glance when I went out, I'll have you know. 'Until 'Mr. Moneybags' comes along you will need to earn some money, that little annoying voice in my head reminded me.'

'So to add to your sins Granny you were also a gold digger?' I asked flippantly earning a steely glare as she continued, 'so I decided to take a walk over to Wedgwood Manor being only a couple of miles away. Of course if I'd had that wonderful thing called hindsight I dare say I would never have bothered. Anyway I made my way across the fields and down a lane but as I walked past the lodge on the edge of the estate I felt a sense of uneasiness. Something was telling me to turn back. I paid no heed and even quickened my pace heading towards the large imposing mansion fronted by four great pillars and three large stone lions.

On looking around the vast room I had been ushered into, by the young servant who had answered my loud knock, I noticed why it had been aptly called Wedgwood Manor. Different hues of blue and green Wedgwood framed the large paintings of the family's ancestors as well as the colourful murals on the walls. Beautifully painted, fine Wedgwood china was displayed pretentiously in cabinets, on tables, in fact, almost everywhere one happened to glance.

'Why couldn't my house have looked like this', I mumbled to myself. Suddenly the door swung open and a woman, I mentally placed in her late forties, marched towards me. Peering over her spectacles she looked me up and down before snapping 'SIT!' as if I were a dog. After a few perfunctory questions I was eventually told 'well I suppose you'll have to do! I hope you can do book keeping the last woman was absolutely hopeless!' I nodded quickly in response.

'Be here tomorrow at five thirty am on the dot and in future kindly remember to use the back entrance' she barked leaving the room. Later I was to learn that the woman's name was Mrs. Alice Jayne Thornton-Woods and in her youth she had been a debutante enjoying a series of admirers, though it was hard to believe now as her face resembled more of a road map than a beauty.

There was also a husband on the scene that I was about to meet unexpectedly.

The role of housekeeper came with my own quarters, though they were not particularly to my taste. I hated the dark brown walls, tiny window and lack of space. 'Not even room to swing a cat,' Charlotte would have said. It will have to do, till something better comes along.

For some time I had tactfully tried to dismiss the playful slap on the bottom or a mischievous wink as I walked by but I'm sure Alice Thornton-Woods hadn't failed to notice his behaviour as he could not have been more blatant. It was obvious from observing their body language that his wife found him disgusting, irritating and according to gossip had been rejecting him between the sheets for some time. Therefore, he turned his intentions towards others.

One day remains burned into my memories. That was the day I was to discover Mr. Thornton-Woods had a dark side. It was late in the evening when I returned to my quarters, my feet were aching, my head throbbing and I was longing to rest my weary bones. As I approached my room I noticed my door was slightly ajar. 'How strange I could have sworn I had locked it' I said to myself pushing it open. I stood frozen, blinking twice on seeing a man whom I instantly recognised, lying half naked on my bed.

In his early forties, greying at the temples with rugged handsome looks and a firm physique Matthew Thornton-Woods would not have been a bad catch if it wasn't for his arrogance and roving eye.

'I've been keeping the bed warm whilst I waited for you my dear' he said with a charming smile while stroking the top cover.

'Well now sir I would be obliged if you would get right out of it and kindly leave my room. Whatever do you take me for sir? How dare you think I would...' I spluttered.

'Oh shut up woman!' He barked as he leapt from the rickety wooden bed then picked me up and roughly flung me on to a nearby chair. 'Now understand this maid, I am the master of this house and you will do as I say or you'll be sorry. I could make things very difficult for you round here.' At first I was taken aback at this but then I had a cunning thought, the power behind a man's throne is usually a woman. Only a clever, ambitious woman allows the man to go on believing that he holds the reins. It was then I decided to change my tactics. However, my hand was soon to be exposed. You see when I entered the room, in a state of shock, I hadn't thought to ensure that the door was tightly shut.

He held out his hand. Seductively I moved towards him employing all my womanly wiles, passionately succumbing to his lips, running my fingers through his hair and allowing his wandering palms to caress my body, cupping my breasts. I started whispering in his ear, hinting that if I were to be his mistress I needed beautiful clothes, fancy jewellery and a house, preferably one without a leaking roof or a population of rats and spiders.

After having taken me for a few brief moments into seventh heaven, he promised me the sun, moon and stars, little did I know then that his promises were merely piecrust, easily made and easily broken.'

'Oh! Do you really want me to write that down Granny, the umm... taking you into a seventh heaven I mean?' I asked hesitantly, interrupting her.

'Why ever not Mary, I am not so old that I have forgotten what it feels like to have an orgasm dear. I told you that I led a rather colourful life and I do not regret one single moment of it well... that is apart from well you know.' She said avoiding my stare.

'Yes Granny, I do', I replied wondering if my cheeks were bright red from embarrassment at the mention of orgasms.

'Now you've made me lose my train of thought Mary.' She snapped, huffing in frustration.

'Umm... Mr. Thornton-Woods,' I prompted.

'Ah! Yes! Him! Well a few hours later I received the summons and the sack. Alice Thornton-Woods stood facing me with her eyes blazing, clenching her teeth as she spoke. 'How dare you behave so appallingly under my roof and with my husband then lie so blatantly. You've brought shame to this house; you're nothing but... a common whore, now pack your bags and get out of my sight.'

Having nothing to lose with anger pulsing though me, I retorted 'you must be blind if you cannot see that your husband thinks you are cold and frigid, you have only yourself to blame if he strays.'

However, I wasn't going to give him up for I had found my 'Mr. Moneybags' and was determined I was not going to lose him. Even if he did have a wrinkle faced, sharp tongued wife, but nevertheless still a wife until death or the courts released him from her. Then that little inner voice intervened whispering 'Wilhelmina perhaps there's a way you can hasten things up a bit there ...'

'Oh! My! God! Granny please tell me you didn't… you couldn't have… you …' I froze in shock, wondering what my great grandmother was about to say next.

'Whatever are you babbling on about Mary and kindly refrain from swearing I have told you before I…' Before she could finish a familiar voice belonging to Mildred interrupted us as she poked her head round the door to ask if her aunt would like some stewed apple and custard for dinner. 'Need to eat plenty of fruit Aunt Wilhelmina, good for the bowels remember, and I'll do you a nice stew with some dumplings, your favourite. Need to fatten you up a bit, get some meat on those…'

'Mildred can't you see I'm busy? And I don't need fattening up, thank you very much!' puffed Granny indignantly.

'Right stewed apple, custard and dumplings it is then,' her voice echoing down the hallway as a clock somewhere in the house struck eleven.

'Now where were we again Mary?' I decided to evade the number of questions buzzing around my head and replied 'Umm…'Mr. Moneybags' I believe.' 'Ah yes! Mathew Thornton-Woods! Well after that little episode in the bedroom I decided it was time to put my little plan into action, so I packed my case and headed back to England and thank goodness I did too, as I learned something incredible.

When I returned, I happened to bump into Constable Tommy Wilson. The same policeman, it turned out, who many months before had helped search Agatha's house, you know after my unforgettable visit with Dr. Johnson. Tommy Wilson had a keen observant eye and diligence to duty, which made up for his lack of experience. Well on that day he explained his concerns;

'There was something bothering me Mrs. Potts, I couldn't put my finger on it but something was definitely not right in that house. So I returned and questioned the occupants further, taking them back to the station, and eventually one of them opened up about your daughter.' Bit by bit he had learned they had used Juju, a form of witchcraft thought to have originated in West Africa. Apparently a Juju priest had been asked to perform an appalling ritual on your girl. I listened in sheer horror as he described how the priest had informed his victim he had access to her soul and had threatened her with death if she did not obey his obscene and barbaric demands. The pair of them had stripped Mollie naked, bound her arms, shaved off her blonde locks and body hair then repeatedly slashed her skin with razor blades. Her blood was then collected and placed in a coffin as the ritual demanded. The horrifying abuse had not stopped there as their victim was then forced to eat the raw heart of a freshly slaughtered chicken before being thrown into another casket where she had lain in agony.

Apparently in parts of West Africa still embedded in the Dark Ages this abhorrent and appalling abuse is still practiced today on young, vulnerable girls before being sold into another living hell, the dark life of prostitution somewhere in Europe, Constable Wilson informed me. As soon as all this had been revealed an ambulance was quickly dispatched to the house where they had found Mollie on the brink of death. Just a few minutes later and it would have been too late. Though eventually her body had recovered, sadly the trauma she suffered had taken away her sanity and she was now a sad, pathetic patient in a psychiatric hospital destined never to leave its institutional life. Upon hearing this all the guilt that I had tried to push away, came flooding back and it wasn't helped by a dream I had that night.

I was stood in a cemetery, looking at my mother's headstone when a white feather suddenly landed out of the blue on my shoulder. As I stared at it she suddenly floated up from the grave then wrapped her arms around me and whispered something in my ear. 'Wilhelmina my dear you will never find happiness until you learn to give it. What has revenge ever brought you all these years but misery, heartbreak and tears? Have you lost your mind my sweet child? I could see what you were planning, you were going to poison Alice Thornton-Woods weren't you? So you could step into her shoes and take over the Manor with all its wealth and opulence. She'll never give him a divorce and you know it. He is too weak to stand up to that woman. He's just using you all he wants is your body, nothing more and nothing less, certainly not another wife. When are you going to learn Wilhelmina? My dear, do not let your past dictate what you are but let it mould you into what you can become. You need to change your ways help others, not manipulate them. I too saw what happened to Horace Fortescue by that waterfall in Black Gorge Woods. Now dear girl you must do what is right. Only then shall I be proud of you.'

I awoke with a gasp, tears streaming down my face. That dream had a profound effect on me; it became a turning point, making me take a long, hard look at my life. How could I have let myself sink so low? Shame and guilt once more enveloped almost suffocated me. It was time to make some important decisions. There was nothing for me in Ireland. My house was barely habitable. I had lost my job, and Mr. Thornton-Woods, well I certainly didn't want an arrogant, selfish, manipulative philanderer. So I decided to make a new life in England, to be near Mollie. Hoping one day she would open her eyes and recognise me so I could tell her how I had searched for her, how she meant the world to me and how I was so desperately sorry for everything that had happened. That was not to be.

Having sold my inheritance for a pittance being all it was worth and relinquished my dream of owning my own manor with all its fine possessions, I conceded that Alice Thornton-Woods was the 'rightful owner' of Matthew Thornton-Woods, wishing her best of luck with him and never returned to the Emerald Isle.

My mother's words constantly haunted me and I was determined to regain her pride. So with the sum of money I received from the sale of Hector's cottage and the small piece of land accompanying it, I decided to buy a cheap little two bedroom terrace house, down the road from Mollie's hospital, then advertised for a lodger to help make ends meet. I also took in the town folk's laundry, visited the sick, carried out umpteen errands for those confined to their own four walls, made clothes for the poor and went to church every Sunday. Yes, my dear mother would have been so proud. My busy agenda also included visiting the women's wing of the county detention as I strove to be 'a light to the blind, speech to the dumb and feet to the lame.' There was only one person who knew I was hiding a dark secret, me.

The dreaded nightmares would not stop; frequently I would wake up in a cold sweat having seen the two old wizened faces, whose voices I recognised from the dreadful day when I had found Mollie. No, I couldn't forget that pair no matter how hard I tried, those faces had to be avenged. I needed justice. That was the day I knew I would never redeem myself in my mother's eyes, because she had seen into my heart, looked into my soul, she felt my need for revenge.

Brownhill Jail, despite its Governor's best intentions, was not a place that inspired much hope. Indeed most of its detainees were almost beyond it, some having murdered members of their own families. I shall never forget on one of my visits when I witnessed an inmate being abused and threatened, but what stuck in my mind was the abuser. She was an old woman, the very same old woman who had abused me many years ago, when I had been pregnant with Mollie. I rushed to alert a prison officer who reacted by saying 'Oh! It's her again is it making trouble, might have known. Never a day goes by without her upsetting someone in here.' I realised that the old crone had made a few enemies in Brownhill who, like me, thought it was time she paid a price for her actions.

Not long after that day, I bumped into the same inmate who mumbled quietly under her breath 'thank you missus, things were now sorted. The old hag got a sugar bath, pulled into the showers, stripped naked then had boiling water mixed with sugar poured all over her.'

I enquired 'why use sugar' and learned it helps increase the intensity of the pain because sugar adheres to the skin. Apparently her assailants had all sung at the tops of their voices to drown out the screams, but the prison wardens had merely turned a blind eye.'

'I believe that horrible maltreatment still happens in certain prisons today Granny', I interrupted in horror. She went on, ignoring me, 'yes I could now cross another name off my list.'

As usual that Saturday I had gone to visit Mollie in the hospital. As I was about to enter the ward a young doctor brushed my arm and asked if I would pop into his office for a little chat.

'We had a little incident this morning and I'm afraid we had to sedate Mollie. You see she became extremely agitated when this man came to see her.

She started screaming at him to go away and leave her alone then she attempted to jump out of the window, barred of course. Then to everyone's horror the stranger suddenly drew a gun, picked Mollie up, threw her over his shoulder and threatened to shoot if anyone approached him. 'She belongs to me, she's mine and I'm taking her out of here', he kept yelling. We called security of course but somehow he got away when he ran downstairs into the hospital basement, although we managed to get him to drop Mollie first thank goodness. The police have been informed but as far as I know the man is still at large. Would you by any chance know who he might be Mrs. Potts?'

I felt sick. The description fitted someone I knew only too well, someone whom I had prayed would never see again. I certainly didn't need the police asking me any awkward questions, so just mumbled, 'Umm... I believe he had met my daughter a long time ago and had taken a shine to her but she didn't reciprocate his feelings.'

Later at home I was sitting by the fire, mulling over this conversation when I was startled by a loud noise, a crashing sound that sent my nerves into panic mode. I knew it definitely was not my imagination. I sat up straight eyes and ears alert, heart pounding furiously. 'Just pull yourself together Wilhelmina,' I told myself sharply,' My stomach was lurching and beads of sweat began to pool on my brow. My mouth had suddenly gone very dry. I left the fireside and quickly made my way to the kitchen where I grabbed first my ten inch carving knife and then a claw hammer from the drawer. Then with trepidation I slowly opened the door, which lead into the dark hall and called out in a faltering voice 'who's there? Come on out. Show yourself. I know you're hiding. I have called the Police!' Then brandishing my lethal weapons in sweaty palms, pulse racing, heart in my mouth I took a deep breath and practically ran to the end of the hall to switch on the light cursing whoever had placed the wiring there in the first place.

To my horror I noticed that the door to the cupboard under the stairs was slightly open. 'Don't go looking in there Wilhelmina, it's dark and full of cobwebs, and suppose someone' but then brushing those thoughts away, I bravely slid my fingers around the knob, took another deep breath and yanked open the door. A streak of orange fur suddenly shot past me, almost knocking me off my feet as it sped away. Fumbling around for the light pull, I sighed with relief seeing broken pieces of pottery all over the floor, along with the contents of two boxes that had been tipped upside down when the cat had tried to jump onto the shelf at the back.

'So that's what that noise was and you got yourself all in a dither for nothing'. I laughed at myself as I placed the knife and hammer back in the kitchen drawers where they belonged.

After that night I decided it would be best to lie low for a while until the furore over my son had died down. It was at that point I received a telephone call, 'Hello I understand you have a vacancy for a lodger. Could I come and view the room today' and that's how I came to meet Harold Williams.

In fact he was a rather nondescript little man, stocky build, dark haired with sprouts of grey, in his late forties, who had never married, preferring his own company. I was struggling to pay the bills and as Mr. Williams was the only applicant I chose to ignore the niggling thought at the back of my mind saying 'beware, all is not what it seems.' A week or so later Harry Williams, along with a few sticks of his favourite furniture and a noisy parrot which had picked up a few choice words of blasphemy, took up residence in my little house.

About three months after he had settled in I invited him to join me for my evening meal and a glass of red wine although, perhaps if I had known he was an alcoholic, I might have thought twice. I suppose I felt sorry for Harry as neither family nor friends ever paid him a visit. 'Don't need them anyway, rely on myself always have, always will,' I was told when I enquired. Then I caught him staring, undressing me with his eyes. Next he put the fear of God into me when he suddenly rose from his chair, marched over to the back door, turned the key and slipped it into in his pocket. I swallowed hard.

'We don't want to be disturbed now do we Mrs Potts.' I most certainly did.

Then I watched aghast as he went to draw the curtains plunging the room into a semi darkness sending my adrenaline levels spiralling through the ceiling.

'I've… umm… invited one of the doctors over from the hospital; he should be here any time now' I stammered, lying through my teeth. 'So if you don't mind I'll take the key Mr. Williams.'

'That won't be necessary Mrs Potts because you're not going to let him in. You're going to tell him to go away. I want you all to myself.'

'Just give me my door key' I retorted. 'I'm getting quite tired of your stupid games Mr. Williams.' I started to back up to the door.

'I'm not sure I like your tone my dear' he said, pushing me down on the sofa promptly planting himself next to me. A rough hand squeezed my knee, an arm snaked round my shoulders and then to my horror his fingers slipped under my skirt and slowly began to creep up my inner thigh as he leaned in to make a pass. Before they could travel any further I quickly removed them, wriggled out of his grasp and gave his face a resounding slap.

'How dare you Mr. Williams! Now hand over my key then collect your things and kindly leave my house before I call the Police'. I demanded, holding my left hand out, while the other pointed towards the door. He looked up at me as he held his cheek, which had turned a deep crimson. Then he pushed his face into mine and spat 'you're going to regret doing that Mrs. Potts. When folk upset me they have to pay you see, as you will soon discover.'

Just at that point Mildred suddenly burst into the room carrying a large tray interrupting the suspense. 'Now then aunt, I've made you a nice heart-warming stew. Put all your papers away, I haven't been slaving over a hot stove to see you let it go cold. Eat it all up, I want to see a nice clean plate when I return and I don't want to find any food hidden in a plant pot this time. Do you understand?'

'Mildred dear, thank you, I'm not a child, and kindly don't speak to me as if I were.' Her niece just sighed, placed the tray down on the table and bustled out of the room as quickly as she had come in.

'I'll… umm… come back later Granny around two thirty,' I interceded trying to ease the tension. 'Enjoy your meal.' Granny was too busy mumbling under her breath, 'no respect for her elders, accusing me of hiding my dinner in a plant. How dare she!'

9

The Premonition

Six months had passed since Mr. Williams' abrupt departure and the nights had begun to draw in bringing chilly temperatures. As I walked back home down the long, winding lane from the hospital, from visiting Mollie, I suddenly had a premonition. I shivered at the very thought and tried to put it out of my mind. It was so hideous. Don't be so ridiculous, that's never going to happen, trying to reassure myself desperately pushing away the terrifying image of me fighting for my life, begging for mercy from a demonic, twisted human being. Then I remembered I had borne a son who was intent on perpetrating evil and was only too aware his hatred for his mother held no bounds.

I pulled up the collar of my coat in an attempt to keep out the biting cold wind and quickened my pace, every few seconds turning round fearful someone could be following me, having become paranoid since my abduction, but no-one was to be seen.

'Just a few more minutes and you'll be safe at home sitting by a roaring fire' I told myself.

All of a sudden, a car came screeching round the bend, its lights blinding and its horn blaring. Having no other option, I was forced to jump into a nearby ditch or risk being mowed down. Landing in the dirt, shocked and startled I watched as the driver sped away disappearing round the next bend.

'You stupid, idiotic fool,' I shouted after him.

Not long afterwards winter arrived with a vengeance bringing frost, ice and snow. To the old it meant slippery pavements, painful falls and often fractured bones. To the young it meant a joyous adventure having fun skating on the ice, snowball fights, sledging down steep hills while shouting with glee. Unfortunately, by this point I slipped into the old category and desperately tried to wrap up warm.

One night, in the middle of this bitter season, I had been to visit Mollie and was making my way home, deep in thought oblivious to my surroundings, when I was suddenly accosted. I don't remember much except an almighty pain at the back of my head causing me to fall into a dark, bottomless pit of unconsciousness. Sometime later I began to wake only to discover to my utmost horror I had been kidnapped and bundled face downwards into the boot of a speeding car.

Gripped with terror I struggled to be free, moving my arms and hands but to no avail. My arms were trapped behind my back. Masking tape had been bound around my wrists so tight my hands were starting to go numb. It also adhered to my eyelids. My shoulders began to ache and my head throbbed with a relentless pain.

I tried to scream but couldn't, there was something in my mouth, it tasted obnoxious making me want to retch. Then reality hit me with a thunderous force. Someone had soaked a rag in petrol, rammed it down my throat and taped my mouth shut. The nauseating stench from the toxic fumes was overwhelming, suppose they strike a match?

I quickly pushed that terrifying thought to the side.

The car was travelling at high speed throwing my body this way and that. I gagged again, forced to swallow my vomit, retching emotionally and physically, adrenaline was pumping through my veins. I honestly believed that day I was going to die and not a single soul would know I had gone missing.

Suddenly there was a squeal of brakes as the car jolted forward to a halt. I lay there with baited breath as I heard the driver get out and slam the door. This is it, I thought, convinced I was going to be battered again but this time to death.

A blast of icy cold air hit me as the boot of the car was yanked wide open, I felt rough hands grab hold of my body and drop me like a stone on to the cold wet ground. Then I heard his voice, a voice that haunts me every day, a voice that I will take with me to my grave.

'Get up bitch!' He shouted. 'I've not finished with ya yet, we've got some unfinished business. Now get up ya stupid old woman!' he shouted, viciously kicking me with his heavy boot, as if I were a football. Instinctively I curled up my body trying to protect my head from his blows. He bent down and grabbed my hair, yanking me to my feet then proceeded to drag me along with him, yelling in my ear, 'walk slut! Walk!'

I stood frozen; in the distance I could hear rushing water. 'Didn't I tell you to walk bitch,' he pushed me in front of him causing me to lurch forward. The ground was covered in muddy puddles from the thawed snow which soaked into my shoes. Then compounding my misery even further overhanging branches scratched my face as I stumbled along in the total darkness. Survival instincts screamed out escape, for I knew there was only one place, one dark scary, terrifying place he would choose to play his sick and twisted games. An owl hooted through the silence as nocturnal life in the wood began to wake up. Stumbling through the trees, I shivered and trembled from a deep, petrifying fear, as the icy wind blew straight through my body.

'Stop!' He suddenly barked.

I recoiled feeling his coarse fingers touch my face as he painfully ripped the masking tape from my mouth then pulled out the disgusting rag. I tried to spit out the nauseating taste of petrol that was stuck in my throat.

'Hey bitch, ya gonna pay for that,' he threatened. Apparently some of my spittle had landed on him, earning me a sharp kick on the shin. Yelping in agony I tried to rub my leg with my other one to ease the pain. Panic consumed me and I screamed out, 'Help! Please help me! Someone help me!'

He just laughed, a deep raucous sound, 'no-one's gonna hear ya.' He was right, I knew he was, but I refused to give up hope; it was all I had left. That soon deserted me as my blood ran icy cold.

'I've waited all me life for this night.' He said slobbering and smacking his lips against mine. Then he pushed his hand into my blouse and grabbed a breast sinking his long sharp and no doubt filthy finger nails into my skin. I screamed out again as his other hand suddenly shot up my leg and began to tug at my underwear.

'No! Maybe I'll have dessert bit later I've still got main course to work through yet' guffawing at his little joke as he pushed me off balance causing me to fall heavily on my knees. I could feel blood trickling down my leg but that was the least of my worries. I was mortified. Oh! My! God! He's going to rape me! What man rapes his own mother? I desperately tried to remove the sticky tape biting into my flesh, pulling on the little hairs on my arms.

'Ya see,' he shouted over the wind, 'I was brought up to believe in an eye for an eye, I mean if someone should stab you then it's only right you stab them back. Don't you agree?'

'I'll not waste my breath on the likes of you,' I spat struggling to be free. 'Saving it then for your dying day are ya, like today maybe?' He hissed.

He went to grab my arm pulling it so hard it felt like it would dislocate as I desperately did my utmost to resist and quickly sat back down, determined

I was not going anywhere. Even fleeing from my nemesis was fraught with danger with tape blocking my sight and my hands tied firmly together behind my back. I could have easily stumbled and fallen to my death.

The loud crescendo from the high waterfall became almost deafening and instinct told me that I was dangerously near the edge, the same edge that decades past I held Horace over before committing him to his watery grave, and now it was my turn. He sat down next to me, assailing my nostrils with his pungent odour and started fumbling in his pockets for something. Then started to swear vociferously as he struck match after match, striving to light a cigarette in the gusting wind.

'You see mother I've all the time in the world, shame about you though. Maybe an hour, maybe only a few minutes then puff, gone forever', and let out another hideous laugh as he blew tobacco smoke into my face making me cough and splutter. I turned my face away and once again screamed 'HELP!' at the top of my lungs, but the high winds and rush of water, drowned out my hopeless pleas.

In desperation I tried again to wriggle my hands free from the tape only to have the monster stub his cigarette on the back of my neck and laugh when I screamed in pain. Then he…my face….' Wilhelmina Potts paused and looked away slowly bringing her hand up to her cheek letting her fingers gently feel for the old scar, as a tear rolled over it. She fell silent.

'Granny would you like to stop now, no sense in upsetting yourself like this?' I asked, my heart breaking for my great grandmother.

'No Mary! I can't do that. There's no time dear.' She huffed, quickly wiping her tears away.

'We can continue tomorrow Granny after you've had a good night's rest.' I persisted softly.

'Tomorrow may not come for me dear; they have to understand you see before it's too late.' The old lady's gaze fell on her lap, as she let out a deep sigh and closed her eyes, before resuming her incredible story, reliving the hideous torment her own son had inflicted.

'I've 'ad enough of this,' he told me impatiently and for a few seconds I forgot the agony from his cigarette when acute terror replaced the pain as he picked me up and slung me over his shoulder. Convinced I was about to be dropped over the abyss I desperately tried to squirm out of his grasp.

'Put me down,' I yelled, regretting it instantly as he suddenly flung me down to the muddy ground, right in the middle of an icy puddle. Landing heavily air whooshed out of my lungs as water drenched me to the skin. As I began to wriggle and squirm, he grabbed my throat and squeezed hard, pushing me down.

'Now my dear mother it is time to play my little game. It's quite simple I ask you a question and you tell me the truth that is the whole truth and nothing but the truth or, you burn, see, dead simple.'

'Question one, did you or did you not push me father over the high waterfall 'ere in this wood?'

'No! No! He had an accident,' I cried.

'What did you say?' His menacing tone penetrated through the moaning wind as he yelled 'LIAR!' I didn't answer.

Chilled to the bone I struggled again with all my might but it was useless. I could feel his heavy boot on my chest, pinning me down making it hard to get my breath, as he slowly repeated his question adding 'ya'll be wise to remember mother the game is called truth or burn and this is what happens when you lie.'

Then, lifting up my skirt he planted his cigarette on my thigh and began to count slowly one, two, three, four, until unable to take the torture any longer I shrieked 'STOP! STOP! I can explain.'

Emitting another eerie laugh he next grabbed my head and shouted in my ear 'start talking bitch! Unless you want some of this, waving something under my nose equally as terrifying.

'Smell it can ya? That's chloroform' he chuckled in my ear, before adding 'but I reckon I'll save that for later.' My chest heaved and my heart pounded furiously, fearing I would be very lucky to see another day. Somehow I had to escape this monster; I tried putting up another desperate struggle only to be thwarted yet again.

'You evil fiend, I shrieked, you'll never get away with this.' Anger was starting to submerge the fear. 'Why not bitch, there's only you and me 'ere, no-one else gonna know? No-one's punished you yet 'ave they, nobody sent you in prison for what ya did all them years ago, but now I 'ave chance to put that right see. Thought ya had got away with it didn't ya. Well ya were stupid, ya were seen by someone, dead now, but he talked when me mate 'Arry went to pay him a little visit like.'

'Would that be Harry Williams?' I asked, connecting the dots. It was all beginning to add up, I thought recalling my old lodger's parting threat.

'S'ppose it were, what's it to ya? Anyway forget that, we ain't finished our little game yet.'

While he was busy talking, I'd been frantically struggling, wriggling and writhing in the muddy water, but it was no use as all the tyrant's weight was still firmly holding me down making any escape impossible, hopelessness filled me. I needed a miracle to survive this.

'Ya ready for question two? Did ya or did ya not abandon a child, ya own flesh and blood, and leave him to freeze and starve?' I lay still, tears falling down my cheeks; I didn't know what to say.

'Well! I'm waiting…its called truth or burn, remember.' he demanded 'Ah! Just remembered I got ya a little present, thought it might help jog your memory see, 'ere can ya guess what it is mother?'

He then brushed my face with something that haunted my worst nightmares and although I could not see it knew beyond a shadow of a doubt exactly what he held in his hand. It was a twig covered in thorns, probably from the thorn bush he had landed when Horace had run off into the woods with him then tripped and lost his balance having fallen into his own snare.

'This bring back memories mother?' He taunted as he scratched my face with the twig but I never answered him. What could I say?

My teeth began to chatter as I begged him to release me, but my pleas fell on deaf ears. 'Ya know I don't believe I 'eard you say thank you.'

'You're depraved just like your evil father,' I spat between violent shivers, quickly turning my face away to avoid a blow. He grabbed my chin and hissed 'Nobody ever calls me father depraved or evil, ya gonna pay for them words.' With that he removed his boot from my chest then rough hands violently tossed me over so I was lying face down in the freezing water. Spluttering, endeavouring not to swallow it, I could feel his knee pressing hard into my spine as he began to tug up my wet clothes, ripping them in his haste. Then took my breath away, escalating my fear to new heights when he leaned forward and hissed in my ear 'Now mother dear I'm gonna show ya what was in me plan.'

At that point I believed death would be a better option as my heart sank to new depths and my body froze. Hypothermia was also beginning to take hold. He suddenly yanked down my underwear and slapped me hard on the bottom before mercilessly laying into me with the thorny whip ignoring my loud yells, sobs and pleas for him to stop. Over the gusting icy wind I could hear him cackle after each agonising strike as he slowly counted each blow until…

'Shut up bitch! Ya starting to give me ear-ache,' he yelled roughly yanking my head back trying to wrench open my jaw. Ignoring my frantic effort to bite off his fingers, he endeavoured to ram the petrol soaked rag back into my mouth, making my stomach heave and lurch as I tried desperately to spit it back out.

Shouting over the wind he shrieked 'I made a vow to find ya and kill ya a long time ago. I promised meself I would make ya suffer so help me God, an eye for an eye.' Then he raised the sharp, thorny twig again and continued to beat me to a bloody mess. The excruciating pain pierced through my body, only stopping briefly when he paused to spit 'Them thorns jogged ya memory yet mother?' My worst terror was about to evolve into cold, stark reality when he suddenly stopped then threw himself on top of me and whispered in my ear 'and now mother I'm gonna enjoy me dessert.'

Just when I could see only one way out of this petrifying ordeal, my death, I suddenly heard a loud shout. I heard it again a few seconds later; it was a voice that could be clearly heard yelling to someone as the gusts of wind subsided. The monster heard it too. 'Try anything bitch and ya dead,' he hissed as we both listened with baited breath.

'I'm bloody sure I didn't imagine them screams Joe, reckon there's someone in those bushes behind the trees. S'ppose they're in trouble?' I heard heavy footsteps approach nearby.

'You'll be in bloody trouble with boss if you don't get on setting these bloody traps Bill. Now shut up and pass me the spade.' The other voice boomed.

"Ere wait a minute Joe, shine your torch over there, near the waterfall. I reckon someone's over there in undergrowth, s'ppose they've been watching us… Ere gimme ya rifle. Some lead shot up backside, that'll teach 'em to spy on us.' Grabbing his mate's weapon he then let off a round of ammunition.

'You bloody idiot Bill, no-one's s'pposed to know we're 'ere. What if they call police, I tell ya I got more brains in me little finger than what you got in ya 'ead.' He shouted to his mate.

My evil son, on hearing gun shots close by, had panicked mumbling 'gotta get away from here.' Suddenly, his weight had been lifted off me as the coward had taken to his heels and fled. Being unable to see or speak, I slowly struggled to sit up, battling searing pain and utter exhaustion, terrified that one false move would send me hurtling over the edge. I heard someone approach and then a hand gently touched mine, while another carefully removed the gag as I whimpered and shivered in fear. Next the tape across my eyes was removed, whilst a comforting voice kept repeating 'you're all right now lass, you're all right'. Both men helped me up, cajoling and comforting this blubbering, hysterical woman as they guided me away from that horrible, terrifying place.

Joe and Bill were my saviours. Albeit, not in exactly legal circumstances, saying 'no need to get police involved missus we'll sort it, just leave it to us.' They promised. I discovered that my son was also known to my rescuers, being in the criminal fraternity. 'You're lucky we 'ad to set traps tonight missus or no- one might've found you. I tell you he's a bad un, he is, a right nasty piece of work. Yeah, we know him, don't we Joe, we've seen him operate. Don't you worry miss; he won't get away from us. We've got a score to settle with him we 'ave.'

Shortly after surviving that ghastly trauma, agoraphobia set in and took hold of me with an iron grip. I would stay in the protection of my cottage from dawn to dusk, refusing to answer my door without first spying through the nets ensuring it was safe. I would barricade my bedroom each night with a heavy chest of drawers, changed my locks of course, and even put up dark curtains checking the windows were tightly shut not once but maybe five or six times. Eventually I ran out of grocery supplies and was forced to venture out, but never further than the local village shop. They say an English man's home is his castle and mine turned into a fortress.

Then one night I was sitting by the fireside enjoying a mug of cocoa listening to the late night local news on the television, when it flashed up a body, thought to be a male, had been discovered in Black Gorge Woods by someone walking their dog, which had apparently unearthed a half decomposed foot. Could it be my evil son? Had Bill and Joe finally caught up with him? I knew I couldn't rest till I got some answers. Though trying to find two dangerous criminals, only having their first name, wasn't going to be easy. I remembered them giving me a lift home in their van, a white transit which seemed to have little suspension feeling more like riding a rickety wooden roller coaster than in a vehicle, not that I had cared much at the time of course. White transit vans were to be found everywhere and I had been in no state to take note of the registration number even if I had been able to read it.

Then once more fate intervened, when not long afterwards I peered through the nets and saw a man wearing a dark jacket with a hood almost concealing his face, heading towards my house. Panicking and fearing for the worst, I found a hidden strength and pushed my heavy oak table up against the door before rushing upstairs. Next I ran into my bedroom and crawled under my bed, pulling up the loose floorboard to remove the old rifle I had purchased from a local farmer, for protection. Someone was hammering on my door. I rushed back downstairs. The flap of my letterbox was lifted, only to quickly snap shut upon seeing the barrel of my gun. 'Look Missus, there's no need to be scared, it's Bill. I need to see ya see, unlock door and let us in.'

On recognising the rough, familiar voice, I heaved a huge sigh of relief, moved the table back and unlocked the door, I then let him in, demanding he first remove his muddy boots. Bidding him to take a seat by the fire I offered a cup of tea, which he politely accepted, then after checking again that the door was locked, I took the seat opposite him, 'I believe you mentioned you had something to tell me?' I asked.

'Aye lass that I 'ave. Ya remember I said before that Joe and me 'ad a score to settle with you know who, well, ya can relax now 'cause he won't be bothering ya again.' 'Ah! You killed him you mean? He's dead now then?' Bill ignored my question. Now Wilhelmina Potts has always had a stubborn streak and I refused to let him drop the subject. I soon discovered he could also dig his heels in when he wanted. 'I told you Missus I just come here to tell ya you've no need to worry, you'll not be seeing him again, not today, not tomorrow, not ever, see.'

'That's because he's lying dead in Black Gorge Woods isn't it?' I persisted, needing to know the truth.

'Sorry missus got to be off now. Thanks for tea. I'm not sayin' nothin' more.' Then he got up and walked towards the door only to turn round and say 'Oh and get rid of that gun, nearly took me eye out it did.'

Not long after Bill's surprise visit I slowly began to regain my confidence and felt more secure. I started venturing out into the next town, 'the exercise will do you good Wilhelmina' I told myself, 'about time you got out again'. Drinking in the spring sunshine dappling the leaves on the trees, making the river sparkle and spotting the crocus, daffodil and narcissus poking out their beauty from the cold earth, I felt my spirits lift.

'It couldn't be, it's impossible, you've made a mistake Wilhelmina', interrupted that inner voice but I knew my instincts were right. The flaccid jowls around the jaw, the deep lines and furrows around the eye sockets, the nose larger, more hooked, she knew she wasn't wrong. The old woman dressed from head to toe in black, still managed to convey a certain unforgettable presence leaving no doubt in my mind as to her identity. Suddenly she turned and held my stare for a few seconds, neither of us saying a word, both enemies facing one another, both with a burning hatred.

Stunned with shock I watched her disappear into a nearby pawnbroker's shop. Unable to resist I peered through the window and witnessed her hand the shopkeeper a pearl and ruby necklace, after a few heated words both disappeared behind a curtain to the back of the shop. I recognised the jewellery, it had belonged to my mother Kathleen. It had been handed down from her family and, by rights, should have been given to me, when I came of age. I tried to keep calm, struggling to restrain myself from running into the shop and grabbing it off him, aware that if any plan was to work it would require careful preparation and meticulous attention to detail. There was certainly no room for emotion as my obsession for revenge intensified. That little inner voice whispered 'careful Wilhelmina you must bide your time, discover her Achilles, only then can you destroy her.'

Then it came to me, I remembered something I overheard Annie mention one day, to the kitchen staff, which had made me laugh till my sides ached. It had been around Christmas time and Annie had decided to bring a bit of Yule tide cheer into the dour, old house by arranging several large bowls of holly laden with red berries, each surrounded by half a dozen oranges and Christmas roses.

'Looked real lovely it did on the table' Annie said 'till Mistress Fortescue came into the room and ordered 'remove that fruit immediately, they make me violently ill if I so much as smell one.'

At that point Annie picked up her display, marched over to where her employer was standing, then deliberately pushed an orange under Agatha's nose, having split the orange peel with her nail, resulting in a fine spray of juice shooting into the air. Then pretending to be dim had asked 'you mean you want me to remove these oranges ma'am?'

'You stupid girl, of course that's what I meant, whatever did you…'but she never finished her sentence. 'Out cold she were, couldn't believe it, could have knocked me down with a feather,' Annie kept repeating, laughing in surprise. That was it. I had found Agatha Fortescue's weakness; she was allergic to oranges.

She had always been a large woman with a strong sweet tooth which had gradually given her not one, not two, but almost three double chins causing her jaw line to disappear into the creases of overhanging flesh. It wasn't all that surprising that her husband turned to other ladies, who were more than willing to serve his sexual needs. And, like most women who discover that their men have strayed, his spouse wanted revenge.

'No man scorned her,' she had screamed at him earlier, for the whole house to hear, 'none who had not lived to regret it' she threatened. Therefore my father, who had drunk more than a few whiskies that day, merely looked down his nose disdainfully at his wife, who was lying in a heap on the floor. Then calmly walked over to a large vase of evergreens, removed the leaves and tipped the stagnant water over his wife's head mumbling 'that should bring her round.'

Did he not know of what his wife was capable of when it came to taking an eye for an eye? I wondered.

Blinking back into reality, I made my way back towards my cottage, repeatedly checking to see if the old hag was behind me. A familiar icy chill ran down my spine as that overwhelming obsession for vengeance reared its ugly head. I'm sorry to say there was no room for forgiveness in my heart not for her. So I took to spying on her making a careful entry in my diary whenever she left her dank house, whoever she spoke to, wherever she went, taking note of all her movements. Waiting for the perfect opportunity to strike.

10

Shock and Horror

As usual, around quarter to three in the afternoon I donned my coat for my daily visit to my daughter, but on this particular day, as I walked into ward 3 on the busy psychiatric floor, I was intercepted by Dr. Woods who had been treating Mollie since her admission.

'Ah! Mrs. Potts before you go in to see Mollie, could I have a quick word please' ushering me into his plush office and bidding me take a seat as he slipped behind his large, highly polished desk covered in bundles of patients' notes and a half drunk cup of coffee. He then dropped a bombshell, my daughter was being released. How could I explain to him that his plan was not feasible in fact it was actually very dangerous, there was simply no way Mollie could come home, even for a few days. It was completely out of the question but he wasn't paying any attention to my umming and aahing, as I searched for excuses.

Brushing them aside he explained 'we want to see how Mollie reacts away from institutionalised life. It's very important of course that she continues to take her medication or she will suffer more epileptic fits. We would like her to go home this coming weekend if you could arrange it.' Feeling pushed into a tight corner attempting to ignore that little voice within me crying 'don't be so stupid, it's far too risky', I heard myself agree to his request.

If my cottage resembled a fortress before then, that weekend it transformed into a model on Fort Knox, with every door and window barricaded to the hilt with all sharp edges padded for Mollie's protection. Indeed my daughter's homecoming was turning into a major security exercise.

Friday eventually dawned bringing with it the cold, blustery winds and a sense of foreboding. I booked a taxi, intending to bundle my daughter into it and whisk her away. On the journey home the driver suddenly stopped to pick up someone who was frantically trying to wave down his taxi. As the door opened I froze to my seat, the mystery passenger was none other than Agatha Fortescue. I hastily pulled my daughter to me clutching her tightly, whilst eyeing up the woman for whom I held the utmost contempt, who was sitting a few feet away. She turned her face towards me, staring at me with an icy, calculated glare.

What will be her next move? I wondered with fear and trepidation. Ten maybe fifteen minutes later I watched whilst she suddenly started fumbling with the door handle and began shouting to the driver to let her out before we went past her grim, dark house. I nicknamed it Colditz. Having pushed a few coins into the driver's hand she slowly hauled her very large frame out of the car, but not before turning to give me one more fixed stare. Then she was gone, but intuition told me it would not be for long. Just as I had been following her life, she too had been watching mine, as I was soon to discover.

Having Mollie home proved to be a nerve racking and totally exhausting experience, needing to keep a constant eye on my daughter, being unable to converse with her and not to mention coping with her incontinence which the hospital had omitted to mention. Come Sunday morning, things were to drastically change.

I recall opening the bedroom curtains to find the sun shining, spreading its cheer, even giving me a sense of optimism. While listening to the sweet music of the blackbirds, I started to think maybe I had gone a little bit over the top with my Fort Knox security. Perhaps just ten minutes in the garden wouldn't do Mollie any harm, in fact the sunshine would do her good after being cooped up in that hospital ward every day.

Later on when I was hanging out the washing, I got caught up admiring the tulips and daffodils which were boasting their glory and the flowering cherry tree that had come into blossom. Spring was my favourite time of the year; everything was bursting with new life and freshness.

I had been so occupied with my thoughts that I'd forgotten to close my back door, let alone lock it, so when I returned to the house to collect another pile of wet sheets, I almost collapsed in shock to find a visitor in my living room. I looked him straight in the eye, the very worst thing I could have done. His lips curled up exposing large fangs as he emitted a low pitched snarl. Bruno had come to pay me a visit that morning. To my profound relief, the mastiff then stopped growling to lift his head sniffing the air. Realising he'd caught the scent of bacon, that I had left out on the kitchen counter, I slowly edged towards the raw meat intending to quickly grab it from the plate then throw it out of the back door with the mastiff in hot pursuit. The snarling hound barred my way and sprang for the meat. In the heat of the moment I hadn't heard the footsteps or noticed the figure standing on the staircase but Bruno had. Having devoured the thin bacon strips in one mouthful, he then galloped towards the stairs heading straight for Mollie.

I can still hear her piercing screams of pain as the aggressive animal leapt up at her knocking her off her feet then sank his fangs first into her arm then her leg as she frantically tried to kick him away, but the ferocious canine then clamped its jaws into Mollie's head. 'Grab a broom,' I heard a voice from within, remembering how Bruno had slunk off when Agatha's crone had brought her stick down on his back, but it was hopeless he had no intention of giving up his prey. Then I remembered something I had heard many years ago and though absolutely appalled at the thought, I knew I had to do it to save my Mollie.

Flying over to the kitchen cupboards I pushed tins of beans, peas and spaghetti out of the way, ignoring the loud crash, as they landed on the floor and felt for a packet of cigarettes. Where were the matches? Running out of options I turned to the gas oven. Bruno let out a loud yelp as I plunged the lit cigarette on to his back, holding it firmly until he released Mollie from his large jaws dripping with frothy, bloody saliva. A totally horrific deed I agree and something I would normally never condone but I would do anything to save my little girl. Pulling my petrified, hysterical daughter into my arms I felt a searing pain shoot through my leg as Bruno next turned on me.

Suddenly a curt but, horribly familiar voice pierced the air, 'well done Bruno, good dog now get here! Come!' I spun round, shock, fear, anger and intense hatred, pulsed through me, wondering how long Agatha Fortescue had been standing there, at my back door watching the ugly scene. At that point my daughter's eyes rolled upwards into her head and her body started to jerk involuntarily, I suddenly remembered that Mollie had missed not one but two doses of her medication. I had been so busy thinking about Agatha and wet laundry, I'd forgotten to administer her morning dose. As the doctor's words echoed in my ears I suddenly felt her body go limp and a wild idea filled my mind.

Allowing her head to loll back I screamed, then shrieked 'she's dead! You killed her!' With faked hysteria I sank to my knees cradling my child and yelled at the top of my voice 'Get Out! Get out of my house! My Mollie's gone, she's gone. Are you satisfied? GET OUT!' I buried my face into Mollie's neck, pretending to sob uncontrollably. The tears that rolled down my cheeks were genuine. Agatha having been taken by surprise, for it was obvious she had never witnessed an epileptic fit before, started to back out of the room. In a clipped, stern voice I heard her command, 'Bruno!' With ears pinned back and tail between his legs the old hound reluctantly obeyed, fearing the consequences if he didn't.

As I gently laid my poor, bleeding daughter on the sofa an overpowering feeling of failure swept over me for the idea of the home visit had certainly not been to traumatize her further. Having ensured the door was well and truly locked; I hurried over to the kitchen and once more ransacked my cupboards to find the necessary first aid box. As I tended her wounds I didn't need a doctor to tell me she needed stitches and a tetanus injection. So after bandaging the bites as best I could, we headed back to the hospital. I sat beside Mollie watching the doctor stitch her up, I knew then, thanks to my carelessness that she would never leave a life of institution again. I also believed even if I moved one hundred miles away it would make no difference to my nemesis who no doubt now believed she had disposed of one thorn but there still remained another sticking in her flesh.

Guilt enveloped me as I saw Mollie wince and scream, making my obsession for Agatha Fortescue to pay, even more powerful. The little voice in my head started to drown out every normal thought that crept into my mind. Never for one moment did I bother to consider what she must have felt, losing Horace, her one and only son whom she doted on, in her own strange way. No, there was no room in my heart for any sympathy, only cold revenge.

'Incidentally did I ever mention that weird dream I had, dear? It still spooks me out when I think about it. I've never forgotten it, so vivid, so ghastly, but confusing'. Her voice trailed off as she turned her face away.

'I'm stood at a railway station waiting for the three thirty train to... I have no idea where, when I hear a commotion at the far end of the platform. Curious to know what was going on, I moved nearer to witness a man and woman having a fight. Suddenly he throws a punch sending her hurtling backwards on to the tracks, straight into the path of the oncoming express. Bloodcurdling screams fill the air but the train does not stop. Within seconds the woman's legs, arms and head are amputated from her body; blood and gore cover the line.

'Call an ambulance' someone yells.

'No, it's too late she's dead!' I tell them. Tears are running down my face.

'Did you know her dear?' a sympathetic voice in the crowd asks.

'I've been cheated,' I tell her, 'cheated by death itself. It was too quick you see, didn't get enough time to suffer, horrific yes, painful maybe, but the Reaper took her too fast.'

'I'll have words with him then dear,' she replies, 'maybe he'll swap her.'

Then someone taps me on the shoulder and I spin round to see a man staring at me with another behind except the latter doesn't have a face just the remains of one, half bloated and decomposed and around his leg is an ugly, rusty iron snare. The first man wearing a dark scowl was short and tubby sporting a long handlebar moustache. He was also naked and carrying a birch twig. They both stand there, staring at me. Then one whispers in my ear 'the next train for the afterlife will be for you. We're here to ensure you don't miss it... here it comes!'

Then in a cold sweat and shaking with fear I wake up trying to catch my breath and reassure myself it's only a nightmare but so strange because…' Just at that point the door was thrown open and Mildred burst into the room.

'Now don't mind me, I have just come to pick up your tray mother,' I remembered my Aunt Mildred occasionally called Granny Wilhelmina 'mother' though I wondered sadly if her niece even recalled much of Charlotte, her true mother.

'Carry on with your project thing. I see you've eaten up all your greens. What a good girl we are today.' She babied.

'Mildred I have told you again and again I am not a child and I demand some respect. I'm sure Charlotte would turn in her grave if she could hear you sometimes.' Granny puffed in annoyance.

'This room could do with a good spring clean don't you think; it doesn't smell too fresh,' Mildred mumbled, totally ignoring her aunt's angry retort.

'Mildred! Really!' she barked.

Her niece wasn't paying attention her thoughts being elsewhere. 'I have to go out later to my Women's Institute meeting, so for goodness sake don't go doing anything stupid. Don't want to have to scrape you off the floor again now do we, or have the police bring you back home.'

'Well it really wasn't too much to ask dear, all I wanted was a bag of sweets, my favourite jelly fruits but you simply refused to buy them, so I took myself off to the shop and got a bit lost on the way. That can happen to the best of us dear.' She said stubbornly, crossing her arms over her chest.

'Aunt Wilhelmina! No-one gets out of bed and goes to the shops for a bag of sweets at four in the morning.' Mildred retorted.

'Mildred I do not care for your tone! Anyone can make a mistake and you've certainly made more than your fair share.' Mildred was out of the room and halfway down the corridor, mumbling under her breath, unaware that I was behind her.

'Yes, maybe I should think again about that old folk's home in Orchard Street. That would be an eye for an eye, indeed. I've had enough. Anyway it's what she deserves, no need to feel guilty, she would have done same to you.' she muttered under her breath as she balanced the tray with one hand whilst trying to open the door leading to the kitchen with the other. Having declined my offer of assistance I watched uncomfortably as she slammed down the tray then clattered about in her immaculate kitchen, scrubbed the dirty dishes with vigour, then once dried, she put them away, stacking them neatly in their allotted places in the cupboard. Mildred was a stickler for tidiness and organisation. 'An untidy house shows an untidy mind', no excuse for sloth was her firm belief and she wasn't scared to tell folks. Having heard Mildred's mutterings I decided to have a few quick words.

'Let's have a cup of tea and a chat auntie.' I suggested.

'No time for chatting dear, have to...'

'You can make five minutes placing a hot steaming brew and a plate of biscuits on the table', I interrupted. 'I couldn't help overhearing you, saying something about a home in Orchard Street being an eye for an eye and ...' I hesitantly asked.

'You shouldn't have been listening Mary. It's nothing whatsoever to do with you, eavesdropping on me like that, ought to be ashamed, well just kindly mind your own business in future.'

The next day when Granny Wilhelmina, as usual enquired 'now Mary dear just remind me again where we finished off yesterday?'

'Oh! I believe you were going to talk about Aunt Milly,' I hastily replied.

'Umm... No! It's best not to talk about Mildred; she may overhear me you see and I don't want to risk upsetting her again.' She hushed, watching the door in case Mildred decided to burst in at that point.

'She's gone out Granny; I saw her leave the house.'

'Well, in that case but watch for her coming up the path dear.' She said tentatively, but before she proceeded to delve into her past once more, she took out her handkerchief and started to wind it round her finger.

'If you recall I talked earlier about my sister Charlotte being sent abroad after ...' she paused, '... after what that cruel bitch did', referring to the branding.

'Well, Lottie, that was my nickname for her, though I don't believe she cared too much for it, I remember she had said in her diary how …'

'What happened Granny, to Charlotte I mean when she was in France?' interrupting her in case she was about to set off on a long tangent.

'Well I was about to say …' she glared at me '…that I never saw my sister again. She never returned to live in England, not even after the war, but we did keep in touch. I remember the letter she wrote telling me she had met this wonderful man and he had proposed to her. Sounded like an excited school girl she did. Then another note arrived twelve months later to say she was going to have a baby. While rereading the letter, I sensed there was something else, something she was hiding. If I had been able to see her I would have known immediately for the dark bruising around the eyes, the cuts, the change in personality, would all have been obvious…if only I was there.' She sighed heavily.

'Anyway, later another letter arrived out of the blue asking me to do something for her, before it was too late, which naturally sent alarm bells ringing.

'I have made arrangements for my darling Milly to come to England to live with you Wilhelmina. It's not good for her to stay here and I know she will be well cared for in your hands. You need to go to Dover to the Grosvenor Hotel on Albert Street and pick her up for me.' Well dear Mary I was shocked, a hundred questions filled my mind.

So the following week I set off for Dover and made my way to the hotel. When I arrived I recall someone directing me to a room towards the back of the hotel. It was clean though somewhat shabby, with its threadbare carpet and badly worn upholstery. In a chair by the window sat a young woman rocking a small child to sleep whilst softly humming a lullaby. I remember her looking at me with such sadness in her eyes, aware the time had come to part. I could see her heart was breaking as she tenderly planted a kiss on the child's face and whispered 'au revoir'. Then she gently placed her charge into my arms and hurried away not wanting to be interrogated or for anyone to see the tears rolling down her cheek. As I looked down into the child's face I could see Charlotte's pert little nose and high forehead.

She soon settled into my routine and I kept her mother informed of each milestone she passed and mischief she got up to. Until … I knew something was amiss when four months had passed as she always wrote back religiously. Eventually I did receive a letter but it wasn't from Charlotte. I anxiously tore it open and read the first line, then realised it had been penned by the child's maid, the one I met in Dover; I sat down numb with shock, reading the words over and over, hoping they would change.

'I am so very sorry to have to tell you this news, but the monster your sister had wed, the man to whom she had given her heart, he put her in hospital and she never recovered.'

Apparently the nursemaid had been tending her young charge when she heard my sister's screams, followed by her shrieking,

'Marie call a gendarme!' Only this time the Police were too late.

I never told Mildred and still haven't to this day. Some day she'll find out I expect when she reads my words when I lie in my grave. You see Mary I have walked down that path and have never forgotten the pain the day I learned the truth, the ghastly, dreadful truth that my own mother had been cruelly cut down, murdered in cold blood. How could I give that agony to my niece? It made me into the person I never ever wanted to become and changed me forever. My heart filled with hatred, bitterness and revenge, it destroyed my life. I couldn't allow her to follow in my footsteps and I wasn't prepared to take that risk.

'Granny' I suddenly interrupted, 'I cannot help but notice that nowadays things are somewhat strained between you and Aunt Millie.' I knew I was treading on egg shells but ploughed on, trying to ignore the glare and asked 'Has something else happened?'

'Poking that nose in again are we dear?' she replies with a raised eyebrow.

'You are right. Sometimes Mildred makes me feel I am a burden. Shouldn't be surprised if she's planning to get rid of me.' My face goes red, did she already know? I wondered.

'You see Mary something did occur, a long time ago now, but Mildred has never forgiven and refuses to forget. I'm afraid I have to admit to doing something of which I'm deeply ashamed and, neither can I excuse myself by saying my niece asked for what she got nor, that I was unaware of the consequences of my actions. I knew only too well but convinced myself I was doing the right thing. It will only end in tears I kept telling myself and if you don't take action it will be too late. In her eyes I totally destroyed her life… You see Mildred used to be a little minx when she was younger and liked to um… well let's say give a man the 'come on'. Hard to believe it now of course, she's a real Miss Prim and Proper.

When she was only fifteen years old your aunt Millie became involved with this man, a real fly by night who went by the name of Jack Robinson. I believe that was one of the names he used. Twenty years older than Mildred and had previously done a stretch in Her Majesty's Prison at Strangeways for grievous bodily harm, a mean man who dealt in drugs and ran a sex racket. Not exactly the best choice for my young daughter but she was completely besotted with this man. When he said jump she jumped and, as it happened, into his bed I was to discover. Of course when the inevitable occurred he could not give her the time of day and she found out the hard way what he really wanted, babies being most definitely not in the equation. I found her in floods of tears when she confirmed my fears but I am afraid she received little sympathy. I believe I told her 'you made your bed my girl and now you must lie on it.'

I decided to pay a secret visit to old Mrs. Rogers, who had helped me when I was carrying 'the boy', agreeing to pay the midwife to deliver the baby then dispose of it making it clear that under no circumstances was Mildred to even hold the infant. Indeed she was not even to see the child. After three long days of arduous labour she finally gave birth to a baby girl who was immediately whisked away and placed in the arms of a woman waiting in an adjacent room. When Mildred asked for her baby she was informed it had died in the night. It was God's punishment for her wanton behaviour.

Though secretly so paranoid had I become, I was absolutely terrified that Mollie's fate might await Mildred's child and was not prepared to see my niece's offspring abused in the name of revenge. But how could I tell Mildred that without having to divulge my past. She would ask questions I couldn't answer and had no stomach to even attempt. Suppose she discovered her aunt had committed murder. No matter how I tried to twist the turn of events that fateful day the cold stark fact still remained I killed him and the knowledge he would have put some other poor soul through purgatory still did not diminish that but there was absolutely no way on earth I could ever tell Mildred. These skeletons might destroy her life as they had mine, and she would never understand. How could she? She was not there. So I vowed then to keep them safely from her hidden tightly away in the closet. However, there was something else, something I have deeply regretted ever since I placed my pregnant daughter in Mrs. Rogers care.'

Suddenly Granny Wilhelmina paused and looked away fearing I would notice the quiver of her bottom lip or the tear starting to roll down her cheek.

'I'm sorry dear but I'm afraid it still chokes me to talk about it and I have lost count of the times I have looked back and yearned to change the past but nobody can do that can they? I truly believe that you have to learn from your mistakes and move on, so I buried another dark secret.

You see when I paid Mrs. Rogers that day I also did something totally unforgivable…I left instructions for the midwife 'do whatever you must to ensure she never bears another child. This must never happen again.' I later learned she had used her knitting needles and irreparably damaged my niece. It was a miracle she did not die, but however could I confess that sin?

So I kept quiet punished by my own guilt and watched Mildred later yearn for a child, knowing it would never happen remembering how she had placed her trust in me, only to deceive her, albeit with good intention, but still deception. Even adoption was out of the question when the authorities discovered from the neighbours of her husband's violent streak. Mind you I believe she did whisper once that he did have a problem with well umm... you know what, in the bedroom department that maybe a spot of vinegar might have sorted.' I laughed.

'I believe you mean Viagra Granny!'

'Anyway, the years passed then something happened that in Mildred's eyes totally destroyed her dreams leaving her devastated. I believe I mentioned Mildred used to be a little flirt and liked to um … well let's say display her voluptuous assets on occasions. She began to arouse my suspicions when I spotted her one day getting very cosy with a friend's husband. A friend who was very dear to me I might say and I certainly was not prepared to stand by and see her betrayed, so I decided to teach my niece a little lesson. Did I mention that Mildred had been married to her husband for nearly five years by then, although what she ever saw in him, I shall never know?

One day I overheard Mildred and her lover arranging to meet and decided it was time this was nipped in the bud so an anonymous little note was left for Mildred's husband to find detailing where, when and whom with he would find his wife. Needless to say the affair quickly ended though I was surprised to discover later it had lasted almost six months. Mildred's lover's reputation proved to be far more important to him than any feelings he may have been harbouring for my niece and he soon returned to the fold, in an effort to save his marriage. Mildred was to find out that her husband did not like being made to look a fool and inevitably took his anger and humiliation out on her, when he beat her with his belt. Then I didn't know she had been so desperate to have a child she hadn't cared that she'd stolen someone else's husband, convinced her own was not able to give her children. Apparently she had planned to end the affair soon as she had given birth then endeavour to make her husband believe the child was his.

'Do you know how it feels to want a child of your own so much that you even consider the unthinkable taking someone else's from its pram when its mother's back was turned?' she had yelled at me when I later confessed about the letter. Unsurprisingly this killed any thin shreds of bond that had been between us. And now I truly believe she hates and despises me, although who can blame her? I have tried on countless occasions to apologise and explain but my words just fall on deaf ears every time. I couldn't tell her the real facts then, either. She still refuses to even discuss the subject but maybe when she reads this she will begin to understand you see and maybe even find it in her heart to forgive me.

I did try to make amends you know. A couple of years after her baby was born I went back to visit Mrs. Rogers hoping for an address to trace the whereabouts of the infant and learned the child had been whisked away to London. Mildred had not even got a photograph of her own daughter.

'You know my baby girl will be two years old today' I overheard her telling someone.

'And I can't even give her a card to let her know her own mother remembered, can't even wish her a Happy Birthday. She will grow up thinking her mother doesn't even care, and will believe that she was abandoned. She will never know she is in my thoughts every day, every night, every minute.' So off I went to London on a secret mission hoping to return with a photograph, reassure her that her child was in good hands and, last but not least, attempt to quell a guilty conscience.

I remember looking for 10 Westminster Street which I found terraced among rows of other houses, some with grimy net curtains and peeling paint, some immaculately kept with scrubbed doorsteps and polished windows but, to my dismay, 10 Westminster Street fell into the former. I must have stood ten minutes or more knocking on the door before I spotted a net drape suddenly move behind a window, from the house adjoining. Then the door opened and a young woman with a cigarette dangling from one corner of her mouth, looking rather annoyed, asked my business. In her early twenties, she was dressed in a scruffy, stained brown dress, with a scarf tied round her head, from which short dark wisps of hair escaped.

'I'm looking for a Mr. and Mrs. Harris, I was wondering if you could help me?' Looking faintly surprised, she then looked me up and down whilst she took a long drag on her cigarette.

'Oh! them pair left 'ere six months ago, headed for States I be ieve, kinda kept themselves to themselves if I remember. Didn't really fit in round 'ere, gave me impression we weren't good enough for 'em. Sorry dunno much more I can tell ya. The kids were always clean and well dressed mind; that's more than you can say for some in this street, anyway, why ya asking?'

I chose to ignore her questions, being none of her business and said 'well if you should hear anything more, anything at all, please let me know. Here is my address,' pushing a scrap of paper into her hand.

'Umm… yes Mrs. but, like I said, I 'eard they sailed off to America so don't 'old your breath.'

'I know, thank you Mrs..?'

'Ferguson, I be Amelia Ferguson. Sorry gotta go now and get my hubby his dinner' and on those words she shut the door. So, with a heavy heart I headed back home bitterly disappointed, I had achieved absolutely nothing. There is more.

You see Mildred happened to be present the day Agatha chose to pay me another visit, a visit I would never forget. On answering the door I saw my nemesis was not on her own with Bruno at her side, but there was also someone else.

'There you are constable, that's 'er. Wants hanging for what she done to my son, arrest her man. She's a murderer.' Panicking, I look towards the policeman.

'Now then you can't go throwing accusations like that Miss.'

'It's Mrs. if ya don't mind, I be Mrs Crabtree the second.'

'This woman is completely deranged Officer,' I quickly interjected. 'I mean who on earth would go out at midnight with a chicken and prance about in a wood calling malevolent spirits to come to her! I tell you the woman's totally insane, Officer!'

'Nevertheless Mrs Potts she has made an accusation that you were involved in her son's disappearance. He was last seen in Black Gorge Woods and we have to investigate. There's a high waterfall …'

'Well maybe he just lost his footing and slipped over the edge. Goodness me Officer you surely don't believe her? I told you she's mad. Her son could be anywhere and, if you ask me, he just wanted to get as far away from her as he could. He's somewhere in Australia if he's any sense. She's evil you see. Reckons she can put weird spells on people you know, thinks she's a black witch. Frogs, voles, birds, even dogs and cats have been strung up by her, demonic that's what she is, I mean who …' I rambled on 'Thank you I get the picture Mrs Potts.'

'Well, I've never heard of anything so ridiculous coming out of her mouth in all my life. Whatever next! Now if you'll excuse me officer I really have not time to stand here listening to this nonsense, I have things to do,' endeavouring to close the door as I spoke.

'Thank you Mrs. Potts, we shall be pursuing our enquiries and will be in touch.' I shut the door quickly and immediately rushed to the kitchen to make a cup of tea, in an attempt to calm my jittery nerves, almost dropping the kettle when I turned to see Mildred in the doorway.

'Well now, are you going to tell me what all that was about or, do I have to drag it out of you?' she asked with a sly smirk on her face.

'Just like your Uncle Edgar Mildred, he could never resist poking his nose in where it was not wanted. I haven't time to stand chatting, got far too much to do. Oh dear! Seem to have run out of milk,' trying desperately to take her mind off anything she might have overheard.

'Oh! Why do you always have to bring up Uncle Edgar every time?' Her Uncle Edgar was of course not her real uncle and long out of the picture after I found him in the bedroom one day, parading in front of a mirror dressed in my clothes, even my stockings and suspenders would you believe! No doubt he was wearing my corset probably even my frilly knickers. I can still see him now standing there with his chest all puffed out just like a male dame in a pantomime begging me not to tell anyone. Shocked to the core I was. So I kicked him out and told him I needed a man not a pansy.

'You had better find somewhere else to play your sordid little dressing up games Edgar Hughes but it certainly will not be under my roof.' He had reacted with an angry parting shot 'Wilhelmina, open your mind. For goodness sake woman I have not committed a crime' but he might as well have.

Nowadays I believe that kind of behaviour is acceptable, I mean it's on the television isn't it but, in my day, it most certainly was not and ignorance lead to prejudice. Later someone told me Edgar had gone under the knife and had the operation, you know given a vagina, grew a pair of breasts and… well I'm sure you get the picture dear. Apparently he changed his name to Edwina. Looking back I really should have been more sympathetic; after all, Edgar was not such a bad old stick. He didn't have an unkind word to say about anyone bless his old soul.

I remember our eyes met across a crowded room, as that old song goes, and we danced the night away. Enveloped in a cloud of euphoria I believed I had finally found the man of my dreams, a real gentleman, who was kind, caring, had strong, handsome features and a lovely warm smile. Yes I really believed I knew all there was to know about Mildred's Uncle Edgar. My niece once told me 'you know Auntie of all the men you have had and there have been a fairly long line, I believe Edgar Hughes is the best.'

'Time will tell dear', I told her and of course time certainly did. We were together a long time, never married just lived over the brush but we were at each other's side through thick and thin. It came as an almighty shock to find I did not really know him at all. Edgar was a good man and Mildred was devastated when I broke the news to her that Uncle Edgar had packed his bags and left us, but to this day I never explained why. How could I make her comprehend that I could not handle that part of him that was a total stranger? It was so unnatural to me you see. Eventually Mildred's sadness turned to hatred and when Edgar later tried to contact her, his shame having prevented him before, she told him she didn't have an Uncle Edgar any more, in her eyes he had died the day he chose to walk out of her life. Then she began to blame me when he told her to ask her aunt why they were not all together, I still could not bring myself to tell her the truth and, even then, would she believe such a story? I very much doubted it. While there is breath in my body I still have to try to make my niece somehow understand the past for only then can we mend broken bridges. Then I can go to my deathbed hoping when she has read my words and seen my reasons she may judge me differently, I must try to remain optimistic.

11

The Gift

Not long after my stepmother's visit something happened. I'd been busy doing a bit of late spring cleaning when suddenly I heard a loud, insistent knocking on my front door. Nervously I peeped through the net curtains, terrified only to heave a huge sigh of relief.

"Ere you are Mrs. Potts, careful now don't drop it, might break.' It was old Tom who delivered the post; he pushed a package about the size of a shoe box, wrapped in plain brown paper, into my arms.

'Now wonder what be in there Mrs. Potts? Ya gonna open it then, looks interesting don't it. Is it ya birthday?' his old eyes looking between me and the package, as a curious smile brightened his face.

'No Tom it isn't my birthday. Thank you I shall be opening it in due course. Now I'll wish you goodbye, and by the way Tom that nose of yours will get you into trouble one of these days,' I said rather sternly.

'Only doing me job Mrs. Potts.' He said as he tipped his hat and then walked back up the pavement. I quickly closed the door and curiously started to peel away the brown wrapping paper and tape. A tingle of excitement ran through my body, wondering whatever it could be and more importantly who had sent it. Carefully I removed the black tissue paper and exposed its contents then my heart sank as I stared at two long black thin candles. A little familiar voice whispered in my head 'aren't they used in the occult to summon evil spirits'? I shivered. Attached to one of the tapers was a small tag, similar to a luggage label, on which someone had penned;

Count the days that you roam free
For soon they will be lost to thee
For off to hell you will be
Soon to taste what you gave me.
Like your soul from me you cannot hide
For I shall hunt thee down
Not rest till you've died
Upon you and yours I place this curse
Before next solstice you shall lie in a hearse.

After many minutes pondering over and over who had penned those vile words, the penny dropped. My instincts told me it was not the work of my stepmother for she liked the element of surprise and I was to be proven right. At first I thought it was written by my son, who hadn't befallen the fate I thought he had. Maybe his body parts had not been scattered far and wide. Then I remembered that literacy was not exactly his forte. Although he may have had cause to curse me I still believed it was someone else and a gut instinct told me I wouldn't have to wait too long before they slipped up and exposed their hand.

I stared at the note. Could someone else have been employed to write those words, probably another inmate I asked myself. Just as a whirlpool sucks one down into its depths so can revenge until it is satisfied. What was the plan? Could it be abduction, extortion, intimidation before going for the kill? I shuddered. Hatred has no bounds.

'Take that note into the police station Wilhelmina', whispered the little voice in my head. 'Leave it to them to find the culprit' and I set out to do just that. The next day I changed my mind fearing it would be me not the author of the note they would lock up in a cell.

Once again my house took on the resemblance of Fort Knox. Once again I was looking over my shoulder whenever I ventured out and, once again my fears were to evolve into ice cold reality. I began to scrimp and save every penny that came my way, often going without proper meals, in order to afford the daily luxury of a taxi back and forth to the hospital to visit Mollie, who would often just stare at me, but no longer with that familiar vacant expression to which I had grown used. Instead terrible memories of pain and suffering were now associated with my visits, often causing her to pull away from my touch, breaking my heart. The terrors of the unknown prayed on my mind, plagued with the possibility of what was to happen to me.

As time passed and nothing untoward had occurred, I gradually started to allow myself to be lulled into a false sense of security, even telling that little voice in my head to be quiet as it persisted, intervening my thoughts, sending shivers down my spine.

'Now then Wilhelmina Potts, you're getting yourself into a right old state. Pull yourself together woman', I sharply told myself, refusing to heed the voice whispering in my head louder and louder

'don't leave the house today, you're in danger, stay at home!'

Shivering I pulled the collar of my coat up around my neck as an icy blast of wind slapped across my face. I hastily locked my front door, placed the key into my purse and bundled myself into the waiting taxi. As I sank into the well worn leather seat I suddenly realised the man at the wheel was not Mr Hopkins my usual driver.

Sitting in front of me was a greasy, long haired, scruffy looking individual, probably in his late thirties, wearing a dirty, olive green jacket. He had not even bothered to shave and preferred to use his sleeve to wipe his dripping nose. A familiar sense of foreboding began to overwhelm me when my questions were met with a glare and stony silence.

Staring blankly into the distance, my thoughts turned to Mr Hopkins whose chivalrous manners were as impeccable as his appearance . A widower who, despite his advancing years, always held himself tall and looked the world right in the eye. I had gotten to know George Hopkins, being treated to his life story on more than one occasion.

'I can practically see my face in your boots' I told him one day as he held the car door open for me.

'Spit 'n shine, Mrs. Potts, can't beat a bit of old spit 'n shine. They taught us that in the Guards you know, Grenadiers I mean. Oh yes, Mrs. Potts, they were good old days.' He said with a wistful smile.

A jolt accompanied by a few choice oaths suddenly brought me back to reality as the unkempt driver swerved to avoid a reckless motor cyclist. Distracted by the commotion, it took a few moments before I suddenly realised we had driven past the turning for the hospital and were now heading down an old bumpy road. I shouted for him to stop, to pull over and turn round, but he never answered. I yelled again but it was to no avail, his response being to increase his speed as we careered past houses and a school at a dizzying pace.

'Don't worry Wilhelmina the police will catch him now; they'll stop him you'll see', I whispered, desperately trying to reassure myself whilst looking out for any sign of help. It wasn't the sound of a police car siren that filled the air a few minutes later, it was the high pitched squeal of brakes as the driver abruptly pulled into the side, throwing me on to the dirty floor of the taxi which was littered with cigarette butts and sweet wrappers. Next thing I knew, the door suddenly flew open and an old bent woman hauled herself in, taking up the seat opposite me. Again, I shouted to the driver to turn around, telling him he was on the wrong road for the hospital which was now miles away. Once again he ignored me.

Acting on impulse I reached for the door handle not caring that I had the faintest idea where we were; I just knew I had to get out before we were all killed. The car sped off once more, making my plans for escape nigh impossible. My thoughts turned to the other passenger who was now sitting staring at me with an unnerving expression.

She was wearing a long, black shabby coat with fraying at the cuffs and dirty brown woollen gloves. A matching scarf was wrapped around her head, half concealing her face and tucked into her neck. I placed her into her late seventies but there was something else.

Something about her that felt familiar. For a second we each held eye contact before I looked away, feeling the hairs stand up on the back of my neck and a shiver run down my spine.

It was then that I remembered the woman had given no instructions to the driver as to her destination just a mere knowing nod had been exchanged between them. I stared helplessly out of the window as alien scenery rushed past us; I was now trapped in the middle of nowhere with no hope of rescue.

'Where are we?' I asked addressing the driver, anxiety bubbling up into my throat, but he remained silent. My mouth started to go dry and my heart began to beat rapidly. A dreadful feeling of de j' vu enveloped me as my attention once again fell on to the old woman, who tightly clutched a brown carrier bag to her chest as if all her worldly goods were contained within it. Just as I was about to question her, the taxi driver suddenly slammed on his brakes throwing her with an almighty bump onto the dirty floor, scattering her belongings under the seats. She uttered an oath lost to the driver, who was busy revving up his engine as he waited for an old man to cross the road. I bent down to assist her.

'Take your hands away! I don't need your help!' she snapped viciously.

Taken aback I obeyed her turning my attention instead to the cameo brooch, hat pin and an old leather black purse that had escaped from her carrier bag, along with a vial containing a greenish black powder, which rolled under the driver's seat together with a few pennies. It was none of those things that left me open-mouthed with shock as I stupidly ignored the old woman's words in an effort to be a Good Samaritan. Out of the corner of my eye, I spotted a scrap of paper, as I instinctively reached for it a claw-like hand gripped my arm and a croaky voice spat 'that's mine, give it 'ere.'

Catching my breath I stared at the hand no longer protected by a glove. Long, spindle-like fingers wrapped in skin that was covered in scars, contractures and weeping sores which reminded me of something out of a horror film or, maybe... Could I be right? I wondered. Staring at the small shred of paper I noticed something had been written on it in illegible text that bore a strange resemblance to my riddle.

'Give it 'ere and mind your own business!' she screeched.

As scratching talons tore it from me, I suddenly felt a wave of nausea sweep over me and my stomach began to lurch. A stream of green projectile vomit spewed out of my mouth splashing onto the old woman. Bits of undigested food lay clinging to the wisps of grey hair, spattering her coat and legs wrapped in thick brown woollen stockings, while a pool of bile covered her feet. Another trickle of vomit dripped off the leather seats onto the littered taxi floor. The old woman looked aghast, sheer horror and disgust plain to see, however I couldn't summon enough will to care.

The driver definitely could. Jamming on his brakes he stormed out of his seat, flung open the car door and started shaking his fist at me, as he uttered a string of expletives. 'Ya stupid bitch get that bloody mess cleaned up now or I'll make ya eat it. Ugh! It stinks!' he said putting his hand over his nose to avoid the stench as he turned to grab his keys to open up the boot to find some rags.

With the drivers head buried in the boot and the old woman distracted by the vomit and attempting to retrieve the vial from under the driver's seat I grabbed my chance. Quickly climbing over her I practically threw myself out of the car then ran across fields. Keeping close to the cover of high hedges and stone walls, I kept on going until my legs couldn't carry me any further.

I paused under a large tree, the sweet taste of freedom intoxicating, as I struggled to breathe. Paranoid that they would find me I kept looking over my shoulder. Could he be hiding, perhaps lying in wait? Had he been part of a plot along with the old woman?

My thoughts turned to her. That hideous limb looked as if it had been in a fire or maybe boiling water, and that voice, when she told me to mind my business the voice had been so familiar, worryingly familiar. Was I adding two and two together and making five instead of four? I did not think so and the more I thought about it the more convinced I became. I still needed to get to the hospital so puffing and panting I made my way towards the road unaware I was shortly to receive the shock of my life.

Upon rounding the next bend in the lane I came to a level crossing and was surprised to see a fire engine and ambulance complete with emergency blue flashing lights. The vehicles attracted a small crowd of onlookers and it was soon clear why. The mangled wreckage of a car lay on the unmanned railway crossing as the emergency teams struggled to free its occupants. Curious I joined the others who were morbidly staring at the scene and asked a young woman if anyone had been hurt.

'Hurt you say, dead more like! I mean ya don't expect to live when a train smacks into ya, doing two hundred miles an hour, now do ya? Need a flipping miracle to survive that. I heard one of them firemen say it was a taxi and driver had picked up a woman passenger but there's not much left of either of them!' Nodding I moved away from the morbid scene and then remembered I had no idea where I was or even if I had been running in the right direction.

'Umm excuse me', I approached a spotty teenager, 'would you happen to know the way to the bus station from here? I must get to Black Gorge Hospital.'

'Black Gorge, 'ere ain't that the looney bin?' he smirked.

'Well you might call it that but I prefer to call it a psychiatric unit. After all minds can get broken just same as bodies can, you know, only difference is there's no stigma when you break your leg is there. A nervous breakdown and admission to a special hospital ward can set some folks tongues wagging.' I ranted, shaking my finger at the bewildered teen.

"Ere anyone know way to bus station?' He shouted to the crowd. 'She wants looney bin.'

Wishing at that moment the earth would suddenly open up and swallow me whole, I hastily thanked the young man and set off on a wing and a prayer, just as an ear-splitting crash of thunder came from above, followed by large raindrops spattering the pavement. I sighed heavily remembering I had left the house in a rush and my scarlet umbrella was still in its stand down the bottom of my hall.

'Just typical, that's all I need' I said aloud past caring that I was talking to myself. 'Ere! Watch out Mrs.! Nearly ran you over. Should look where ya goin'!' Startled I looked up to see a broad shouldered, burly farmer looking down on me.

'Oh! My goodness! I didn't see you I was ...'

'Well ya better get glasses Mrs if ya canna see tractor coming right in front of ya.' He interrupted, frowning at me. I had been so deeply engrossed in my thoughts I hadn't noticed the farm vehicle shoot out of a gate and straight into my path as it headed for a field opposite. I chose to ignore his comment about my eyesight as I tried to recover my equilibrium and dignity. Then I pulled myself up straight and enquired if I was on the right road for the town centre.

'I need the bus station could you please direct me?' I asked politely.

'Town ya say, yeah keep right on till ya get to crossroads then, let me see?' He removed his cloth cap, scratched his head and said in a gruff voice. 'Take right, no left it be at end like then ya need Robbins Lane or is it Ash Tree Road, anyway one or t'other and there's a roundabout somewhere at bottom of hill. Then y' want Market Street or could be Moon Street. Bus station is round there somewhere I believe.'

Having thanked him for his confusing directions, I continued forward following my instincts and a few other more helpful souls, I happened to meet on the way, to guide me. I heaved an enormous sigh of relief when ten maybe fifteen minutes later I came to my destination. Then having ascertained I needed to get the number twelve bus, which would drop me about a hundred yards from the hospital, I hauled myself on to the vehicle. As I put my hand into my coat pocket, to pay the two pound fifty pence fare the driver requested I felt my heart drop. Where was my purse? A long queue was beginning to form behind me as I desperately searched every single pocket, nook and cranny. I tried to ignore the puffs and sighs from the grumpy, bald headed bus driver and someone shouting 'come on Mrs I wanna get home today, not next year.'

A minute or so later I finally admitted defeat and with crimson cheeks was forced to reluctantly disembark. Then a thought popped into my mind. 'Could you tell me where I can find the Police Station? I must report my purse is missing; perhaps some kind person may have found it.'

'Yeah spent it more than like' huffed the bus driver.

'No! Wilhelmina,' that familiar little voice interrupted. 'You probably lost it in the taxi when you were thrown around by that lunatic driver.

'Police station, did you say my dear?' Pulled out of my thoughts, I looked round to see a middle aged woman dressed in a bright red mackintosh with dyed locks to match, wearing heavy make-up and a stressed expression.

'You're miles away from there, but believe number fifty one goes past it dear. Get yourself over to stand eleven. Best hurry it leaves in couple of minutes and if you miss it be another hour before you see another one.' She pointed into the distance.

' I have no money. I've lost my purse' I replied looking down in defeat. 'I am going to have to walk there.'

'Here you are dear take this' she said gently, pressing some coins into my hand. 'A couple of pounds dear, that should cover your fare.' She smiled

'Thank you but I...' I held the coins out to her.

'Just take it dear, it shall be my good deed of the day.' She closed my fingers and patted my hand tenderly.

'Well please can I have your name and address so I can at least pay you back for your kindness.' I asked.

'Just go dear before you miss it.'

After thanking the lady profusely, I rushed to find the stand for the number fifty one bus service which was revving up its engine to leave. Embarking quickly then taking a seat at the front I suddenly remembered with an almighty shock that when I left home that morning I had hastily tucked not only a five pound note along with a few coins into my purse but also the key to my front door. My back door key was just as inaccessible being in a dressing gown pocket hanging up behind my bedroom door, and my spare set of keys were with a neighbour, who had just taken himself off to enjoy six months of sunny climes on the Costa del Sol. So now I have to break into my own home.

'Can this day get any worse?' I asked myself.

'Yeah! No doubt it will', answered the little voice in my head.

About twenty minutes later I found myself stood staring up at an old stone faced building. Above it was a sign bearing the name 'Church Leigh Police Station 1901'. It looked quite pleasing to the eye, that was until I remembered that somewhere inside there would, no doubt, be cells holding unfortunates who had strayed off life's highway. After procrastinating a little longer, I took a deep breath and walked up to the heavy wooden double doors, slid my hand around the shiny brass knob and turned it to the right.

Upon opening it I could hear someone shouting 'I'm innocent officer. I tell you I'm innocent. You've got the wrong man'. On walking up to the large oak desk I was just in time to see two burly, poker faced policemen escorting a prisoner whose hands were cuffed behind his back, but as I looked up to the criminals face, I was shocked to see it was none other than Joe they were holding. Something in me snapped, remembering that I owed Joe my life. He and Bill had been my knights in shining armour and would always be placed on the highest pedestal as far as I was concerned, no matter what deeds they had committed. I ran over to them.

'Here, that's my Joe. What's he done? Why have you arrested him?' I demanded as Joe froze at seeing me.

'Caught breaking and entering old Mrs Jones farm last night Miss that's what he's done.' After giving Joe a quick glance, I turned to the policeman.

'He can't have officer. You see Joe was with me last night. You've arrested the wrong man. It must have been someone else. He was with me I tell you. He's a real gentleman is Joe, he would never put a foot wrong outside the law.'

'Umm… he was with you, you say, all night?' the officer asked suspiciously.

'Yes, it was my birthday and Joe came over to mine about teatime, we shared a bottle of wine and then umm…. we went upstairs to the bedroom.' I replied defiantly.

'And what happened then?' he asked curiously, raising an eyebrow.

'You're a man of the world Inspector what do you think happened?' crossing my arms over my chest.

'Joe is innocent. Let him go.' I again demanded.

'Nay Miss, you see he was caught on camera. Mrs Jones had special camera surveillance fitted recently after someone tried to steal some farm equipment and the camera doesn't lie but… maybe you are?' the policeman looked to his colleagues.

'Well! It could have been someone who looked like my Joe, officer.'

'He's guilty as charged Miss. We caught him red-handed this time not only on camera but he also kindly left us a few matching finger prints, not too bright is he Miss.' Realising my efforts to help Joe were proving futile I shot him a look that hopefully read 'I did my best to save you' and then headed over to the desk leaving justice to take its course. g, seeing Joe had brought back the hideous memories I had so desperately tried to bury, I began to tremble and my mind started to swim. Clutching my head I headed for the nearest seat.

'Are you all right Miss? Can I get you a cup of tea? Why it's Mrs Potts isn't it? I remember you.' Looking up I recognised the face of the young police officer who had long ago brought my Mollie back to me. If it had not been for his instinct and sharp mind when he had returned to the house and made an arrest, then things could have turned out very differently. Agatha Fortiscue's accomplice had cracked under interrogation and revealed everything.

I learned to my horror that my daughter had been Agatha's slave, kept on a chain and made to beg for food. Some days morsels would be thrown in her direction, others she would go hungry.

I had ensured the crone received her own comeuppance in prison when she was given that sugar bath, I refused to allow my mind to go any further. The more I reflected on it the more convinced I became that my fellow passenger in the taxi now lying on a mortuary slab had been my stepmother's old crone and the death threat had been her revenge for days spent imprisoned and abused. Her twisted, scarred gnarled hand, the strange vial containing some potion, maybe even poison, that she had quickly tried to grab from me. Then the scratchy, high pitched voice, the very same voice I had heard when Dr. Johnson and I had gone back to the house to search for Mollie. Yes, it all fitted together like pieces of a jigsaw.

'Now then Mrs Potts, take your time and tell me why you have come here.' His voice brought me back to reality and I looked up into his face. I wanted to tell him all of it, everything, but knew I couldn't. It was my secret and would remain so until I took it to the grave.

'Oh I've gone and lost my purse officer, must have dropped it out of my bag and was wondering if a kind soul had handed it in you see. I'm in a bit of a pickle as my house key was also in it along with a bit of money. Umm… you know that chap I saw being taken away when I came in umm… what's going to happen to him?'

'Expect he'll be charged, remanded in custody then tried by the courts.' He replied with a shrug.

'He is not a bad man Constable. Do you know he saved me from a torture worse than death?' I knew my loose tongue had said too much.

'Whatever do you mean by that Mrs Potts?' Well versed in the art of placing questions he gradually coaxed the whole sorry saga from me as I slowly and painfully revealed events of that dark day in Black Gorge Woods held prisoner at the mercy of my evil son. Wild horses however would not have let me tell the young policeman how Horace had suddenly disappeared without trace.

After I had finished he passed me a tissue to wipe away a tear and then announced 'we will investigate your son. Have you any idea where he could be? Are you prepared to stand up in court and testify all that Mrs Potts?' I hesitated. I knew that if I testified, all would be revealed.

'I shall think about it officer, after all he is my flesh and blood. Oh goodness me! Just look at the time, I must get home and I have no means of getting there.'

'Well! As it just so happens Mrs Potts I am going your way shortly so I can give you a lift. Is there a window you might have left open by any chance?'

'I'm afraid not. Don't believe in leaving windows open when I am away for burglars to take my stuff.' I answered, shaking my head.

'That is very sensible Mrs Potts. Now if you would like to follow me.' He gently smiled at me and held out his hand.

Thirty minutes later thanks to the assistance of the very kind constable, helping me gain access to my little cottage, I sat by the hearth watching the flames dance as they leapt up the chimney reflecting on my close brush with death. If I hadn't escaped from that taxi, no doubt my body would be lying in the mortuary along with that awful taxi driver and the old ghoulish woman. I shivered at the thought.

12

Forgiveness and Retribution

The next morning I woke up from my restless sleep with heavy eyes and a pounding head then remembered what I had to do today. I looked out of the window to see that my mood matched the grey cheerless sky and I became filled with a familiar sense of foreboding. Desperately trying to find a shred of optimism, I dressed and went downstairs for breakfast. My stomach was tied in knots and I barely had any appetite for anything other than half a slice of toast, which I managed to burn.

'The sooner you get this done and dusted the happier you will feel Wilhelmina', I told myself trying to find some conviction in my own words.

I went into the hall and grabbed my coat. On catching sight of myself in the mirror was horrified to discover I hadn't even removed my curlers let alone combed my hair. 'Pull yourself together' I snapped, snatching at the rollers, wincing as I quickly yanked them out and dragged a comb through the mess. Then searched through my old brown leather handbag for lipstick and rouge to add some colour to my face. After arming myself with rashers of bacon in case fate threw me face to face with Bruno again and remembering to grab my scarlet umbrella in case things turned for the worst, I took a deep breath, locked my front door and set off towards my stepmother's.

Twenty minutes later, on rounding a bend in the road I could see four tall chimneys, shards of brick jutting into the leaden sky, which represented the dark landmark belonging to Agatha Fortescue. As each step took me closer to the unknown I could feel my heart starting to pound, beads of perspiration gathering on my forehead, my body began to tremble and shake as a wave of nausea swept over me and my knees turned to jelly. An icy cold flush chilled me to the bone while an overwhelming fear of doom fell upon me as I felt in my pocket for a small brown paper bag and quickly breathed into it, trying desperately to calm myself down. Ever since my horrific kidnap, I had developed anxiety attacks when forced to confront stressful situations.

Maybe today wasn't such a good idea after all, I thought, I did pretty well to get this far, now turn around and go home, try again another time. I started to back away and headed for my little cottage before anyone saw me.

'Ah, home sweet home!' heaving a deep sigh of relief I rummaged in the depths of my bag, my fingers tripping over this and that until I felt the cold sting of metal that was my house key, at the same time through the door I could clearly hear the insistent rings of my telephone.

'No! Not again! Don't stick now!' I begged, wiggling and tugging at the key. Finally it yields and I burst through the door, just as the phone stops ringing.

'Oh! For Goodness Sake! Well if it's important they will call again' I tell myself, wondering who on earth it would be, as I pick up the phone and dial to see if anyone has left a message.

'Mrs. Potts this is Sister Jenkins from the hospital. I am afraid Mollie has had a bad seizure and a heavy fall. We think you should come straight away.' My heart stops. I hang up fast and while trying to control my trembling fingers reach for my address book for a taxi number, taking deep breaths trying to keep my fear and panic at bay.

Suddenly a flash of lightening lit up the room followed by a loud clap of thunder. I hated storms. They always unearthed horrible memories I had tried to bury.

'I am sorry Mrs. Potts but our nearest taxi driver is half an hour away. It's the bad weather, every man and his dog wants a taxi you see. You might try Mr. Coates. He may be free.' The gruff voice suggested. Luckily he was right and fifteen minutes later I relaxed into the comfortable leather seats of John Coates car, my thoughts taken over with Mollie. She had been such a happy, beautiful child, how I wish I could go back.

As I walked over to the bed, guilt plagued me eating away at my flesh, leaving a gaping hole of sorrow and remorse. My eyes welled up and I tried to swallow a huge lump in my throat as I stared at my beautiful daughter who lay attached to a life support machine. Her little face was ashen, her eyes closed and was surrounded by technical equipment that beeped and flashed every couple of seconds.

I knew the doctors were having problems controlling my daughter's epilepsy, but I'm ashamed to admit that I had been too busy working on my revenge to give her condition much thought. Standing at the head of her bed in a daze, I tried to concentrate on Dr. Matthew Wilson, a Consultant Neurologist as he explained that this seizure had been prolonged, lasting six and a half minutes apparently and including other injuries sustained she had cracked her skull when she fell.

'Has Mollie ever had a traumatic head injury in her past, Mrs. Potts? On the X-ray there was evidence of an old fracture.' I mumbled 'no' as my mind reeled with thoughts of Agatha; what did that evil bitch do to my girl?

'Umm is Mollie going to be all right? When did this happen? Why didn't someone tell me immediately?' I demanded taking my anger out on him.

'We tried to call you several times but there was no answer.' Just as fast as my fury arose, it quickly deflated.

'No! I was out' I mumbled shame warming my cheeks recalling how my obsession with my arch enemy had once again taken over my mind as I stared at my daughter, through a blur of tears.

'I am afraid to tell you Mrs. Potts there is a strong possibility that Mollie could have suffered permanent brain damage.' The doctor said, placing a gentle hand on my shoulder. He guided me towards the chair beside her bed; I sat trying to absorb the doctor's words, permanent brain damage, three life altering words. I grasped Mollie's hand tight, willing her to squeeze back, for her hand to move, eyes to blink, something. I begged her to fight, to come back, I whispered promises, into her ear, telling her I would do better, be better if she just came back.

A little while later silence cloaked the room, the only thing to be heard was the beep… beep… beep… of the cardiac monitor and my gentle sobs of despair. I sat and stared at the intravenous equipment, watching each drop of medication drip…drip… drip…when suddenly I was startled by a friendly voice, I shot up in my chair to discover it belonged to a plain but homely face.

'Would you like a cup of tea dear?' she smiled gently.

'Are you staying overnight? We have special rooms for relatives you know.'

'Umm yes, thank you.' I replied, trying to blink the tears from my eyes. She smiled again and left the room, a few minutes later she returned with my tea, a biscuit and instructions as to where I would be sleeping tonight.

At around ten that evening, having found some plain white sheets and a couple of slightly lumpy pillows, I made my way to the small room just off the ward and snuggled down for a couple hours of rest, having instructed the ward staff that I was to be woken should my daughter's condition change.

It wasn't long before my thoughts drifted as I slipped into a light sleep, only to be disturbed by dreams of Agatha Fortescue trying to strangle me with my mother's necklace until a loud crash suddenly broke my nightmare. I jolted from my bed bathed in sweat, to find my bedding and pillows lying on the floor and my alarm clock flung across the room.

'So that's what that noise was, I said aloud to myself relieved to find there had been no intruder in the room as I inspected the clock face then noticed the hour said five thirty am.

'Go back to bed' my body screamed in annoyance at being woken too early. I glanced at my mess of pillows and sheets and decided instead to find some tea and breakfast. So I headed towards the kitchen. Two nurses were sat at the table, discussing my daughter.

'Molly was making headway, real progress until her mother took her home. Now look at her! Doctors are not holding out much hope. It's criminal what happened, just criminal. If she dies it will be because of her you know. How could she…'

They fell silent as I walked into the room. It wasn't much to look at a table and few chairs with a small counter top which housed a kettle, toaster and small microwave. I made my way towards the kettle, feeling the women's eyes stare daggers at my back. After making a cup of tea and stealing a muffin, I muttered 'good morning' but they sped away averting their eyes, bearing red faces. Mine too was scarlet as my eyes flashed anger at their assumptions and gossip.

'How dare they criticise me! They have absolutely no idea what they are talking about and it is none of their business' I huffed storming out of the room. Having made my brew, I headed back, sat on the bed and allowed my thoughts to wander.

Later having ascertained there had been no change in Molly's condition I made my way in the rain to the nearest stop for the number 78 service, assuring myself that I would be back at her bedside by noon. I sat on the bus near the front, watching the rain drops chase one another as they trickled down the glass, when a stout, elderly lady suddenly landed heavily into the seat beside me and continued to invade my space as she wriggled and fidgeted to make herself comfortable. I jumped as her cold wet umbrella brushed my leg and gave her a disapproving look, though she failed to notice and much to my annoyance shuffled even further into my personal territory.

'Hello dear, terrible weather we're having today. Wilhelmina Potts isn't it, if I'm not mistaken?' she suddenly ventured.

'By God! It's been a long time hasn't it dear! Tell me how are Charlotte and Hector? I heard about poor Harry. God rest his soul.' I half turned in my seat and squinted at her face trying to place her.

'Umm I'm afraid they have both passed away' I replied as I struggled to recall her name. I didn't have to worry though as I wouldn't have got a word in edgeways and before I reached my destination I had practically heard her entire life story, but strangely it bore similar co-incidences to mine.

She too had been a mere infant when she had lost her mother, had been brought up by a hard, insensitive woman who happened to have borne eight children of her own and clearly had no time or inclination to take on another despite her husband's wishes.

'You know Wilhelmina dear I can still remember clear as day what she did, you wouldn't believe this. She waited until I turned fourteen you see, the day I left school to get rid of me. On my birthday my stepmother pushed a note into my hand. At first I stupidly hoped it was a present but when I opened it I discovered it was an application for a servant's post, a scullery maid I believe, in a house somewhere miles away from home. Not five minutes later, I was bundled up in my best clothes and sent off to the interview, but before I left she made it very clear what was to happen.

'Emma-Jayne, if you fail to impress and are not offered the position then not on any account are you to return to this house. Do you understand? You're not to set foot here ever again do you hear?' I told Emma I had also heard those same words from my own father however she wasn't interested in my woes and continued with her tale.

'As it happened Wilhelmina I did not get the post, but luckily the posh woman who interviewed me knew of someone who needed a governess to look after her son. I remember his name was Timothy. He was six years old, precocious and completely ruined by his mother. She indulged his every whim you know, be it a new expensive toy or later when he turned eighteen she even gave him five thousand dollars to buy a flying field would you believe and paid for a course of flying lessons. He might have been alive today if she hadn't, got killed flying a plane, you see.

Of course Timothy's mother had always known wealth. If I recall her father was a shrewd business man and owned his own shipping line.

I heard she had been a rebel in her youth who had brought shame to her parents smearing the family name with scandal when she had ran away and married a stable lad, beneath her station, you see. So she was punished, sent abroad, excluded from her family, friends and the exciting social life that London offered the rich in those days. Her father didn't see her penniless mind you, far from it, and she used her money to buy a farm and build a vast mansion on the land.

My mouth fell wide open you know Wilhelmina, could not believe my eyes when I first walked into that house. It had electricity you see, no oil lamps to light, no candles to burn, and it had hot water heating, sheer luxury in those days. There were thirty rooms and no less than fourteen bedrooms, fourteen would you believe it. All of them contained en suite bathrooms, tiled too they were. I remember overhanging the grand staircase there were six huge chandeliers, beautiful they were and lots of paintings of her and her husband lined the walls then there... Suddenly the bus swerved round a bend in the road sending my companion almost flying into the aisle. 'Goodness! Gracious! Wilhelmina, now where was I? Oh yes, I remember, she was passionate about animals particularly Persian cats and they all had their own special decorative accommodation. Then there were her horses, by the time I left no fewer than ninety would you believe. Couldn't send them to market you see. Wilhelmina even the servants' quarters had escaped the normal Spartan appearance of dark brown paint and meagre furnishings of comfort.

You know all that wealth and status never brought her happiness, real happiness, I mean. You see apart from her house much of the money just dribbled through her fingers as she financed her husband's wild schemes and dodgy deals which invariably turned sour. Then the ungrateful man went off to look for greener pastures, the lecherous fool. Never could stand him. Good riddance I said.

Abandoned his own flesh and blood, he did too, though by then I had won Timothy's affection. Well I thought I had but it didn't last long mind. He was a strange child, never knew quite what he was thinking but he certainly had his mother well and truly wrapped around his little finger. I can still remember the day he suddenly sprung at me and deliberately scratched my arm, drew blood he did, when I refused to give in to his demands. Then he tried to scare me, would you believe. 'I've only to click my fingers he said and my mother will send you packing along with all the others.' He was a clever, manipulative boy who would even inflict injury upon himself but ensured others took the blame. I wanted to wallop the daylights out of him but knew his mother was totally against corporal punishment having made it clear when she took me on her little darling was never to be put over my knee, not a single hair on her son's head was to be harmed. So I knew there was absolutely no way on earth she would believe her son had purposefully clawed at my arm.

Anyway by then I had had more than my fair share of him and decided it was time to move on, so I left and joined the Land Army. However Wilhelmina I heard…'

'Oops!' Just at that point the bus hit a large pothole in the road and for a few seconds my companion stopped talking but my relief was short lived.

'Oh! Dear! Lord! I fear I shall soon be seeing my breakfast again at this rate! Now where was I dear? You seem a little distracted Wilhelmina; I do hope I haven't been boring you. I can talk the hind leg off a donkey I'm afraid. Now what was I saying? Oh yes! my charge, couldn't believe my ears you know when I heard it was his offspring though don't suppose I should have been surprised.'

'Um why couldn't you…' I tried to interrupt.

'…Well dear, you remember that woman, you know the prostitute, she was all over the papers in the sixties? Now what was her name, Christine something, my memory is dreadful these days. Anyway Timothy had a son you see who went to work for her would you believe! Well that was after the Chickenpox took his father.'

'The chicken pox?' I asked in surprise, I thought she said he was killed in a plane crash? Did she mean Smallpox? I wondered. Nobody got taken by the chickenpox.

'Jacksons Corner.' Was suddenly shouted down the aisle as the bus jolted to a stop.

'Oh! That's my stop dear. Goodness! Gracious! Shouldn't be allowed on the road he shouldn't. Think I might tell him too. Anyway been nice chatting Wilhelmina.' She started to get up and hurry away.

'Actually it's mine also' I mumbled to her retreating form, remembering why I was on the bus in the first place. I stumbled onto the pavement and turned round to see my grey haired, gregarious companion having words with the surly bus driver, each slowly becoming as red-faced as the other, but I was on a mission. Now where was that pawnbroker's shop?

I turned left and headed for the village main street as my thoughts started to wander, trying to remember that children's nursery rhyme 'Pop goes the weasel' it had something to do with a pawnbrokers I think, 'pop' being a slang term for pawning and 'the weasel' being a shoemaker's tool. So lost in my thoughts I almost missed the familiar three golden balls sign only a short distance away and soon forgot about nursery rhymes as my mind turned to more important things.

I walked up to the shop and peered through the window, my eyes caught the red glint of my mother's ruby necklace lying in its case, given pride of place in the centre of the display. Then I saw the price tag, 200 guineas, however could I afford that? I continued to stare in shock, feeling my mother's despair weighing on me, at the thought of that witch wearing such a cherished treasure. There had to be a way to get it back, but what way for I had nothing to pawn, certainly nothing worth anywhere near 200 guineas. I stood in front of the shop for a good ten minutes as an idea, albeit a wild one began to form. Slipping my fingers around the shiny door knob I entered the shop crammed full of personal possessions. You could feel the misery and sadness cloak the room, radiating from this collection from which folks had been forced to part. As I walked up to the counter a little man with a brown wizened face and sharp beady eyes, wearing a monocle, appeared from behind the curtain that lead to the back of the shop.

"Excuse me sir but are you aware that ruby and emerald necklace inset with pearls you have in the window is stolen property. I know the woman who pawned it you see. She stole it from me.' 'Umm... No!' looking slightly astonished and a little annoyed in case my words had been overheard by a nearby customer perusing a platinum ring.

'You wouldn't want stolen goods on your premises now would you sir', endeavouring to carry my voice a little louder.

'Have you reported the theft to the police then madam?' his monocle eye squinted in suspicion.

'Umm no... not yet but I intend to sir. That woman, the one who brought it in, is a black witch, worships Satan you know, you want to have nothing to do with her I tell you. She could put a curse upon you. Your shop could be set on fire, anything could happen.' I insisted raising my voice a little more.

'Look Miss all sorts of folks come into my shop and I give them a service. Now if you can give me 200 guineas you can have it.' He outstretched his hand awaiting payment.

'Umm I don't suppose you could mark it down to say 50 guineas and hold on to it for me?' I asked hopefully.

'Look Miss I've a business to run. Who do you think I am, Lord Rothschild? It is worth no less than 200 guineas, now take it or leave it! And if you don't mind I am a very busy man so please hurry up and decide.' He snapped, slapping his hand on the counter top in frustration.

'I shall get the money and return for it but whatever you do sir, I beg you not to let that witch get hold of it.'

'Get the money then madam.' And with that he then disappeared back behind the curtain, leaving me to wonder where on earth I was going to find 200 guineas. I had nothing of any value or, had I? Racking my brains I recalled an old brooch Fred had given me years ago saying he had found it in the street but reckoned it was only a bit of tat but pretty tat like you Wilhelmina. He had a talent for giving back handed compliments had Fred but suppose it had been worth something. I vowed to find it and return the next day.

When I did, my face fell when after peering at the brooch under a special magnifying glass, I heard the shopkeeper say 'Nah its worth maybe ten bob and that's my final offer.' With a heavy sigh of disappointment I put it back in my pocket and left the shop at a loss of what to do next.

Granny suddenly paused, looking me straight in the eye, 'Mary I believe I mentioned earlier that I had led a rather colourful life and done certain things umm … I fear you may be shocked by what I have to say next but …' with a deep breath she continued, 'say it I must!… do you remember earlier my mentioning a prostitute called Christine Keeler?'

After a quick peek at my note book for a reminder I replied, 'Umm yes…' I paused hating myself for asking this question, 'Granny I hope you are not going to tell me you were planning to sell your body to get that money!' I scrunched my face up in anticipation, feeling slightly sick.

'I had no choice!' she stated.

'Whaaat!' I shrieked in horror.

'Well how else could I quickly get my hands on such a large sum? Now you needn't look so disgusted Mary, close your mouth and kindly hear me out before you start judging me.' I was shocked, how could she scold me right now, I could barely look her in the eye.

'Umm… perhaps asking the bank for a loan isn't that what most people do?' I retorted.

'I tried. They turned me down flat. 'Two hundred guineas Mrs. Potts', they said, 'is quite a tidy sum and just how and when do you propose to pay off this debt on such a small wage?' You see my weekly paltry earnings, cleaning the local village store, was spent on feeding, clothing and keeping a roof over not only my head but also my young ward Mildred. There was nothing left to put aside and I no longer had a spare room to take in lodgers though, after my brush with Mr. Williams that was my last desire.

Mary I was not going to be any common call girl. Just as Christine Keeler had, I was going to achieve fame or maybe notoriety. I had ambition you see so set my sights on pleasuring certain individuals of the upper class in English society. My imagination had been set alight when I had read the exploits of a beautiful English lady called Cora Pearle, born 1835, who lived in France. You see Cora had many wealthy and connected lovers, all eating out of her hand, vying for her amorous attentions. They would shower her with chateaux, exquisite gowns, money for casinos and jewellery. It is said Cora became famous all over France for her erotic entertainment and amorous affections.' She had once teased fifteen male guests at a dinner party defying them to eat the next course. Naked apart from a light sprinkling of parsley she had curled up on a large silver platter and been carried aloft by six servants who had then placed her in the middle of the table, much to her guests amusement. What fun that would have been.'

I took a deep breath and tried to swallow the lump in my throat. Just when I thought my grandmother couldn't shock me anymore, she announces a penchant for whoring. What else was going to come out of this woman's mouth? Or maybe her alto ego's, I wondered, silently shaking my head in disgust.

'Of course to get to the top one has to start at the bottom' she continued, smiling as she realized the double meaning to her words. I was beginning to see Granny Wilhelmina in a slightly different light as I pictured the scene of prostitution. Male and female sex workers can be found in every city in every country; it is violent, abusive and disrespectful with many stuck in this life because of drugs, alcohol or necessity. It is often said that some do not choose prostitution but their addictions do.

'Anyway in the daytime … Mary did you hear what I just said? Really you must pay more attention dear,' hearing Granny's voice break into my thoughts.

'In the daytime I would don a skirt, classic twinset and a pair of sensible shoes. Then I would catch the bus to the hospital and sit beside Mollie, who had sadly fallen into a deep coma, stay until visiting time was over and then head back home. When the dark arrived out came the blonde wig, hitched up skirt and revealing blouse along with a pair of fishnet stockings, high heels, a saucy garter and scarlet lipstick. You would never find me standing on street corners to hook a punter, in the cold and the rain. No, instead I used to do what a few sailors wives did, when their husbands were away at sea, and resorted to a packet of washing powder being strategically placed in my front room window with the sign 'OMO' stuck to the front as this was code for 'old man out'. Also a certain card I had placed into one or two telephone booths, which read 'Call me if YOU yearn for Adventure and Ecstasy', produced some clientele.

So slowly but surely my little black book began to fill up and more importantly so did my purse. I called myself Dolly and if I recall one customer nicknamed me Dolly Dimple but I'm sure he wasn't referring to the dimple on my chin.' She chuckled, choosing to ignore my raised eyebrows of disapproval.

'I had to make a few changes of course, a warm red light replaced the stark white bulb in my bedroom and strategically placed red cushions and satin sheets covered the bed, at the top end of which, swinging from a hook on the wall was a leather whip and matching handcuffs. After all, I did promise to suffice all needs. Half an hour for missionary or oral relief, and then fifteen minutes for anything on the kinky side, I told them and charged them accordingly. I remember one young man asked me to put him across my knee and then spank him one hundred times, then handcuff him to my chaise lounge and give him another hundred strokes with my whip!'

I sat fidgeting in my seat blushing with embarrassment from head to toe, face as red no doubt as that man's buttocks by time she had finished with him, I could not help thinking how easily this stuff was spilling out of my great grandmother's mouth. Indeed most old ladies who had reached the grand old age of ninety six would never have dreamt of disclosing such things but Granny Wilhelmina was a law unto herself.

'I tell you there are some weird people in this world Mary.'

'Umm yes Granny' I agreed, inwardly including my great grandmother in that statement.

'Of course every action has a consequence and sometimes they can be dire. How long she had been standing there watching, I have no idea. I blamed the punter for if he had not made such a racket screaming and yelling every time that leather whip struck his nether regions my ward would never have woken and crept out of her room to investigate.' I froze at her words, glancing at the door for Mildred.

'I told him to be quiet. It had been him who first spotted her as he lay across my chaise and suddenly pointed to the door. Her eyes were like saucers and mouth agape as were the punter's who quickly slipped his shackles and grabbed his trousers he had discarded earlier in gay abandon. Then struggling to do up his zip he ran past my little ward, down the stairs and out of my front door. Hey! Where's my money? I shouted after him as I heard the front door slam.

'Go back to your room this minute Millie!' anger covering my acute embarrassment, my face as red as my satin sheets and no doubt my punter's behind as I berated my young ward for having left her bedroom. I must have forgotten to lock her door, how careless of me. Guilt and remorse suddenly washed over me like a great tidal wave as I recalled Charlotte's words when she had placed her child in my care.

'I know my darling Millie will not want for anything with you Wilhelmina. She will be showered with love and affection and I know you will guide her along the right path as she slowly blossoms into a young woman.' How badly had I veered off that path! Charlotte would turn in her grave if she knew. 'Maybe she does! Maybe she was also watching that little scene' piped up my conscience. I had not only let my sister down but I had probably damaged her nine year old daughter for the rest of her life.

Later when Mildred was throwing one of her frequent tantrums rebelling against my authority her disgust poured out in a torrent when she announced she was going to search for her father whom she planned to live with, saying vehemently 'Anywhere, just anywhere, on God's earth, would be better than here, living with a whore!' Biting my lip hard I chose to ignore the word 'whore'. After all she had seen it for herself so it was pointless to deny the fact. More importantly, however, could I tell her that she couldn't go to her father that he was serving a life sentence in a French prison for murdering her mother. I simply couldn't and did everything in my power to prevent Mildred from ever finding out the truth, at least until she was old enough to deal with the emotional fallout. Unfortunately, when she reached her early teens she came across a newspaper cutting of the trial.

'Is it true Aunt Wilhelmina? It says here this man killed a Charlotte Dupont in a house in France. That's my mother isn't it' she demanded pointing to an old picture of my sister taken in happier times.

'It's her isn't it? I know it is because she looks identical to the woman in here' she insisted, opening the locket hanging on a thin gold chain around her neck.

'Was... was he my father? I nodded as she showed me the paper then tears streaming down her cheeks she ran out of the room and upstairs to her bedroom. The report of the trial had revealed the sick, horrifying facts how Charles Dupont had used a machete and barbarically stabbed his wife repeatedly in the head, face, arms and stomach severing her main abdominal artery... Apparently her body had been discovered the next morning by the cleaner who had suffered a stroke brought on by the shock. I prayed every day that evil twisted man would get to suffer indescribable agony, that his body would be sliced into, perhaps by another maniac in the prison. I believe like all psychopaths he was very manipulative choosing to go on hunger strikes, trying to influence other inmates to follow. If I recall his defence for the murder was that his wife was having an affair and had to be punished. When he was shown the photographic evidence of her injuries he had displayed not a shred of remorse.

Anyway to return to the episode of the punter's acute embarrassment, not to mention mine of course, it was then, to ensure complete privacy, I decided to discreetly visit my clients in hotel rooms, some seedy, others quite plush, lying to Mildred about where I was going on each occasion. I still needed fifty more guineas to afford to buy back the necklace and every day I would make time to walk past the shop to check it was still sitting in the pawnbroker's window.

Before long, dentists, architects, bankers, even a lord were all my clientele and just like Cora Pearle I too specialized in giving my guests erotic surprises getting to know all their little likes and dislikes. Ice cubes followed by hot candle wax dripped over his erogenous zones was one man's request or painting such zones with maybe ice cream and champagne, to be slowly licked was the banker's idea of heaven. I got to hear their innermost thoughts and perverted fantasies but also became their friend and it was one such friend whom I turned to following Mildred's shocking exposure to my world.

I believe he came from the Punjab if my memory serves me or was it Bengal? Saheed was a lovely man, well at first, real salt of the earth and affluent. Anyway one day he said to me 'you know Wilhelmina we would make a good team, you and I. We should go into the sex business together.' It was Saheed who introduced me to that famous book you know. Now what is it called 'Kama something or other?'

'Umm the Kama Sutra' I ventured, inwardly praying Granny was not going to choose the topic of pornography to go off on one of her tangents.

'Yes that was it Mary, the Kama Sutra, a wonderful book, simply fascinating. Ever read it dear? You should, you can learn a lot from it. Did you know it describes over one hundred ways to …' I quickly interrupt.

'Umm Granny that's a really pretty skirt you are wearing today', desperately trying to change the subject.

'Oh thank you dear. Now about that book it…' I tried again.

'Granny how was …'

'Mary please do not keep on interrupting me dear. The Kama Sutra was not just a bible of sex positions and techniques you know …' by this point I would have been happy to jump out of the window.

'Granny is that relevant, surely …'

'Hush Mary' receiving a glare this time, I snapped my mouth shut.

'Now Kama of course as everyone knows was one of the Hindu goals of life meaning aesthetic and erotic pleasure but you see the book was also written as a guide to virtuous and gracious living for those born in India many centuries ago. As was the custom in those days it particularly embraced the marking of the body with the nails and teeth but in a certain fashion you see. During the height of passion the man's nails should be driven into the woman's flesh. It was immaterial where he dug them, could be into the breasts, thighs, throat or neck so long as it was hard enough to induce pain and leave a lasting mark. This sign was highly regarded and respected by both the wearer and other citizens in the community serving to ward off any aspiring strangers. Of course in those ancient times Indian women left their breasts entirely exposed you see, including royal ladies. I remember how Saheed pressed his nails into my throat once then he…'

'Oh Granny, look it's almost lunch time. What do you fancy to eat? How about a nice Spanish omelette' I asked desperately trying once more to get away from that book, or any information about my great grandmother's sexual exploits.

'Totally ignoring my question she continued 'Now Mary you may or may not be surprised to learn that in a certain town on a certain road in a certain two storey house there is a certain massage parlour belonging to me. My partner in crime died a long time ago but Saheed was never a well man, had this persistent cough you see. They said it was the Tuberculosis that killed him, but personally, I think it was the Syphilis. Anyway, going back to my …massage parlour. I was the Madame and in charge of no less than ten girls I'll have you know, and highly respected too I might add. I ran a decent, respectable establishment where we gave relief and performed our ministrations in tastefully furnished rooms decorated with red flocked wallpaper, heavy red velvet drapes and gold gilt furnishings.' Respectable did she really just say that? I wondered.

'Wilhelmina's Wicked Wares still brings in the profits today dear although of course I no longer manage it myself, but one day Mary it will all belong to you, although there are one or two provisos. You must not change anything. Everything must be kept exactly as it is and you must never get rid of any of my girls. It was my way of helping those who had fallen on hard times, you see. I gave them food, clothes and a roof over their head and in return they brought in the business. I saw it as um… well charity you know. Where else would these young women have ended up, many had already turned to petty crime before coming to work for me?'

'Umm… I see Granny and um … just where is this brothel?' I asked, not really wanting to know the answer.

'Oh! It's a massage parlour dear not a brothel and Wilhelmina's Wicked Wares is nowhere near these parts, it's not even in this country. It's in Holland, Amsterdam to be precise. The laws there are so much more lax you see. I also own another smaller parlour called Sugar and Spice which is in London, it's down a little side street in So Ho to be exact.

You know I remember coming down the stairs there one night when I heard a familiar voice. Saheed was trying to pacify a man who had become angry and impatient.

'I'm sorry sir but all our young ladies are busy at the moment so if you would like to wait in the red lounge you can get a drink and then choose…'

'I will look after the gentleman Saheed', I told him. The client spun round visibly shaken as our eyes met, mine displaying a genuine happiness to see my dear friend, his displaying utter disbelief and astonishment seeing me in this new light so alien to what he had witnessed before. Then he began mentally undressing me with his eyes, removing my tight fitting low cut, satin emerald dress, matching laced corset and fishnet stockings.

'Joe' I whispered breaking the uncomfortable silence then flashed him a warm smile and asked him to follow me upstairs. After we made love, we sat and talked. I knew I could tell Joe anything and I would never see that look of disgust that I now see in your eyes Mary. He didn't sit there judging me as you do, how could he? Although he didn't appear so happy when I asked for his help.

'Oh, dunno 'bout that Wilhelmina, just come out prison see. Judge gave us twelve months but they let us out just gone seven see 'cause of good be'aviour. If I don't keep me nose clean they'll send us back and lock us up for another five see.'

After a few whiskies I got him to see things from my point of view. Sex and alcohol can be very persuasive you know. My obsession with revenge still continued to blind me, making me totally unaware of the jealous rivalry between my partner and Joe. I should have noticed the dark looks, the set mouth and the attempt to turn Joe away or charge him six times more than our other clients, but I didn't and it became inevitable that Saheed and Joe would lock horns one day.

I remember the fight well, chairs and fists were thrown, tables overturned and the floor became awash not only with beer but blood for Saheed had produced a knife. It was only when one of my girls quickly exposed her large breasts to distract Joe and I managed to smash a bottle on the back of Saheed's head did it finally end though I nearly put him in hospital. He forgave me, then not long afterwards my Indian friend shocked me to my core, when he got down on one knee and proposed marriage. Told me I was his sun, moon and stars and he loved me with a burning passion but I turned him down despite the fact I was carrying his child having no wish to be shackled to his jealous fiery temper the rest of my life. Although when your grandmother Eliza arrived I soon discovered it was not only her father's olive skin and dark, sultry eyes she had inherited from Saheed. From knee high Eliza knew exactly how to use those assets. It was almost a natural progression when the time came for her to follow me into the business and she was good, very good, the punters liked her a lot and always came back for more. Then when her time came to bear a child, the right side of the blanket I might add, she soon passed the tricks of the trade down to your mother.'

'Did you just say my mother?' I spluttered.

'Yes dear, Amy was a natural at the art of seduction, had a good head for business too until her riding accident. So tragic but we will not go into that now, it was a long time ago. You know Mary, to look at Amy was just like looking at a mirror image of my own mother Kathleen with her ebony locks, porcelain skin and those forget-me-not blue eyes.'

I just sat there stunned with a gaping mouth, still trying to process what my great grandmother had just revealed. My mother, my own mother had sold her body and I not only came from a line of prostitutes but what is more would be inheriting a brothel in the not so distant future. What else had been hidden from me. I dare not even think. It couldn't possibly be any worse than this or could it?

13

Best Laid Plans

Having finally accumulated the two hundred guineas, the next morning I sat on the bus smiling to myself, believing that in no less than thirty minutes my mother's beautiful ruby necklace would be safely tucked inside my handbag. Fate intervened and my life went awry once again!

I stood staring through the pawnbroker's window; tears pricked in my eyes, seeing not my beloved inheritance but instead sitting front and centre was a gaudy old vase.

'Well I hung on to it long as I could madam, but been over six months you know, and I have a business to run.' The owner peered down at me looking over his monocle.

'I begged and pleaded with you sir not to let her have it.' I took a step back feeling uncomfortable from insistent leering.

'I didn't madam. I sold it to a man who said he wanted to surprise his wife with a little romantic token'. So that was that, my heart sank, I would have to accept that I would never see my mother's jewellery again.

'Well believe you did mention madam that it had been stolen and I don't want anything suspicious in my shop, I am glad to be rid to be honest madam.' He nodded his head and turned to help another customer. I left the shop in a haze of anger; this was all Agatha's fault. On that day I vowed to do whatever it took to get my jewellery back, as bitter hatred surged up in my throat choking me. I would never ever be able to forgive Agatha Fortescue for the devastation she has brought to my family. Since she came into our lives she has savagely murdered my mother, beaten and tortured my sister, banished my dear brother Hector to Ireland and abducted my daughter when she was only five years old and who was now lying in a coma fighting for her life.

Also wasn't it her who had given birth to that sorry excuse for a man, Horace who had sadistically killed a sick foal then beat and repeatedly raped me, not forgetting how he carved into my flesh. The hideous memories just like the scars I bore would never disappear. So, you see if it wasn't for my arch enemy and her evil offspring I wouldn't be trapped in this need for retribution. My hatred held no boundaries, nor did my obsession to reap an unholy revenge on this woman.

Six months later I was to learn that the man who had bought my necklace had returned to the pawnbroker's as his gesture turned sour when he discovered that his spouse had betrayed him. Therefore once again my mother's fine, elegant jewellery ended up being given pride of place in the pawnbroker's window, except now it wore a price tag of three hundred guineas!

However this time I was determined it was not going to slip through my fingers and a bit of bargaining on my part would not go amiss. So with a firm grip I pulled the door knob, took a deep breath then stepped inside the musty old shop and glanced around for the shopkeeper. Spotting his assistant a thin, wiry man in his late forties who was bald as a coot and wearing a frowned, exasperated expression. I strolled over to the counter and told him that I wished to speak to the owner.

'You can't. He's not in today. I'm in charge. What can I do for you?' He huffed, clearly not in a very good mood.

'You have a ruby, pearl and emerald necklace in the window that happens to be mine. It was stolen from me.' I stated, pointing in that direction.

'Look Madam, Mr. Turner has told me all about that necklace; just take my advice and let the Police deal with the matter.' Having had a few brushes with the law, I had no wish whatsoever to involve the local Constabulary in this matter.

'Umm, I'll give you one hundred and fifty pounds for it.' I bargained

'Sorry madam but it's priced at three hundred guineas.' He said with a shake of his head.

'It's very strange that it was only worth two hundred guineas not so long ago, thought he would earn himself a nice little profit at my expense, did he?' I asked with a sickly sweet smile.

'I think you ought to discuss this with Mr. Turner. I really have no idea what you mean. I can tell you madam you are not the only customer interested in the jewellery.'

'Very well, I'll increase my offer to one hundred and seventy five guineas', becoming extremely annoyed, begrudging having to pay for my own inheritance.

'If Mr. Turner says it's worth three hundred guineas then three hundred guineas it is madam' He insisted.

'Two hundred and that is my final offer.' I countered.

'Three hundred and that is mine madam. I suggest you come back and discuss the matter with Mr. Turner or the Police. Funny though that PC Wilson didn't know anything about it being reported stolen because he knows everything that goes on in these parts?' This stubborn man wouldn't give an inch.

'Oh very well, I will be back tomorrow with some more money but here is fifty guineas deposit so don't you dare sell my necklace to anybody else do you hear. It's mine.'

'Yeah did you 'ear the lady? It belongs to 'er.' Shocked I spun round to see my good friend Joe standing behind me. He caught my elbow and ushered me out of earshot.

'Been thinking what ya said Mrs. Potts about that woman and reckon that maybe I could do summit to help ya.' I gave him a suspicious questioning look.

'How did you know I was here? Have you been following me Joe?'

Ignoring my question he said 'I'm gonna go and break into 'er house and strangle 'er with me bare hands then chop 'er up and feed 'er to pigs. Or, maybe I'll gag 'er, tie 'er up good and proper and shove 'er in that cellar she locked ya sister in all them years ago and throw away key. What do ya think to that then Mrs. Potts?' I stood there stunned with a gaping mouth, maybe my decision to ask for Joe's help had been a little rash, after all he wasn't exactly the greatest thinker of Great Britain, but what Joe lacked in intellect he could redeem in other ways. After all how many friends are prepared to commit murder and take the consequences?

I so wanted to tell him yes take that evil woman out of my life along with my troubles, let the pigs digest her, but instead I said 'Joe if you are caught it will be you they'll lock up for life! Just how do you think that your hare-brained schemes will ever work? Have you forgotten that she has body guards with her day and night? You'll be lucky to get near her, they will shred you alive,' suddenly recalling my childhood and how I used to run as fast as I could whenever I saw her one eyed black cat nearby. I remember once I witnessed it attack, seeing the bloodshed from its long fangs, hearing the ghastly screams as it embedded its thick piercing claws into its victim's head refusing to release its prey. And then there was Bruno, can't forget about that nasty, vicious mongrel.

'I'll be all right Missus; I've got me rifle and me knife. It'll be ok Mrs. Potts, that woman don't scare me nor 'er animals.' I started to shake my head in denial, couldn't he see that her evil knew no bounds, her use of dark magic and sacrifice taught by previous generations . It was probably best not to mention that, fearing he would think they were crazy rants of a desperate woman.

'Umm, are you planning to do this alone Joe or will you have accomplices?' I asked, fearing he might have told someone about my dark and dangerous past, whilst also worrying for my friend's safety.

'Na might take Bill with us.' He said with a shrug.

'I think maybe you should sleep on the whole idea Joe.' I pleaded.

'Well I'll tell Bill and if he says it's ok then I'll do it.' he nodded, said a quick goodbye and a promise to help.

That night after I had collected Mildred from my next door neighbour, Mrs. Jackson who had kindly offered to look after her when I went to visit Mollie, I thought about Joe's plan. It must have played on my mind because when I went to bed I dreamt of Joe strangling Agatha with his bare hands, her hands struggling to pry his fingers apart, when Bruno suddenly jumps onto Joe's back then sinks razor sharp teeth into his neck whilst the cat draws torrents of blood from his face, clawing at his eyes. All the while Agatha looks on laughing as her animals tear him apart. His screams for help, still rang in my ears as I jolted awake. I lay there the rest of the night, trying to forget his pleas and cries for me to save him. However, fate was also going to play her trump card.

14

Justice

The chimes of the ward bell rang out loud and clear announcing the end of visiting time, distracting Sister Jenkins who hesitated before repeating 'I called you into my office Mrs Potts because I wanted to tell you that Mollie has been taken off the respirator and is making good progress. In fact she has surprised us all and if she continues to do so we may even consider sending her home. I cannot stress enough how important it is that Mollie receives her medication. She must not miss one single dose do you understand? We don't want any repercussions that we had last time she was discharged now do we?' She looked down at me with a disapproving tone.

'It was most irresponsible of you and I sincerely hope it will not happen again.' That woman had an incredible ability to make me feel small and insignificant. How dare she talk to me like that! I suddenly had an urge to slap her face but I resisted. I had been so busy thinking of Sister Jenkins' words that Sarah Jackson's had been completely forgotten.

'Now dear any time you want to go up to the hospital to visit your Mollie you are welcome to leave young Mildred with me but do not forget today I have to be at a very important meeting so kindly collect her before three thirty please.'

However as I knocked on Sarah Jackson's door I was sternly reminded.

'You are late Mrs Potts I told you I had a meeting to attend today. I am the Chairwoman of our local Voluntary Society and punctuality is extremely important.' She barked while putting on her old worn blue coat.

'However, you can redeem yourself. We are very short staffed on the meals round and would certainly welcome another pair of hands. Come along and help, you can bring Mildred with you. The old dears always like to see children well, most of them, maybe not Mrs C but we'll not worry about her.' She said with a dismissive wave.

'Who is…' I started to ask but Sarah Jackson was not listening.

'…Now let me see I'll put you down on the roster to cover Mondays, Tuesdays and Thursdays Mrs Potts and when someone is off on holiday or goes off sick I'll put you down for then as well. I want to see you on the round every week, no slacking you understand…'

I was beginning to see why she had earned the nickname 'Mrs Bossy'. My guilt from my past still sat heavily upon my shoulders and seeing this as a way of redemption I agreed to volunteer my services. Before long I got to know the people behind their wrinkles and warts and even started to enjoy dishing out their meals whilst listening to stories of past glories and adversities and occasionally their haemorrhoids and high blood pressure.

One Tuesday however things suddenly changed when another name was added to the list of recipients requiring a hot meal.

'Mrs Potts we shall be going to see a lady who lives down Cherry Tree Avenue today' Sarah Jackson informed me as she started up the motor of the old van.

'I understand she is still quite frail, only came out of hospital last week, I tell you it's a sheer miracle she is alive at all after what happened! She was in an accident, hit and run would you believe! Apparently a white transit van just ploughed right into her at about eighty miles per hour. Both of her legs were broken, her spine was damaged and she fractured her pelvis. Two weeks later she suffered a stroke and then on top of all that the poor woman contracted that dreadful bug, you know the one you pick up from dirty hospitals.' I nodded.

'Anyway they should bring back hanging if you ask me for scum that knock down little old ladies and blind too, not that they cared she had a white stick.' I glanced up at Mrs Jackson in shock, who would try to hurt a poor old blind woman?

'You know Mrs Potts some people really do seem to get more than their fair share of trouble and I reckon she must be one of them.' We finished packing up the car and started to leave for our rounds.

'…You see about three weeks before she was mown down, some men broke into her house, tied her up and then threw lime in her face. Went right in her eyes it did. Then not being content with having blinded her, those evil thugs then stripped the poor woman and slashed her body with razor blades before proceeding to ransack her house smashing everything they could lay their hands on and more. The district nurse told me she has some ghastly burns and cuts, poor dear.' I started to get a bad feeling, something about this story was making me very uneasy.

'Crikey! Have they caught these barbarians?' I spluttered.

'No, not yet they haven't. I believe the Police are still searching but Constable Wilson told me they will not rest till they do.' All the blood drained from my face, damn it Joe!

'Umm…Who is this lady Mrs C? What is her name?' I tried to ask casually, but my question went unanswered as the van came to a stop, having arrived at our first port of call. Carefully placing a slice of thin meat, a spoonful of peas, carrots and a ladle of mashed potato Sarah Jackson balanced the plate on a tray and handed it to me. 'Oops! I forgot the gravy dear. That is for Mr Banks at number three. He'll be expecting you and he will probably tell you off for not having brought his dinner yesterday but he forgets you see.'

About an hour later it was time for us to turn down on to the council estate into Cherry Tree Avenue; I could feel my heart racing. Would my instincts be right? Is Mrs C who I think she is? My mouth felt dry, I was jolted out of my thoughts as the van stopped again, this time drawing up beside a row of ill kept council houses and flats. I looked out of the window to see 58 Cherry Tree Avenue. The exterior had been rendered a mustard yellow colour, which was dirty and cracked and like the rest of the estate it had a depressing atmosphere. As I walked up the path covered in weeds and moss, bearing a tray of food being careful not to slip while telling my thumping heart to be still, a sudden strong gust of wind blew down the path and the paper thin slice of spam flew right off the plate leaving behind just a small spoonful of vegetables.

'Oh! Dearie me! Mrs C will not be too happy about getting half a dinner Mrs Potts. You best get back to the van for some more or she'll be clocking you one with her stick.'

Having hurried back replaced the spam, calmed my flustered nerves and taken a deep breath I was about to knock on the scruffy door when Sarah Jackson shouted 'No need to knock just put your hand in the letter box and reach for the key, should be hanging on a piece of string' I did as I was told. The first thing to hit me as soon as I stepped inside was the overpowering stench that emanated throughout the house. The second thing I noticed was the oppressive darkness as all the curtains had been tightly closed. Only a single candle in the corner of the room allowed me to just make out a figure huddled in a wheelchair. It was as if I had gone back a century in time. I felt a shiver run down my spine as a familiar voice chilled me to the bone. 'Is that my dinner? Bring it 'ere and 'urry up about it.'

'I'm just coming.' I squeaked as I rushed to her side. Remembering her sight loss I was about to tell her the location of the food on her plate when

'… Ouch!' She lifted her stick and suddenly struck me on the arm.

'That's for being late!' she snapped.

Placing the tray in front of her as quickly as possible I resisted the strong urge to wrench the weapon out of her hand and smack her on the head with it. After taking a few deep breaths, I made my way over to the kitchenette and suddenly had a feeling of de ja vu remembering when I stood in a similar kitchen at Hector's filthy cottage in Ireland. I recalled the abundance of spiders, earwigs and cockroaches that had taken up residence and wondered if this kitchenette at 58 Cherry Tree Avenue was also hiding the same.

However, a low pitched growl making me jump and shudder suddenly brought me back to reality. On lifting the greasy net curtain I recoiled in horror, recognising the black mastiff straining at its leash and baring its teeth. It must have seen the movement of the curtain and knew someone was in the house. I quickly backed away and turned to look at her. Why did she still fill me with dread and foreboding, that something dark and sinister was going to happen whenever I was near her? Or, maybe it was because I wished something dark and sinister would happen to her. That little voice in my head which until now had been surprisingly quiet suddenly chirped 'Wilhelmina Potts just when is your obsession to avenge ever going to be satisfied? The woman is blind, confined to a wheelchair, and you know why.

What have you lost Wilhelmina because of this stupid, pointless exercise you called revenge? Your heart is now enveloped in bitterness and hatred. Didn't Fred abandon you in the end because of this obsession? Would Mollie have been abducted if you had not committed that unforgivable crime in Black Gorge Woods? Would she have suffered such appalling neglect as a result? You lost Mildred's love not to mention a string of others? One day she may just begin to understand your motives but she will never forgive you for denying her the chance of children. You showed little tolerance with Edgar and pushed him out of your sorry life. Don't you see all of that is the true legacy of your will for revenge Wilhelmina?' I tried desperately to ignore that little voice but it refused to be subdued.

'Take a close look Wilhelmina and search your soul. Can you not see Agatha Fortescue is trapped within her own body? The stroke has left its mark. The paralysis will always confine her to a wheelchair.'

Did she know it was me who had brought her meal, I wondered? No doubt she recognised my voice. Despite her physical disabilities there was still something to fear, something intangible, something that made my skin crawl an evil presence. Endeavouring to shut out that annoying little voice in my head and waiting in trepidation for the expected reaction I slowly leaned in towards her body and whispered in her ear 'Hello, this is Wilhelmina, your step-daughter. Did you enjoy your little visit from my friends? I guess that makes us just about even now.' A smile crept up my face as I watched her jolt with shock. It was obvious she felt vulnerable, aware that I was so close. About to strike out with her stick in retaliation she suddenly changed her mind, instead she grabbed me with her good arm then took me down memory lane. I was back in the woods facing my sadistic step brother who lay trapped in his own snare, he threw back his head and aimed a disgusting glob of thick green phlegm straight into my face, just like the spittle Agatha Fortescue had just aimed.

'Oh! How disgusting! You poor thing! Here is a tissue dear, but I think you had best come and look at this Mrs Potts.' With the intensity of the situation I had not heard Sarah Jackson come into the room. Following her into the tiny kitchen I watched her open a cupboard and then point to something. The stench was overpowering. Coughing and spluttering she quickly closed the door again saying we need to get the Environmental Health people in here.

'I am certainly not touching that, even if you paid me.' Had the old woman killed it? I wondered. The half decomposed cat was barely recognisable.

'I think maybe the RSPCA is also required Mrs Jackson.' Lifting up the filthy net curtain to show her the mastiff chained up in the yard, he had no access to a bowl of food, a kennel or even water. Bruno was now a sad emaciated specimen, no longer demanding my fear but my pity. I could not bear to even think what that poor feline had suffered but at least it was now out of its misery. How long had it been trapped in that cupboard? I reflected. Much as I had hated that cat, no animal deserved a demise as cruel as that.

'I think we need to call in the Authorities to do something about Mrs Crabtree dear,' said Mrs Jackson, breaking into my thoughts.

'I shall get in touch with her doctor. She is obviously unable to cope living alone… The place will need to be fumigated. Ugh! Let us just get out of here dear. I cannot stand this stench any longer.' I nodded in agreement, as we rushed out.

About three weeks later as we made our way down Cherry Tree Avenue searching for the address of another unfortunate soul, when I noticed outside number 58 was a large board that read 'To Let Contact Wilson and Hambrose.'

'Where has Mrs C gone?' I asked.

'Haven't you heard Mrs Potts?' one of the other volunteers on the round suddenly interrupted. I shook my head in confusion.

'She's dead.' There was a few minutes of silence as I processed the information.

'Dead? Did you say dead?' unable to believe my own ears.

'Yes, that's right, gone up there she has' pointing to the sky.

I tried to ignore a certain little voice in my head doing a dance and singing 'hallelujah', as I replied with suitable reverence whilst lying through my teeth, 'Oh dear, I'm sorry to hear that. How did it happen?'

'They say she had another stroke, a massive one apparently. She went into that old folk's home in Orchard Street you know after she left Cherry Tree Avenue. Shouldn't laugh but they say she was sitting on the commode when it happened, the stroke I mean. Anyway she had plenty of miles on her clock and some say it's a blessing she went what with all her trials and tribulations.' The volunteer said with a slight smile on her face.

'Well I say good riddance to the old bag. She was a woman without a conscience, satanic, mendacious, wicked through and through, indeed they don't come more evil than that witch,' I ranted giving way to feelings I could no longer subdue.

'Now then, Mrs Potts you should not talk ill of the dead dear and whatever made you spurt all that?' I ignored her rebuke, it was none of her business.

Later that day as I stared at Mollie in the hospital, wondering how much longer her frail body could withstand the fits the doctors seemed unable to stabilise. Convulsions caused by me after I had carelessly left my young daughter alone on that fateful stormy night when the witch came seeking to take her pound of flesh and stolen my child damaging her forever. I still hear her calling out to me in my dreams.' How I wished I could turn back the clock.

My thoughts turned to Mildred recalling Charlotte's faith in me when she had passed her lovely innocent, unblemished child into my arms, how I had failed her, failed them both. I thought of the day I …'

Granny suddenly looked away into the distance with that familiar expression, biting her bottom lip, fidgeting with her wedding ring and I knew she was about to reveal another skeleton she had closely guarded down the decades. Tears filled her eyes as she stumbled over her words, reliving the memory.

'I remember drawing the bedroom curtains that morning seeing a cloudless blue sky. Opening the window I deeply inhaled the fresh air catching the scent of new mown grass and roses, allowing a surge of optimism to sweep over me. Then after a few moments reflecting on the wonders of nature and with a spring in my step I ran downstairs to prepare a hearty breakfast of sausages, bacon and eggs.

'I must go and awaken Mildred' I said to myself as I put the food on the plates but just as I placed my foot on the bottom step I realised it was me who needed to wake up not Mildred as reality overwhelmed me replacing optimism with a sudden pang of loneliness and anxiety.

For Mildred was not lying in her bed upstairs asleep you see, a few weeks ago we had argued and she had stormed out of the room in a huff playing her normal drama queen card, her parting shot being 'this place is like a prison! Indeed it is worse than a prison! I have had a bellyful of living here with you, a bellyful of this life and a bellyful of you playing 'mother hen' over me every five minutes. Aunt just when are you going to get it into your head I am not a child anymore? I am sixteen not six and plenty of young men have kissed me too I'll have you know. I can look after myself so, for Goodness! Sake!, will you just leave me alone to get on with my life,' she screamed at the top of her voice.

Of course I tried to run after her, reason with her telling myself it was just another teenage tantrum and she would soon get over it so I didn't worry too much when she packed a suitcase and walked out of the door. Deep down I knew she had been right. I did play mother hen over her and I did curtail her freedom even though she had given birth herself. To me she was still a child, only nature saw her as a mother, but it was hard to fight maternal instincts.

One week passed then two, then three, until eventually six months with no sign of my ward. I searched for her high and low of course and so did the Police. Eventually she became just another sad statistic on the Missing Persons Register. Five years was to pass before I was to set eyes on my niece again. I shall never forget that day as long as I live.

I had just sat down to eat my lunch you see when there was a loud insistent knocking on my door.

'All right, I am coming, give me chance, I'm just undoing the bolts' I told them as they continued knocking. I threw the door open and froze.

'Mildred! You've come back!' I gasped overcome with joy and then shock on noticing the handcuffs clasped around her wrists, attached to a burly six foot policeman standing on the step beside her. My niece was doing her best to avoid any eye contact with me.

'I believe you know this young woman Mrs Potts?'

'Yes, she's my niece. What has she done?' I asked glancing between the gruff Policeman and my Mildred.

'Can I come in Mrs Potts, I don't want to discuss this on the doorstep and I think maybe you should sit down before I go on. Perhaps a cup of tea if you're making one?' he said politely, gesturing towards my house.

'Yes officer, come in' I told him, directing him to the kitchen table.

'I'll just put the kettle on, make yourself comfortable.' I remember I almost dropped the cups, my hands were trembling so much. I handed him a strong brew as he began 'I am afraid to tell you Mrs Potts that we have reason to believe your niece abducted a male five month old child with intent on keeping the infant. We believe she was planning to take him abroad as we discovered her passport in her pocket.'

I had seen the police investigation on the evening local news never believing for one moment it could be Mildred, my Milly, who was the culprit.

'Umm what is going to happen to her? Will she go to prison officer?' I asked refusing to look at Mildred, angry and heartbroken over what she had done.

'Well if you can put up the bail no, she will not be remanded until the trial but if not, then she will be taken into custody to await the court case.'

'I see, and exactly how much are we talking about officer?' adding up all my money, hoping I had enough.

'Bail has been set at £985. Are you able to pay that Mrs Potts?'

'£985 did you just say officer?' almost choking on my tea.

'Yes that's correct the case should come to trial in the next six months.'

In an effort to temper my guilt for Mildred's troubles, I agreed to pay the bail, explaining how my niece had fallen off the rails when her own child had been taken for adoption. As I wrote out a cheque for the princely sum of nigh a thousand pounds, courtesy of Wilhelmina's Wicked Wares, I could feel Charlotte's presence looking over my shoulder. I knew only too well what she would have said had she been alive and my sister would not have minced her words.

'Wilhelmina if you had never permitted that old woman to use a knitting needle inside my daughter ensuring she would never again conceive a child then this would never have happened. Indeed it is a miracle my Milly was not killed. How dare you play God like that? This situation is entirely your fault. I hold you accountable not her, you.'

Around seven months later I found myself sitting on a pew in the Visitors gallery of the old court room, adjacent to the Police Station, listening to the prosecution endeavouring to tear my niece's reputation to shreds. She stood her ground and thankfully the judge was lenient, awarding her a two year suspended sentence plus court costs. Just when we thought it was all over and could get on with our lives she received notice that the baby's parents were not happy with the outcome. It was their opinion she should serve at least five years at Her Majesty's Pleasure and so they appealed.

I decided to go and see the couple myself who obviously wanted an eye for an eye, feeling justice had cheated them. Eventually I tracked them down, discovering they lived in an imposing mansion, causing worry to shake my body. Determined to do my utmost to help Mildred and ignore my sister's presence, I pressed the door bell, took a deep breath and waited. A servant opened the door, looked me up and down and ushered me into a room off the main entrance, saying the Master would see me when he was ready.

Five minutes later as I was busy perusing the pictures and family portraits, covering the walls, I jumped on hearing a man's voice saying 'Ah! You must be Mrs Potts. I am Ernest Fitzgerald. I believe you asked to speak to my wife but she is currently unavailable so whatever it is you have come to say you will have to address me. This has been a dreadful business and to think this is how we're repaid for giving that girl a chance to make something of her life.' He signalled for me to sit down in a nearby chair.

'Now I will not beat about the bush both my wife and I feel strongly that the girl needs to be punished. She has to learn she cannot go around stealing people's children. Have you any idea of the desperation your niece put us through? We feared we would never see our child again. My wife needed tranquilisers she was in such a state. Do you know we waited nearly fifteen years for Samuel, fifteen long years for him to be born? The girl needs to be taught a lesson; the sooner she is locked up the better.'

I stared at the man who bore a striking resemblance to Humphrey, from my past. He seemed to command my presence with a calm, understated authority indeed he gave one the impression that he carried that ability to an entire room of people. Perhaps like Humphrey he too had undergone military training. I became increasingly grateful that his wife was unable to join us, I was having a hard enough time trying to convince her husband not to go through with the appeal case. That was until I discreetly showed him my bag, which I had stuffed with hundreds of notes. Yes! Money can definitely talk.

I was reflecting on this fact on my way home and suddenly had an idea; I decided to throw all my energies into making it succeed. You see through my business I had become acquainted with many influential people. So just when certain clients were let us say, at a slight disadvantage, I demanded their help and before long I had not only an address but also a contact number. This time I was determined to leave no stone unturned. The contact number proved useless and there was another problem.

'You see Wilhelmina the people who had taken away your niece's child were very religious and joined a commune somewhere deep within the Bible Belt of America', I was informed.

'Plus have you thought you could be upsetting the stability of the child? In her eyes she already has a mother. Then, supposing we do find the parents, just how are you going to convince them that Mildred will not be taking them to court for custody or access? Didn't your niece desperately want to keep her baby?' I knew my client was talking sense and suggested I should rethink my plan, but I also knew I owed it to Mildred to try every avenue possible.'

Granny suddenly paused, looked into the distance with a far away expression and mumbled to herself 'but never in a thousand years would I have believed something like that was going to happen, such a dreadful shock.

'Whatever do you mean Granny, something like what?' I asked confusion colouring my voice. She sighed and looked at me before letting out a wide yawn.

'I am feeling a wee bit tired now dear. Would you mind if we continue this tomorrow Mary? Shall we say eleven o'clock?' Although bursting with curiosity I took the hint and left after saying a polite goodbye and giving her a kiss on the cheek. 'A dreadful shock,' she had said, whatever could that be?

15

The Commune

As part of my mission to put things right for my niece, not to mention perhaps quelling a guilty conscience, I took the difficult decision to rake up the past. What and where had fate taken Mildred's child, I needed to know? Had she been happy? The answer to that would later make me wish I had not turned over that particular stone. For nothing, absolutely nothing could have prepared me for what I was about to learn.

'Wilhelmina I'm not sure how to tell you this, so I'm just going to come straight out with it.' My informant had told me as he took out a flask from his back pocket handing me the alcohol. I took a swing as I watched him replace his shirt and trousers, after having given him one of my 'specials!' They were very popular you know. I would first ask the client to…'

'Umm Granny what did you find out about Mildred's child?' I quickly interrupted, not needing to know the particulars of my grandmother's exploits.

'Oh yes, that …Umm… Do you recall my telling you Mary, that I went to an address in London hoping to see the infant? To find out if she was being cared for satisfactorily and hoping to obtain a photograph to give Mildred, but was informed that the couple had moved to the States. Well, apparently the adoptive parents had split up not long after they emigrated and each gone their separate ways. The woman, I forget her name, Jayne Harris or was it Janet Hargreaves, had moved to Arizona in the sixties, where it is thought she had come under the influence of a self proclaimed prophet and leader of a cult, I believe they called themselves 'the Children of God'. Anyway, Jayne had gone to live communally in the Preacher's house and had taken the child with her.

Apparently in those days the children in the Commune received vicious beatings if they tried to rebel, child sex abuse being openly encouraged and commonly practiced in the Commune. It is said this man even exposed his toddler stepson to free love practices and apparently made him engage in perverted sexual play with several women in the Commune including his own mother. Unsurprisingly the boy had grown up so deeply scarred that in revenge for the appalling abuse he had suffered, he later became a murderer and told the world in a spine-chilling video, whilst brandishing deadly weapons, that he intended to kill his mother whom this self acclaimed prophet had called his queen. However, tragically when he was just twenty nine years old, the Preacher's stepson put a gun to his head and pulled the trigger.

I am afraid it's possible that Mildred's child had also been exposed to this terrible evil as her adoptive mother like the rest of this man's followers, had been completely brainwashed. I am so sorry Wilhelmina … it is believed that around thirty people who spent their childhood in the Cult, later committed suicide, and… and very sadly there is strong evidence that Mildred's daughter may have been one of them. I am sorry to bring you this news.' I sat on the bed in shock; I don't normally like whisky, but after everything I had just heard, I all but emptied his flask.

There and then I decided to do everything in my power to prevent Mildred from ever knowing what had happened, knowing it would destroy her. There was something else, something my niece didn't know I had seen.

Poor Mildred, fate had not been kind to her, a father that turned out to be a savage killer, a mother whom she could barely remember murdered by his hands, then being forced to abandon her own child who may have taken her own life to escape the demons of her childhood.'

'Did Mildred ever find love Granny?' I asked curiously.

'She looks so sour nowadays, I have never seen her smile and if you should happen to mention the opposite sex well, you would think it was a mortal sin to even speak to a man, let alone bed one.'

'No! I'm afraid Mary; hell will freeze over before that happens. You see sex is a taboo subject in her eyes. It is dirty and unpleasant. Well, that's what she told me after… You know Mary I should not be talking about Mildred behind her back in this way. It's not right. How would you like it?'

I persisted through sheer curiosity keen to know why Mildred disapproved of sex so strongly and why she had trapped her heart in barbed wire in case anyone should try to touch it.

'I'll tell you what I think Mary. I imagine the answer to that lies in her past, for it came out in that dreadful murder trial. You see Charlotte had apparently and understandably, been rejecting her violent husband between the sheets. He believed it was his conjugal rights to do anything he wished with her body. So he punished his wife by forcing her to do something so totally obscene that it made her physically sick and he didn't even care if his young daughter had witnessed his depravity or seen her mother screaming for mercy when he attacked her. That, my dear Mary, is why Mildred later saw sex as dirty and wrong.'

How strange I reflected, remembering that Mildred had run off in her youth with another woman's husband, no doubt she did not see sex as something sordid and unpleasant then. No! There was something else, something that had turned Mildred into the cold, unbending prude she was today. Needing to get to the bottom of this I gently repeated my earlier question.

'Did she ever find love? I mean real love, you know the kind where you love someone more than you love yourself?' Granny looked into my eyes for a while as trying to decide if I should know, after a deep breath she nodded.

'Yes but please don't write this down Mary. I would not wish to offend my dear niece… There was a man, Richard Sykes her 'silver fox', that's what she called him and she was smitten well and truly. Although I am not sure whether he was, there was something about that man that I didn't like. He had this habit of looking through you rather than at you and the condescending tone he would produce when he bothered to speak to you. I did hear a rumour once, that he had a shady past dealing in drugs, cocaine I think. Anyway she threw her line out and eventually she hooked her fish. He put a sparkle in her eye, a spring in her step and a bun in her oven! Isn't that what they say nowadays Mary?'

'Umm well some folks might but…'

'Anyway, that is what she believed and nothing and nobody could dissuade her otherwise. Then one day I found her doubled over in agony, holding her stomach convinced it was labour pains. She collapsed and was rushed to hospital where she learned the truth. There was no baby of course, that old midwife Mrs Rogers had seen to that, but there was a tumour growing in her uterus, which had slowly caused fluid to build up in her abdomen.

Believing she was pregnant, Richard agreed to marry her and to my amazement, he turned up at the altar. When the truth was revealed, that was when he showed his true colours'; Granny shook her head in anger and disgust.

'I knew deep down he was a rat, but she would always defend him, until the day he left her totally devastated. I can still hear her crying 'Aunt I gave that man everything; now he has taken my heart and shattered it into a thousand pieces, I hate him I shall never be so foolish as to fall in love again'.

Later when her divorce came through I overheard her say to someone, who enquired if she would ever remarry, 'I see marriage as a deck of cards. In the beginning you need two hearts and a diamond but in the end you wish you had a club and a spade.'

'Granny you said earlier there was something else, something you had seen.' I pushed, not able to take the silence any longer.

'Umm yes but perhaps it's best not to talk about that Mary.' I scrunched my face up in annoyance. Was that yet another question to go unanswered, another secret to be left in the shadows? I wondered.

Suddenly Granny Wilhelmina pushed her face close up to mine and placed a finger on her lip, 'Now then Mary, this is strictly confidential between the two of us, you understand?' I nodded, trying not to break eye contact.

'Mildred liked a drink, well more than one or two. In fact she had been a secret drinker for years. She would keep a bottle under her mattress and believed nobody would notice. Later, when she lost the love of her life, she sadly evolved into a full blown alcoholic, often being asked to leave the public houses she frequented. Then she would stumble through the door, shouting and swearing and I would try and put her to bed. Every time, I could hear Charlotte whispering in my ear 'and whose fault is this Wilhelmina? Who made it impossible for her to bear children? Who allowed her to fall down this path, where she turned to alcohol and drugs to shut out her pain? Soon you will have to face your consequences and be judged on your actions, soon you will be punished.'

16

Worms and Revelations

'It must be nigh twenty years since I set eyes on you Eliza.'

'I have told you again and again mother I have a business to run, it won't run by itself.'

'Ummph! I could be dead and gone before you even notice!' Granny huffed indignantly.

'Don't be ridiculous mother!'

'Umm... Would anyone like a nice cup of tea?' I asked, desperately trying to defuse the tensed atmosphere. As I headed towards the kitchen, I noticed that Eliza had also gotten up from her seat and started to follow me out of the room.

'Let me give you a hand Mary, I need to have a word with you about this stupid project mother is making you do for her,' this all being said within full earshot of Granny Wilhelmina, to my acute embarrassment.

'I am not deaf and I am certainly not stupid! Whatever you have to say Eliza you can say to my face, I have no time for folks creeping behind my back.' I glanced at the door, debating on whether I should put on the kettle or stay and listen to the coming argument.

'Well it's about this book you have decided to write mother. Amy told me you were writing stuff about us and...'

'And you thought you had best rush over to see what I had to say about you. I can read you like a book Eliza Crabtree.'

'I'm Eliza Foster now, remember? I have been for the last ten years' she said, anger building up, turning her face red.

'Oh Yes! You wed that layabout didn't you? I told you that man would bring grief but you wouldn't listen, thought you knew best didn't you. I always knew he was a slippery eel that one.'

'Look mother what John did is in the past. He has paid for his crime and apologized a hundred times…' Eliza insisted.

'Really, I don't recall him showing any remorse, not a shred, or have you forgotten that he robbed me of nearly ten thousand pounds? If Amy hadn't caught him when she did then Wilhelmina's Wicked Wares would now be facing bankruptcy.' Granny screeched.

'Yes mother and we all know what you did don't we!' Eliza shouted back.

'I only ensured he got what he deserved.' Granny said, a smug little smile lifting her face.

'Spite mother that's what it was, complete and utter spite; he still hasn't recovered, you know!' I stood by the edge of the room, doing a good impression of a wall fly. My head twisting to and fro between Granny and Eliza. Ignoring her comment, Granny turned her head towards me.

'Mary where is that tea you offered?' Giving her daughter a withering look as she spoke.

'I'll just make it now' I murmured, discreetly beckoning for Eliza to follow as I left the room.

'Oh! And if you look in the cupboard you will see a packet of ginger nut biscuits and a box of my favourite fruit jellies' Granny called out to me.

Once we reached the kitchen and having checked that we could not be overheard, I asked 'umm what exactly did Granny Wilhelmina do in the past that was so spiteful?'

Eliza stared at me for a few seconds before answering.

'You mean you don't know, or, has my mother just given you her own version of what happened?' she looked at me suspiciously.

'No, I…I simply have no idea what you are talking about' I told her, staring at this tall woman standing in front of me, with a slight air of arrogance, recollecting the flattering remarks Granny Wilhelmina had used to describe her daughter. A real beauty, olive skin, high cheekbones, now not so well defined, ebony hair now peppered with grey, framing her sultry mysterious eyes that still held an air of dark mystery. She had aged well and no doubt could tell a tale or two. How on earth could she not visit her own mother in twenty years? Had Granny Wilhelmina crossed swords with Eliza as well?

'It's a long story Mary and now is neither the time nor the place dear. I think you should certainly have all the facts if she is intending to leave this project for posterity. I haven't told mother yet, but this is really just a flying visit I am afraid, but perhaps we could meet one day next week and I will tell you everything, in all its nitty gritty detail.' I nodded eager for more information.

'I believe Amy mentioned a quaint little tea shop in the village where they do the most delicious home-made clotted cream scones?' She asked.

'Ah! That will be Florrie's Fancies near Jacksons Corner.' I exclaimed, knowing the place she was talking about.

'Shall we say eleven thirty next Tuesday?' knowing it was the only time I could make it.

'Yes dear, but you will be punctual won't you because I shall be leaving for Amsterdam later and I would not want to miss my flight.' Worry creasing her face.

'Do not worry I'll be on time.' I reassured.

The following week as I made my way to the cake shop my mind was buzzing with curiosity, imagining all kinds of things quite far-fetched and almost unimaginable, after all Granny Wilhelmina was an extraordinary lady who had a penchant for shocking people, Wilhelmina's Wicked Wares for one.

John Foster was also an enigma. He only got what he deserved she stated but whatever had she done? I licked my lips with anticipation at the forthcoming tale and quickened my pace, seeing Florrie's sign up ahead.

Pushing open the door, I was met with a wonderful aroma of home cooking, gingham tablecloths and dark oak beams, the building being so old even the floor was on a slant. As I looked around for Grandma Eliza feeling twenty pairs of eyes on me but none of them belonging to her, a waitress approached. Gently ushering me to a table for two in the window she then pushed a menu into my hand saying, 'I'm sorry duck we're clean out of the cream scones I'm afraid but I can recommend the carrot cake.' Thank you I'll try some with a pot of tea, I told her. Where was Grandma Eliza, I wondered, noting my watch now read eleven thirty five? Whatever could have happened to her?

After a further fifteen minutes had passed with neither sight nor sound of her I decided it was time to ask for the bill and leave. Just as I was putting on my coat the waitress suddenly approached apologizing profusely

'I'm so sorry dear, have been run off me feet today and I clear forgot to give you this' pushing a note into my hand.

'Mrs. Foster asked me to give it to you. She was in a rush, you see and couldn't stay.' She then dashed off, to attend to another customer.

Sinking back into my seat, I quickly unfolded the paper and read.

'I am so sorry Wilhelmina something came up and I had to rush back to the airport. In short this is what I was going to tell you in the café.' I stared at the writing, taking a deep breath, preparing myself for what I was about to discover.

'You see Mary, mother has always had a distaste for my husband John from the moment she met him, said he wasn't good enough, 'a fly by night' I believe she called him, who would disappear once he had enjoyed his oats!' She told me rather bluntly one day. Said I could do a lot better and was a fool if I did not try. Truth be told there wasn't any love lost on his part either; 'I cannot stand being in the same room as that woman' my husband once informed me.

Anyway your Granny hatched a plot to get her revenge after he was caught stealing from her, but that is another tale and he intended to put back every last penny. You see Mary, your great grandmother may be very old but my goodness she was sharp as a new pin when it came to balancing the books and, anyone who tries to take her money would live to regret it, which my dear husband was soon to discover. You'll never believe what she did to John, despicable that's what she is!

Not long after his crime was discovered, his mother Agnes died suddenly and left him with a fairly substantial inheritance. When your great grandmother heard of this she had him believing he could double it, even treble it, by investing the entire sum in the stock exchange.

She knew the shares which she had advised him to buy wouldn't make a profit; they weren't even worth the paper that they were printed. She had contacted a friend of hers who happened to be an employee of the firm in which she had advised John to invest you see and learned the business was failing, would soon go under, just a matter of time.

'A fool and his money are easily parted my dear' was Wilhelmina's comment when John became penniless. If it wasn't for my money Mary, I really don't know how we would have coped. I'll bet Granny Wilhelmina hasn't mentioned that in her pet project!

Oh and don't get me started about poor dear Amy. I expect she has brushed her under the carpet as well, maybe you should ask Granny Wilhelmina yourself, about what happened to her. She should be the one to tell you not me. You know, I believe she still gets flashbacks of when your grandmother used to lock her in the attics at the brothel, for being impolite to the customers. Amy hated the business with a vengeance, you see, made her feel dirty she used to say. I bet Wilhelmina hasn't mentioned that.'

Thinking back, I recalled Granny Wilhelmina saying 'Amy was a natural when it came to seduction.' What more could she be hiding, I wondered.

'Ask Amy about that heated argument they had, when she yelled for the whole place to hear.

'You have taken everything from me mother my dignity, my money, my clothes, I have nothing left, nothing except these horrid, gaudy costumes that leave nothing to the imagination and my shame. How can you treat your own daughter like this? Do you have any idea how much I detest having men leer at my body and then abuse it.' Pulling her bodice up she told her 'don't you know mother, a little bit of mystery can be alluring.'

'No! That is what the punters pay for Amy' she told her as she tugged at her bodice until her nipples were exposed.

'Breasts, buttocks and spankings, my girl excite our clients not mystery. We have to keep the clientele happy, what you like is immaterial to me, just lie on your back and do as you are told' she retorted when Amy tried to tell her about the foul smelling, six foot wrestler who had forced her to do something unspeakable. All your great grandmother cared about was the money it brought.'

So much for my great grandmother's charitable Cause I reflected with a snort.

'Oh! And another thing Mary', Eliza added, 'don't forget to ask your Granny Wilhelmina about a certain horse called Gold Sovereign and then wait for her reaction.'

I sat in the café for a good hour, unable to move, my mind reeling. It was only after the waitress came over and politely asked me to leave, that I started to gather my thoughts and head home. Wondering how on earth I could face my great grandmother knowing all of this.

17

Orchard Villas

The next morning as per usual I went to visit Granny Wilhelmina's flat armed with my notebook and pen, wondering what surprises and no doubt shocks would be revealed today. To my surprise, I was met at the door by Mildred, who greeted me with a finger to her lips saying 'hush Wilhelmina is sleeping. She had another fall in the night and bruised her ribs; I've had Dr. Johnson over to look at her. However, I reckon, Mary the time has now come to think about moving her into that Home down Orchard Street.'

'Does she know about that?' I asked. Never did I believe for one moment that she would calmly agree to go there of all places!

'Didn't Granny say that was where Agatha Fortescue had ended her days?' I exclaimed, hardly believing this turn of events.

'I'm going to get Adam Johnson to talk to her, make her see sense. She listens to Dr. Johnson. Did you know she wanders off, day and night and I cannot be doing with it? I have lost count now of how many times Constable Wilson has brought her back home and told me to take better care of her. No, Mary, I have had enough, done my bit and much more, I have made my decision.' She said with the same stubborn look in her eye as Granny, not that I would ever tell her that.

'So I telephoned the Home this morning and it just happens that they have a vacancy.' Was this Mildred enacting her revenge? I reflected.

'Auntie Mildred maybe Granny Wilhelmina's short term memory may leave a lot to be desired but you would be surprised at what she has told me to write about her past. In fact you would be truly astounded!'

'And why is that Mary?' her eyes tensed in suspicion.

'Umm…her project will reveal all, I suggest you make time to read it but be prepared because you could be in for a bit of a shock.'

'Whatever has she told you? I hope there's nothing insulting about me?'

'Ummm…'

'That woman has an acid tongue and can be as sour as a lemon when she wants to be. I've seen her reduce a man to a blubbering wreck before.' Fleeting thoughts of Granny Wilhelmina's prostitution days suddenly came to mind.

I remembered how desperately she wanted to be forgiven by her niece, or at least for Mildred to understand her actions. I wondered would that ever happen? Were Granny's hopes too high? After all she pretty well destroyed any happiness in her niece's life, when she already had such a tragic start.

Even so, I had to stop Mildred from seeking her revenge on the woman who had taken her in, given her a home, a better life and affection, though perhaps misplaced at times, but I knew she truly cared, in her own way. Maybe if Granny Wilhelmina hadn't been consumed by her obsession with Agatha Fortescue. Then things could have been different, but no she had to have her pound of flesh and it didn't matter to her how she took it.

I still couldn't bear to think of her trapped in Orchard Villas. It would kill her for sure. I heard from various people, whose relatives had been living out their days in that dreadful place, that the care there depended very much on just who could be bothered to give it. Basic needs like the toilet or having a wash frequently went unanswered. There was even talk that some poor souls passed away from mal-nutrition on account of food being left for helpless residents with no assistance offered, then removed, untouched, no-one caring whether they had eaten or not. And those who were lucky enough to get fed received very little, as a three pound chicken couldn't go too far when it's shared between nineteen people.

No, I wasn't going to allow such a proud old lady, my Granny, to be treated with such cruelty and degradation, no matter what she'd done in the past. All I could do was help her finish her little project; Mildred had to know as soon as possible then maybe she would reconsider.

Although on account of her present condition, I knew she was safe for a few days, at least until her iron constitution returned, if it returned? Nevertheless I still needed to say my piece, before Dr Johnson arrived. Then I had an idea. Would it work; would she even believe it? Could I even do it? Do I even have the strength to drop such an earth shattering bombshell in that way? Then she'll have closure, I argued with myself and that, at the very least, she's owed.

I decided the next day was going to be 'D' Day. So after filling the kettle and preparing for tea, I called for Mildred.

'Auntie, would you mind coming into the kitchen for a minute', being a ploy to get her into the room where I had carefully left open Granny Wilhelmina's file and placed a cup of tea on top of it.

'Why? What do you want Mary?'

'Come sit down, have a cup of tea and take the weight off your feet.'

'Well just for five minutes dear. I am very busy you know. Have a thousand and one things to do today… What's this? Is it Wilhelmina's project by any chance? Carefully removing her cup, her eyes scanned over the typed sheets'

'Yes, I was just making some notes. Would you like to read it?' I asked, aware that she was burning with curiosity to know exactly what Granny had said about her. 'Yes I would, I would very much indeed. Thank you.' She replied, picking up the pages, her eyes glued to them.

'First you may need this', handing her a large glass of brandy.'

'Really Mary don't be so melodramatic dear.'

Ten, maybe fifteen minutes later I sat staring at Mildred's face. It didn't crease as I had expected. No tears were misting her eyes, her bottom lip didn't quiver, nor did I once hear her take a sharp intake of breath or try to swallow a lump in her throat. In fact, it was almost an impassive expression that she wore. No questions asked, no emotion, nothing. Indeed, 'I see', was all she commented before closing the file on Great Granny's past and hopes for forgiveness.

'Give her time' I thought, as worry coursed through my mind. Had it been a dreadful mistake to allow her to read it, after all, I hadn't even asked Granny Wilhelmina's permission.

'Well Mary soon I shall not have to worry about Wilhelmina; she will be somebody else's responsibility, the sooner the better.'

'Auntie have you looked, really looked at that place, Orchard Villas? I mean have you ever been there? It might appear bright and rosy on the outside, but on the inside it's riddled with worms. In fact it's nothing short of a disgrace! I wouldn't wish that place on my worst enemy,' then remembered Agatha Fortescue and knew I would. The stony face did not change. Maybe it was all too much to take in for her? I reflected. It was her own flesh and blood, how could she not be emotional?

The following day I accompanied Dr Johnson when he went into Granny's little flat and as I slowly closed the door I overheard him say 'now Mrs. Potts I don't believe in wrapping things up so I am going to come straight to the point. You are not able to look after yourself and your niece I believe is unwilling to help you anymore, so I have arranged for you to move into a home, Orchard Villas to be exact. It's nearby and you will…'

'No! No! No! Over my dead body!' Granny Wilhelmina's screams echoed though the entire flat.

'I have told Mildred, Mary, Eliza and everybody else that when I end my days, I shall be lying in my own bed, my bed do you hear! Not a strange one that someone else has died in. No, I don't care what you say; you will never change my mind. I am not setting one foot in that place and that is final.' She ended on a huff, her arms crossed over her chest and her chin set high and uncompromising.

'Mrs. Potts let me…' Dr Johnson tried to placate her.

'Did you not hear me doctor? Final! Now, if that is all you have come to say kindly leave.' She pointed to the door with a thin bony finger, glaring at him as she did.

'Well I shall leave you to think it over.' He smiled patiently.

'There is nothing to think over, absolutely nothing.' She said with pursed lips, still pointing to the exit.

'I shall be back again in a few days Mrs. Potts and I will bring some photographs of the rooms to…'

'Well, you know exactly what you can do with them doctor, goodbye.'

In view of Dr Johnson having ruffled Granny's feathers somewhat I decided to risk the Grim Reaper paying her a call and postponed my visit for a few days, although I had to admit a part of me was burning with curiosity wanting to know what happened to Amy.

'How are you feeling today Granny?' I enquired. 'Would you like to do some more work on your project?'

'Well Mary I am a lot better than three days ago when Dr. Johnson came to see me. He told me I could not stay here and I told him I could, but would he listen? No! He had the audacity to…'

'So you are ready to continue your trip down memory lane?' I interrupted, preventing a long rant about Dr Johnson and Orchard Villas.

'Umm… Yes dear but you will have to remind me where we finished last time.' 'Amy, I believe you were going to say something about Amy.' I said, trying not to sound too eager.

'Well I cannot think for the life of me why I should wish to talk about her.' 'Umm…Didn't something happen to Amy, an accident I believe?'

'What do you mean by that Mary?' Oh! Dear! This was going to be very difficult, I reflected, but bravely continued.

'Umm… I'm sure earlier in your project you mentioned something about a tragedy and a horse called Gold Sovereign' I coached, hoping I wasn't being too obvious.

'Oh! Did I?' Sadness and anger coloured her voice. Worried that I might have hurt her feelings or over stepped, I tried to change the subject.

'You look tired today Granny, maybe I should come back tomorrow. You need to rest.'

To my relief despite her great age, Granny Wilhelmina's health slowly improved. I was only too well aware that Dr Johnson, just like his patient, had a stubborn streak and would not easily let this go. Having visions of Granny being thrown into a waiting ambulance with him and Mildred getting in beside her then telling her Aunt that revenge has been served, I knew I had to act quickly and decided on a plan of action.

'Granny, how would you like a few days at the seaside, call it a spot of convalescence after that nasty fall?' Granny perked up at the suggestion. 'I was thinking we could go and stay with a friend of mine near Scarborough, well Filey to be precise. It's a lovely town with a beautiful golden beach. You would really love Filey Granny. We could visit Cayton Bay, taking the route along the water's edge providing the tide is out of course.' I continued. Then a vision of Granny plus wheelchair plus me slowly disappearing into quicksand came to mind suddenly remembering how a child and his parents had almost been swallowed by the treacherous beach not too long ago.'

'Umm… well Granny on second thoughts maybe we'll not go to Cayton Bay. Perhaps we could go and see a show and buy some fish and chips. You cannot beat fish and chips eaten straight from a newspaper by the sea with the tangy, salty sea breeze blowing the cobwebs away.' I caught Granny's disapproving expression. 'Umm most unbecoming dear, we shall eat either at a hotel or with your friend but my fish will be on a plate, preferably made of bone china.'

After making the necessary calls I returned a few days later to pack her suitcase. As I threw in skirts, high necked blouses and cashmere twin-sets, plus necessary toiletries, not forgetting several pairs of large red bloomers, I stole a quick glance at Granny. She was busy turfing out a hundred and one things from her handbag on to the bed getting more exasperated by the minute.

'I cannot seem to find my passport dear', she finally announced, ignoring me completely when I informed her we were not flying off into the sunset!

Eventually after a long train journey accompanied by many delays, we arrived at a large red brick house divided into flats overlooking the bay. Margaret Townsend, a small dumpy woman in her fifties who also seemed to be stuck in that era judging by her clothes, greeted us.

'I was beginning to think you had gotten lost Mary, well there's a nice hot meal waiting for you when you have unpacked your bags. Now come in and get warm both of you, I've just stoked up the fire.' She led us through the hallway into a cosy room decorated with chintz furniture and antiques.

'You know Mary you were right this place is like a breath of fresh air' Granny announced later on as I battled with her wheelchair along the beach stopping here and there, watching half a dozen yachts bobbing and dipping in between the waves while sea gulls squawked and circled overhead. We passed a group of ponies huddled around a bale of hay, waiting obediently to take children for short rides along the sea front.

'Mary dear I've been thinking, perhaps you could persuade your friend to let us stay a little longer, after all we still have not done everything on our itinerary yet have we? I would like to visit the Brig tomorrow; you know those big rocks that jut out into the sea, and perhaps a cliff top walk.'

'Umm let's see what tomorrow brings shall we Granny' inwardly groaning at the thought of heaving her up hundreds of steps to the top of the cliffs.

Tomorrow brought a surprising turn of event. Just as the clock in my friend's living room chimed ten fifteen in the morning, there was a loud knock at the door.

'Are you expecting anyone Mary?' Margaret asked, a touch of curiosity in her tone. 'No, as far as I am aware, nobody even knows I'm here' I told her as I walked up the long hallway, feeling a little anxious as I pulled open the door, clad in pyjamas and dressing gown.

'Hello Mary, I must say you have taken some tracking down. Well are you going to let us in then or are you just going to stand with your mouth hanging open? Why on earth are you not yet dressed?' What is she doing here? I wondered as I guided them into the house.

'Umm… of course Auntie but if it's Granny you've come to see, she is still resting at the moment.'

'Well then perhaps you could give her a message. You see, I got to thinking after you let me read Wilhelmina's project thing, I mean it was a bit of a shock, a massive shock really, when I saw what she had said about my baby girl. I now see Aunt Wilhelmina did try to make amends. I'd no idea she had even gone to London to see her or tried to get a photograph, or that she even cared for that matter. So I said to myself, 'Mildred you must tell your Aunt

Wilhelmina that you now understand why she did what she did all those years ago', mind you I am not denying it was a criminal thing to do and neither was she punished for it but maybe, just maybe in time I might even begin to forgive her. I see now that she was just trying to protect me in her own bizarre way.' I stood stunned.

'Oh! I really think you should tell her that yourself Auntie Mildred. She's in her bedroom, just go up the stairs and you will find her second door on the left.' My gaze fell on someone else.

'Umm…Are you going to introduce us Auntie?' I asked, wondering about the handsome stranger standing by her side and clasping her hand in a tight grip.

'Oh! This is Jack dear, a very close friend. He's taking me to France in a few days so I can see where my birth mother lived. I want to visit her grave you see and lay some flowers on it.' As she spoke she looked into Jack's eyes then squeezed his hand.

'Jack and I are going to be wed Mary. We haven't set the date yet but when we do you are invited to attend the wedding, nothing fancy mind, just a small affair. Neither of us are exactly spring chickens are we dear?' There were a few moments of silence, a feather could have knocked me over.

'Oh… how exciting Auntie… I would love to come. Congratulations, I am so very happy for you both.' I gave her a quick hug and her fiance a polite hand shake.

Despite her age my Aunt still reminded me of a teenager caught up in the throes of first love, her face was glowing and there was a sparkle in her eyes I had never seen before.

'Well I think this calls for a drink Auntie and I am not meaning tea so when you come back downstairs from seeing Granny, there will be a glass of sherry waiting for you. I'm afraid we haven't any champagne. Then you can tell me all about your romance. Wherever did you find him? I suddenly spewed without thought for her valued privacy or manners on my part.

'That is none of your business my dear but suffice to say Jack and I have enjoyed a friendship long before you were a twinkle in your father's eye.' Maybe after she has had a few more glasses of sherry she will open up, I thought.

Five minutes later Aunt Mildred swept into the living room announcing 'Wilhelmina is asleep. I have no wish to wake her so will you be sure to tell her why I am here Mary.'

'Yes of course but she's probably only looking at the back of her eye lids you know, well that's what she likes to tell people. Anyway, tell me how did you two meet? You still haven't said.' I smiled encouraging them to take a seat as I handed out the drinks.

'Oh it was a long time ago dear, I believe I had just turned sixteen when a friend introduced me to Jack. Your Granny Wilhelmina didn't approve, saying he was no good and forbade me to see him or anyone come to that. I remember feeling like a caged bird desperate to be free.'

'Jack didn't give up on me, so we began to meet in secret until… well until SHE took your fancy.' She glared at him as he shuffled uneasily in his seat.

'Millie I told you that was a mistake, the biggest mistake of my life. I thought you had forgiven me. Anyway my wife is dead now and I am free to marry, to marry you my dearest. You have to know that I never stopped loving you and I always will to the end of my days just as I told you when I proposed.' Feeling slightly awkward listening to all this, I tried to change the subject.

'Auntie may I ask where you will be living, after the wedding I mean?' She looked surprised.

'Why? With Jack of course, he has a delightful house with eight bedrooms if I am not mistaken?' addressing the question at her fiancé.

'I see. Umm… could I have a word in the kitchen Auntie?'

'Mary dear I have no secrets from Jack whatever you wish to say just come straight out with it.'

'Umm…' feeling slightly uncomfortable being put on the spot, umm

'eight bedrooms did you say? In that case there would be plenty of room for Granny Wilhelmina to come and live with you, right Auntie? And, perhaps you could have a live in nurse to look after her.'

'I was under the impression Mary dear that Dr. Johnson had arranged for her to go into Orchard Villas?'

'Well Granny has not agreed to go there and personally I do not think she should, it's a dreadful place. She would not last a day.' I insisted. How could she abandon Granny now, after everything she just learned, I wondered, shaking my head in disapproval.

'I see.' Downing her sherry as she spoke.

'Well umm I am not sure Mary about your grandmother moving in, I mean it's not my place to say, it's up to Jack and we have made plans. He wants to turn the house into a Bed and Breakfast. It's his dream you see.'

'Oh! Dear! Well perhaps you might consider my suggestion.'

'Well we will talk it over, but we are not promising anything.' Trying not to let my frustration show, I picked up the empty glasses.

'Oh! Your glass is empty here let me top you up Auntie?'

'No dear we have to get going but I shall just pop upstairs again to see if she is still looking at the back of her eye lids.'

'Umm before you go, there's something else I would like to ask you.' I hesitated.

'Well spit it out Mary I haven't all day dear.' I took a deep breath.

'Umm it's about Amy. When I asked Granny she refused to talk about it… but I understand it had something to do with a horse called Gold Sovereign… I believe?'

'Oh! That! She once told me that her lips are sealed on the subject. It's my belief Mary she must still feel guilt about it. After all, they said it was her fault.'

'What was? What exactly happened?' my curiosity boiling over.

'Well you know Amy was… umm… working in that business you know the… umm… the one your great grandmother ran with that Indian chap?' I nodded.

'Well apparently Amy became entangled with a client there and they had a love child, believe she was called Francesca, but I cannot be sure'

'Oh I didn't know that.'

'Well the child's father, a married man, rarely saw her but instead tried to buy her affection and one day he turned up with a horse, a red chestnut mare. It was a highly spirited animal totally unsuitable for Francesca, given to suddenly rearing up or galloping off the moment something spooked it. To Amy it meant the world, a few words from her and it would calm down instantly.' Anyway I remember the day your Granny Wilhelmina said to Amy I am going to teach you how to ride that horse side saddle like a lady would, it is most unbecoming to sit astride it like a man in breeches.'

I believe I heard Amy then mutter 'I've a good mind to really shock her and ride like Lady Godiva stark naked.'.

Amy could be quite rebellious when she wanted you know and a few days later she did just that, except someone in the street who was drunk as a skunk, decided he was going to leap up on the horse and join her.

Well as she fought him off, the horse suddenly reared then bolted, causing poor Amy to lose her balance and fall. Somehow, she managed to get her foot caught in the stirrup. They say she was dragged almost half a mile before she could be rescued by which time she was barely conscious and the skin on her back was hanging in shreds. Then Gold Sovereign fell, broke his neck, and had to be shot. It broke Amy's heart.

You see Mary, that ghastly ride put poor Amy in a wheelchair when she was informed she would never walk again.'

'She has always blamed your great grandmother for what happened, not once attributing any of the blame to herself for the accident and said that she will never forgive her as long as she lives. So nowadays they hardly speak. They're estranged and unless a miracle happens, I don't think it will ever change.' There was a slight sadness in her voice.

'Then perhaps Auntie you could arrange for Amy to maybe come here so they can make their peace and end this before it's too late?' I asked, remembering Granny Wilhelmina muttering to herself when we first began her pet project, 'please Lord, give me the courage to tell them. Help me make them understand, particularly Mildred and also Amy.' Suddenly it all made sense.

'Now don't you go poking your nose in Mary; it has nothing to do with you and anyway I told you all of that in confidence remember. Now I shall pop upstairs and then we must be on our way. Come on Jack, come and meet Wilhelmina.'

'Auntie Mildred no disrespect to your intended but Granny Wilhelmina will have a heart attack if she wakes up and sees a strange man in her bedroom looking at her.' I said, blocking them from the stairs.

'Oh! Mary will you stop being so dramatic. Have you forgotten your great grandmother used to be a 'lady of the night'? I imagine my aunt has had more men in her bedroom than she has had hot dinners.' She scoffed, pushing me out of the way.

'What was that you just said Millie darling?'

'Oh! Nothing! dear.' She called over her shoulder with a dismissive wave.

'Lady of the night did you say?' he persisted.

'Uhh…Auntie was talking about Granny Wilhelmina's charity for fallen girls weren't you auntie' I answered, earning a look of gratitude and relief as she confirmed this. Umm so much for 'Jack and I have no secrets from each other', I wonder what else she is keeping close to her chest? 'Come on Jack, we haven't got all day, put that newspaper down and follow me upstairs.' She barked.

'Yes Millie, I'm coming dear, no need to get your knickers in a twist!' he snapped back.

'Oh! Was she still asleep?' I asked surprised to see them walking back into the lounge again so soon.

'Well Jack said he could have sworn she opened one eye then tightly shut it again, but I am sure my aunt wouldn't have done that.' How well did she think she knew her I wondered? After all it's possible to live with someone your entire life but never really know them. In my mind Great Granny Wilhelmina was indeed a hypocrite being even further convinced after having heard Amy's story. On the other hand she did try to make amends when she became a 'do gooder', I debated. Those thoughts were best kept to myself. Her family would no doubt make up their own minds when she went to sing with the angels.

'Well Mary, it has been short but sweet, take care of yourself dear. Come on Jack, do hurry up, you can read the paper when we get home.' He gave me a quick nod goodbye as she ushered him out of the door. I had no sooner shut it when I heard two thuds on the lounge ceiling.

'Have they gone Mary?' Granny asked on going upstairs to answer her call; I nodded.

'Oh! Thank goodness! Now whatever did she want and who on earth was that man she had dragged along with her?'

'It was…'

'Got the shock of my life I did when I saw him staring at me'

'Oh! He's her fiancé would you believe' choosing to answer the latter question.

'I believe she just wanted to see how you were after that nasty fall you had Granny.' 'No, I don't believe that, Mildred is up to something, you mark my words.'

'She's getting married Granny.' I insisted.

'No, she's plotting; thought she could drag me off to that terrible old folk's home from here, didn't she. Her and Dr Johnson, I don't trust either of them, two slippery eels that's what they are! He wants to see me out of his hair, and she wants to see me six foot under, I tell you!'

Our time at Filey passed all too quickly and before we knew it we were back home again. Just as we had begun to settle back into our mundane routine, a letter arrived out of the blue. As I bent down to pick it up from the doormat, I recognised Mildred's handwriting. Ripping it open I was shocked to read what she had to say.

'My dear Mary,

You will no doubt recall when we last met we discussed the prospect of Aunt Wilhelmina living at our house and how Jack was taking me to France so I could visit my mother's grave. Well, whilst we were there my fiancé received some terrible news. You probably won't know this but he had a family by his first wife and he was the proud grandfather of twin girls whom he simply adored. Well, his daughter and her partner had decided to take a little break and were on their way to join us when tragedy struck. Their car was in a head on collision with a lorry. Apparently the driver was drunk and acting completely recklessly.

Sadly neither survived the crash though the police told John they would have both died instantly. Miraculously, the two children who had also been travelling with them were both found alive. Tragically, the little girls are now orphans and so we have decided when they are well enough to leave hospital they will be coming to live with us and I expect in time we will consider adoption. We shall be hiring a full time nanny of course, who will live at the house.

Nevertheless I shall have my hands occupied looking after the children, so I'm afraid Aunt Wilhelmina is going to have to go into that old people's home near you after all. I'm sure she'll understand dear when you explain everything to her, and let us face it wherever she goes I expect her time will be short. She can't go on forever dear. Anyway Mary I am very sorry but that is how it is. Take care of yourself,

Best wishes,

Mildred.'

I stared at the sad letter as I filled the kettle for a cup of tea. After reflecting on it for a little I thought, finally Mildred could now be a mother. She would have children to love and cherish, something up to now she had always been denied. A little voice in the back of my mind intervened.

'Got her hands occupied indeed when she has been spoilt with a cleaner, cook, gardener, chauffeur and now a full time nanny! What more does she want?' What Mildred wants Mildred usually gets; Granny Wilhelmina had said that fact more than once. Could Aunt Mildred still be harbouring seeds of revenge? I wondered. As I picked up the letter again I noticed she had written something on the back.

'Really Mary first you wish me to care for an old, petulant woman who destroyed my life. My daughter would be alive today if it wasn't for my aunt's sad, pathetic obsession. No! Aunt Wilhelmina can expect no sympathy from me. She got what she deserved and I see now it was merely a cloak of guilt, nothing more and nothing less that made her search for my child. As for that back street abortionist she took me to when I was pregnant it is a wonder we both survived.

Knowing what my daughter later suffered in that atrocious cult tears me apart. And then you have the audacity to tell the doctors that because I am lucky enough to have a large house that I could also take in Mollie whom I hear is now as nutty as a fruitcake!'

'No! She's not and anyway Aunt Mildred if you were sandwiched between the fangs of death wouldn't that leave you just a little traumatized' I said aloud in anger.

'They say she sits and talks to herself Mary dear all day long. Isn't that a sign of madness? I even heard that once she picked up her lunch threw it on the floor and swiped a nurse across the face with her plate, just because she was told to eat her dinner. The poor girl had her nose broken.

In any case how can I be expected to deal with all those fits she keeps having every day? Indeed she is worse than a child when it comes to getting pills into her. I have heard she acts really strange at times, like an animal she will suddenly get down on all fours, try to make a dash across the room then let out a piercing howl. Is that not displaying insanity dear? It certainly isn't normal in my book. I have a friend who works in that hospital, on her ward as a matter of fact, and she told me the doctors were considering sending Mollie home soon being short of beds that she would be put on the list to have a dog, a specially trained Labrador apparently. It would sense when Mollie was going to have a fit then raise the alarm. I have my hands quite full enough now and I certainly cannot be bothered with a canine.

In any case Mary I have to put my husband first and abide by his wishes so dear my answer is no, no on both accounts and it is pointless trying to make me change my mind. Between you and me I don't think I will ever find it in my heart to forgive her for the lies and heart rending pain she put me through day after day, month after month and year after year. All I ever wanted was a child of my own and she tore her from me. I am sorry Mary but I cannot help you.'

I had forgotten that the Lord works in mysterious ways. Feeling sad for Granny Wilhelmina, I watched her constantly fretting that the Grim Reaper was waiting to claim her. Each night she would ask in her prayers to be given more time saying 'you know Lord what I still have to do' but whether that meant revenge or atonement I am not sure.

So the day she told me 'I need you to get the doctor Mary, I have a sharp pain in my chest, call Dr Johnson now, I am finding it hard to breathe' she gasped, panic rising in her voice. I knew then the severe cold that she had been battling for the last few days had possibly turned into pneumonia.

Letters to Eliza, Amy plus a few old friends Granny had kept contact with over the years had been hurriedly written requesting they come at once, informing Amy that Granny Wilhelmina needed to speak to her urgently before it was too late. Amy had now shed her wheelchair and progressed to leaning on two sticks having been sent to a hospital specialising in spinal injuries where she had eventually learned to walk. Her family and close friends gathered around Granny's bedside listening to the old lady gasping to breathe when a faint smile appeared on her face. Then I noticed she was trying to whisper something.

'What is she saying Mary?' Mildred asked me. 'Can you make it out dear?'

At first I thought she was trying to say something about her sister that Charlotte was waiting for her along with her beloved Fred, but I couldn't be more wrong. Granny frowned, slowly, feebly shook her head and tried again to make herself heard but this time there was no mistaking her faint whispers.

'I have left you all a special legacy it's a copy of that book the Kama… Kama…'

'Kama Sutra, do you mean Granny?' I asked hoping I was mistaken.

'Yes, enjoy it my dears, it makes good bedtime reading but when you look through the pages you may find something else. That is all I can tell you dear.

'Well, Mary what did she say?' Eliza asked, seeing the gaping mouth and wide eyed look of shock cover my face.

'Umm you will all be getting something special, she said, but you will have to wait and see what it is' hoping I wouldn't have to explain any further.

'Oh! How intriguing dear! Umm… do you think I could have a private word with my mother, Mary?' Eliza whispered. 'I need to tell her something you see.'

'Yes of course Auntie; we'll go into the garden, it's a beautiful day and a shame to miss the glorious sunshine. Take your time.' I patted her hand gently.

'Umm Mary I too want a quick word in case, in case she…'

When I returned to take my place once again by Granny's bedside I noticed an enigmatic smile playing on Granny's lips and wondered if she had finally heard words she had been yearning to hear for so many years, perhaps she could now finally rest in peace? Or, could it be naughty thoughts of a certain book had put that smile on her face? Whatever it was, it would be her secret, never to tell.

To everyone's amazement, a week later, Granny Wilhelmina's iron constitution yet again resurfaced and her ramblings were dismissed as just that, but I knew different. She had murmured something that day about a heavy mantel she had carried on her back since she had said farewell to her stepbrother Horace. Then she had whispered that her burden not of guilt but an overpowering, necessity to avenge, had only been lifted from her shoulders when she had learned that Agatha was finally dead and no longer a threat to her or more importantly her children. Sadly, it was too late for the damage had been done, she insisted and there was nothing, absolutely nothing that could be done to repair it.

'Only a fool could think otherwise. You see', she murmured to everyone standing around her bedside, 'when I look down the years it is not happy scenes that play in front of me but a litany of broken promises, lies, twisted bitterness and betrayal of those I held most dear to my heart, my very own family. So, Mildred, Eliza, Amy and everyone else I have carelessly trodden on whilst wending down life's long winding road, I pray you will read my words and try to comprehend why I did what I was driven to do but as to whether you will be able to ever forgive me I know that is another matter. I have no right to even ask just a faint glimmer of hope that one day Mildred you will search your soul and realise how desperate I was to protect your daughter from evil, and that Mollie will not look upon me as a foe but a friend who, like most mothers would move heaven and earth for their child, to see them happy. To those waiting for me in the stars there is no need to say anything because you all saw that parasitic tumour greedily devouring, eroding everything in its path spreading out its hungry tentacles, consuming my mind day and night.'

Then to the astonishment of her little audience she had revealed how one day she had become tired of endeavouring to cope with that daily burden which had become heavier as each day passed. She had been overcome by crazy thoughts, except they didn't seem crazy when she had climbed up on to the parapet of the bridge and stood there teetering, staring at the inky depths below where raging torrents were waiting to swallow her body and reunite her with her beautiful five year old child she believed to have drowned.

Try as she might she could never block out that little haunting voice that constantly called out in her dreams 'mama, mama, where are you? Why have you abandoned me?' How many times had Mollie believed she would come and rescue her until finally she had given up all hope of ever seeing her mother? Or, perhaps that hope turned to hatred as each day, month and year had passed? If only she had ignored that insatiable, overwhelming passion to take an eye for an eye in Black Gorge Woods and remembered instead that love conquers everything.

'Love is patient, love is kind.
It does not envy, it does not boast, it is not proud.
It is not rude, it is not self seeking, it is not easily angered, it keeps no record of wrongs.
Love does not delight in evil but rejoices with the truth.
It always protects, always trusts, always hopes, always perseveres.'

The End